PUFFIN BOOKS

SKiNNy B, sKAz and mE

First rule:
what Skinny wanted, Skinny got.

Second rule:
same as first rule, what I had Skinny wanted.

Third rule:
what I wanted, Skinny got first.

John Singleton reckons kids are the best readers: honest, turned on and tuned in. They've been teaching him all his life – the screwed-up and the clued-up – and now it's his turn to write their lives, talk their talk, tell it as it is.

And this is it.

Books by John Singleton

SKINNY B, SKAZ AND ME
STAR

SKINNY B, SKAZ and ME

JOHN SINGLETON

PUFFIN

PUFFIN BOOKS

Published by the Penguin Group
Penguin Books Ltd, 80 Strand, London WC2R 0RL, England
Penguin Group (USA), Inc., 375 Hudson Street, New York, New York 10014, USA
Penguin Books Australia Ltd, 250 Camberwell Road, Camberwell, Victoria 3124, Australia
Penguin Books Canada Ltd, 10 Alcorn Avenue, Toronto, Ontario, Canada M4V 3B2
Penguin Books India (P) Ltd, 11 Community Centre, Panchsheel Park, New Delhi – 110 017, India
Penguin Group (NZ), cnr Airborne and Rosedale Roads, Albany, Auckland 1310, New Zealand
Penguin Books (South Africa) (Pty) Ltd, 24 Sturdee Avenue, Rosebank 2196, South Africa

Penguin Books Ltd, Registered Offices: 80 Strand, London WC2R 0RL, England

www.penguin.com

First published 2005
1

Copyright © John Singleton, 2005
All rights reserved

The moral right of the author has been asserted

Set in 11.5/16 pt Adobe Sabon
Typeset by Rowland Phototypesetting Ltd, Bury St Edmunds, Suffolk
Made and printed in England by Clays Ltd, St Ives plc

British Library Cataloguing in Publication Data
A CIP catalogue record for this book is available from the British Library

ISBN 0–141–31609–8

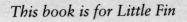

This book is for Little Fin

Contents

1

Ghost Baby and the Ju Ju Men

I grew up an orphan.

I wasn't born that way. It just happened. Dadless one minute. He was on the taxis – nights, weddings, limos. Mumless the next. She was non-stop daft and drooly over Skinny B, my sister, for as long as I can remember.

Yeah, it was all Skinny B's fault. If she hadn't been born thin and then got sick we'd have been an average, ordinary family, right there in the middle of normal.

And nothing like Skaz, Ju Ju, The Tower or Hoodz 5 would ever have happened.

Of course I was a kid myself when Skinny arrived. And still a bozo. Ask me about babies then and I'd have said cribs at Christmas. Ask me about babies now and I'd say sex. Ask me about sex now and I'll say Alison Libidowicz. Ask me about Alison Libidowicz and I'll tell you later.

Well, Skinny B came one summer. No angels, no star – all stick and no stuffing back of a taxi with Mum. I thought she was just visiting and that soon she would go back to her real parents. It was bad news when I was told she was there for keeps.

Right from the beginning it was like Skinny was kept for best, Mum fussing all the time like if she fell she'd break.

Result was, Skinny ruled.

First rule: what Skinny wanted, Skinny got. My Buzz Lightyear? Skinny got it. My strawberry flake? Skinny got it. My life? Skinny got it.

Second rule: same as first rule, what I had Skinny wanted.

Third rule: what I wanted Skinny got first.

So, the big thing about our family is that most of the time B is the main tune and I'm the triangle; the one that ping pings in the school orchestra once in a zillion bars.

Skinny was a long-time baby. She grew dead slow and never made much fuss about it like most normal kids do. Sometimes, when Mum wasn't around, I had to lean over her cot and prod her a bit to see if she still had squeak in her. Made no difference. She'd just stare at me, no no blinks, no no smiles like I wasn't there. Other times she'd hold on to my pinky like she only had one breath left, as Gran used to say, dead tight, as if something was trying to pull her away.

Like Mum, Gran worried too about Skinny not growing much. Skinny, she said, was a ghost baby.

Sometimes I would lie awake at night wondering if she was drifting round the house like ghost babies do, pushed along by their own breath. I imagined her coming through the wall at the end of my bed like kettle steam and turning into baby Bea. I thought she'd float about holding on to my pinkie so she wouldn't get sucked under the door or out of the window into the night.

But she never made it. Not strong enough, I guess.

Eventually, ghost baby started talking and things. Started walking, getting spots, rashes, coughs, sniffs, sneezes, pukes, fevers, aches.

Then Gran was happy. About time that child got normal, she said. But Mum didn't see it that way. First sign of ill, the doc was in. Dad was there and I was kept out of the way like I was the germ or something, like I was at the back of a crowd trying to see what was going on.

And when Skinny got a cold the whole house went red alert. She had pills and drops and sprays, stuff for her throat, stuff for her chest. 'All those medicines,' said Gran. 'Bound to make you ill.'

But Mum would cry over the ironing in the kitchen, certain Skinny was dying.

'What's up, Mum?' I'd say hoping she'd tell; let me in on the secret at last. 'Skinny'll be OK, you'll see. Gran says.'

She'd blink and half smile. 'Don't call her Skinny, Lee,' she'd say with a sniff. 'Not Skinny. Call her Bea. That's her real name.'

Then she'd run the iron over B's pink sweaters and socks, over and over, getting them dead smooth like she was steaming out spots and germs, like it was B she was pressing clean and perfect again.

Yes, my mum ironed socks; B's little white socks. Mine got tied together and dumped at the bottom of the stairs like a bag of dead kittens.

So whenever I was pigged off with Skinny always being the main tune, I'd go round to Gran's.

One day when Dad had refused to take me fishing and Mum was pushing pills into Skinny like she was coin operated, I took Magic Ted and my Man U jamas and went knocking on Gran's door.

She was hair-drying the budgie. Basil was lying on the ironing board, his blue feathers all puffed up, shivering in the blow.

'Why you doing that?' I said. 'You'll kill him.'

She gave one of her looks.

'He's dead anyway. Drowned in the scummy sink.'

She turned off the dryer.

She was trying to give him the breath of life.

Then I asked if she'd foster me, just for a week or two till Mum and Dad started missing me.

'Got one pet,' she said. 'Don't need another.'

I knew she meant her dog, Tig.

Just like Gran. No messing with Gran. Hit you right between the eyes. Dad used to say she had a right tongue on her. Could cut keyholes in concrete. He should know – she'd right lathered him once or twice.

'I'll get myself adapted then.'

'Adopted, you daft little brush.'

Gran was no bozo. She knew all this was to do with Skinny B. 'Look, Lee,' she said, dropping Basil into a plastic bag, 'what your mum wants to see when she

4

gets back from work is a normal kid sitting at home watching normal telly, eating normal, sleeping normal.'

I wasn't so sure.

'She likes Skinny B better than me,' I said, putting Magic Ted on top of the fridge. 'Skinny gets lemon fizzies, I don't.'

Gran dropped Basil-in-a-bag on to the floor and toed him into the corner by the sink.

'Rubbish,' she said.

But she gave me a big hug. Then she poured herself a glass of her own medicine from the usual bottle in the corner cupboard. 'Just a skim,' she said slopping it in. 'Thing is, Lee, your sister was a surprise because yer mum thought she was too old for babies. They can be problems when they come late. Yer mum was scared hers might be born different. So, when B did arrive all skin and grief but not too wonky, she was dead pleased and dead careful of her. Wouldn't take her out of the packaging, so to speak. Skinny was hers. That's the way it's been ever since. Keeps her in a box with a lid on.'

'So does that mean I can stay?' I said.

'Not Lotto likely. You're going home right now.'

When I was coming on eleven and Skinny was pushing five she started following me. Everywhere. She'd pretend to be a duck and come quack quacking after me all day long, up the stairs, in the garden, outside my room. Never stopped.

It freaked me out.

I couldn't shout at her. It wasn't allowed.

5

And when I moaned to Mum she hard-looked me.

'She wants to bond with you,' she said. She reads a lot does my mum so she knows these things. Skinny was trying to bond with me like animals do in the wild.

'But this isn't the wild,' I said. 'This is number three, Far Pastures Close. And she's a girl not a duck.'

'Yes, but underneath, deep down, we and the animals are all the same,' said Mum. 'We're programmed alike. It's called instinct, Lee. It's evolved over millions of years.'

Sure, Mum. I felt like a right duck-brain listening to her.

'So, carry on playing,' she said. 'Play is how we learn about our environment and how to survive in it.'

I nodded.

I went out, into my environment, followed by a duck. I kicked at a ball on the grass. Missed. Duck did the same. Missed.

I growled.

Duck growled.

Give her a red card, ref.

I stared at the sky.

I didn't give a skinny duck about surviving. I just wanted my sister off my back.

So I said to her, 'We're going to play Jungle.'

'What's that?' she quacked.

'It's where we go hunting snakes.'

'What sort of snakes?' she said.

'Big ones, big, slimy green ones, with big fangs.'

'What's fangs?' said Skinny.

'Poisonous teeth.'

'Ducks don't like snakes,' she said.

No, but snakes like ducks, I thought.

'You have to stand there,' I said. 'I'm going to tie you to a tree and we'll wait till the snake comes.'

I pretended to rope her up.

'What happens when the snake comes?' she said.

'I leap out and kill him,' I said.

'Why?'

'Because if I don't kill the big green snake he'll eat you up, feathers, everything.'

'Then I won't be able to quack any more.'

Exactly, Skinny.

Just now you're snake bait, duck.

I told her to wait while I went back to base camp upstairs, in my room. I told her she had to be very quiet and not frighten the snake off. I told her it might take some time before the big green snake arrived but not to worry. He'd come eventually.

I smiled to myself.

You're a dead duck, Skinny.

I sat down in my room and got out my PlayStation. I'd only been zapping away for a few minutes when I suddenly stopped dead still. Outside on the landing I thought I could hear a strange noise.

It sounded like a big green snake hissing.

I opened the door. Skinny B stood there.

'I ate the duck,' she said. 'Even though it tasted bad. Now I've come for you.'

I slammed the door. I needed help. I needed Jigger.

Jigger's been one of my best mates ever since primary.

Still is, sort of but not quite, now we're at secondary and he's with the scalp heads and bozo brains in 3E. Jigger's called 'Jigger' because he never sits still. People think he's thick, even the teachers, but he's not. If you don't count his looks, he's OK is Jigger. He knows the difference between an ice cream and a good licking, my gran says.

He had a sister too – Kelli. A right ball and chain he used to say. That was because he had to nursey nursey her whenever his mum was on overtime at Kwick Pax down in The Feck. And all because his dad had left home.

One day at primary he said, 'Now we're grown up, we should be able to choose our own mum and dad.'

We discussed who we could have as parents. I chose Madonna and Alex Ferguson. Jigger decided he didn't really want a dad. That's because the one he'd started with slapped him about. He thought of his Auntie Alice cos they had great caravan holidays by the sea, but in the end he said he'd stick with his present mum because she'd need him to look after her later on.

I looked at Jig. He was jamming a stick into the soil like he was trying to kill something squirming in the grass. 'My dad hit my mum,' he said suddenly as the stick broke in his hand. He looked up. 'Does yours?'

'Do what?'

'Hit yer mum.'

'Don't be daft.'

'Yer sister then.'

'No. My dad's not like that. He drives taxis days and plays darts nights. He doesn't have time for it.

Anyway, my gran would murder him if he laid a hand on me or Skinny; specially Skinny.'

'Wish I had a gran like that,' said Jigger.

I gave him one of Skinny B's fizzies, the ones I'd nicked from the fridge.

So, that summer before I started secondary and while Skinny played drakes and adders, I played Escape with Jigger. And Tracker and Jungle Warrior down The Swamp. The Swamp was great. It was a hollow full of trees and bushes and a soggy bit in the middle. Everybody's garden backed on to it, and everyday kids ran down the slopes to race and fight and shoot, and every evening before dark fell they ran back up to become bozos again and watch telly. From the air, I suppose The Swamp would look like one of those dead volcano craters, pit-black at night and full of strange life-forms.

It was here, in this massive crater, deep in the African jungle, that Jig and I fought the Ju Ju men. Right in the heart of The Swamp, lived the Ju Ju king. We never saw him. Instead, each day we battled with Ju Ju warriors. Ju Ju have grey dusty skins, white-hot eyes and smoking mouths. If you're down there after dusk, they'll catch you and suck the soul out of you and you become one of them, a Ju Ju boy, hollow inside with skin that's shrivelled like a puffball.

According to Jigger, only the blood of the Coca Cola bird can protect you. While tracking Ju Ju in The Swamp we drank lots of Cola Bird blood. Really it was OK during the day because the snakes protected us, but at night they go blind and are useless. And because Ju Ju can see in the dark we had to binge on Cola or get out when the sun went down.

Thing is, don't mess with the Ju Ju.

Sometimes, when Skinny B was being a pain and doing my head in, I prayed the Ju Ju would come and get her. I told her about them just for a scare.

'They eat little girls,' I said.

'That's horrible.'

'Devour them. Swallow them – whole. In one gulp.'

'That's a lie. There's no such thing.'

'Yes, there is, Skinny. They live in The Swamp.'

'Says you. Just because you and that Jigger kid think so doesn't mean it's true.' She wandered off. 'You're just stupid,' she shouted back.

Skinny was right, of course. The Ju Ju were just in our heads, living in the swamp bits of our brains.

'Well, I've never seen them,' she said, coming back. 'And, anyway, I'm a big green snake. And I could eat Joo Joo for tea. So there.'

'You've not seen God,' I said back, 'but he exists.'

'He's not in The Swamp.'

I shrugged. 'Could be.' I hadn't really thought about that. About God's exact address, I mean. He was more of a sky thing in my mind.

'God's at school,' said Skinny. 'And I've seen him, in a library book. So there! And what's more, God's scared of snakes.' She screwed up her face. 'Everyone is,' she said hissing at me.

I hissed back.

*

One day Jigger brought some mushrooms down The Swamp. Some bozo on the market had sold them to him. Said they were Gandalf's Goolies and they made your brain go wild. 'Boil them up. Make juice,' said Jigger. 'Ju Ju hate it. Drives them mad.'

'What do we do,' I said not believing a word, 'sprinkle them with it?'

Jigger shook his head like I was bozo first class.

'We drink it.'

'Drink it?'

'Take your head for a ride,' grinned Jigger. 'Terrify Ju Ju.' He got out a box of matches.

An hour later we had a kettle full of simmering mushrooms.

'I'm not drinking that stuff,' I said, peering at the frothing goo.

'Wimp,' he said.

'No! It's puke. It's poison.'

'Wimp,' he shouted.

'Wimp yourself,' I said. 'Dare you.'

'Dare you.'

I hesitated. I didn't want Jigger to go one better than me. 'You go first.'

'No, you,' said Jig. 'I dared first. First one to dare chooses. You first.'

'It was your idea. Means you do it, then me.'

'Wimp,' he said and tipped the spout into his mouth. Grey dribble trailed from each corner of his mouth.

He handed me the kettle.

'Drink,' he spluttered.

I trickled juice into my mouth.

'Wheeeehh!' said Jigger.

Five minutes later we were roaring through The Swamp rooting out Ju Ju.

'Seen one,' shrieked Jigger. 'This way.'

We hurtled through the bushes, burst into a clearing and stopped dead.

Opposite us, not ten metres away, was a huge Ju Ju man, his round head lowered, his eyes molten, his mouth venting grey smoke.

I smiled. With one swipe of my paw I knew I could kill him.

I advanced slowly.

Then suddenly he turned and ran back into the dark forest. We raced after him, my fangs out, Jigger's hooves pounding beside me. Mile after mile we chased him till exhausted he stopped and turned.

We faced each other.

He was breathing heavily, small chuckles of flame spurting from between his ashy lips.

We could hear air hissing in his throat.

Then he lowered his head and tilted it to one side. The lids were half-closed over the melting eyes, the mouth lolled open, red sparks cracking and lighting up its dark interior.

Then he charged.

I remember the burning eyes and the scorch of his hands at my throat.

I think we fought for hours.

Jigger said later that I went wild.

I came round hours after with Jigger chucking water over my face. 'Skeffin Ju Ju,' he said. 'You had me worried there, Lee.'

I staggered to my feet. 'You're right. Ju Ju got me,' I said. 'Nearly killed me.'

'Mushrooms got you,' said Jig. 'What happened?'

I stared at him. 'What do you mean, what happened? You were there. We killed a Ju Ju, a giant one. Tore him apart.'

Jigger laughed. 'Not me, mate. I was in a blue balloon. Been to China and back, me.'

Only later, when Dad came looking for me, after I said I'd fallen asleep and when I was back in bed and the stars were blinking, did I wonder if Jigger had actually drunk the goolie stuff or just let it dribble down his chin. Why else would he tell lies about being on some balloon when he knew for sure he and I were fighting it out, hand to hand, with a monster Ju Ju?

That night I asked God to keep the house safe from Ju Ju men. Keep Mum and Dad safe. Me safe and even Skinny B.

No one really knows what happens at night, out there in the jungles and the swamps and the forests. I began to wonder if the Ju Ju would seek revenge for their lost mate. The one I'd killed. A life for a life, that was the law of the jungle.

For ages after this I feared the Ju Ju might come and take me at night, catch me unawares. And whenever I heard the wind whispering outside my window I knew it was the Ju Ju trying to get in.

Then I'd jab the light on and thank God.

And when I woke and found I was still there in the morning, I'd thank God again.

That's what happens if you become a Ju Ju junkie like Jig and I did that summer.

2

Assault, The Feck and Alison Libidowicz

Once we were at secondary it wasn't the same with me and Jigger. We still went down The Swamp at weekends and stuff. Now and again we hunted rhino, riding our elephants through the high grasses of the Borneo swamplands. Occasionally we knocked off a few Ju Ju, but most of the time we scorched about on bikes or played Tiger Bait with some of the younger kids from Saint Joseph's.

'Look, Dad,' I said one day, 'I need a new bike.'
  'What's wrong with the old one?'
  'Just that. It's old.'
  'So? Still works, doesn't it?'
  'So did your old Volvo.' Dad had just bought a new Ford.
  'Watch yer lip, Lee.'
  'But, Dad, the brakes are knackered, the saddle kills yer bum and half the cogs have stripped their teeth. All the kids in my form have got these off-roaders with shock-soak suspension, kiss-hiss pneumatics and stuff.'
  'I don't care if they've got booster rockets and skid-pan brakes, the answer's no. N. O.'

I tried Mum. I really was tired of riding twosomes with junk wheelers like Jigger.

'You know that dangerous old bike of mine . . .'

She listened as I laid it on about how it was a hazard looking for an accident. 'I'm not safe on it, Mum,' I said, frowning and looking responsible.

'If you wore a helmet like I keep saying,' she said.

I knew that was NO in capitals.

'I bet if Skinny asked she'd get a cutie cutie horse with little pink ribbons.'

Mum hard-looked me.

That night I heard them arguing, so I crept down and listened at the bottom of the stairs.

Dad seemed to have changed his tune.

'And what happens when a car hits him or it gets stolen? All that money!' Mum was saying.

'Why should it?' said Dad. 'And, anyway, these modern machines have got anti-skid tyres.'

I smiled.

'It's not anti-accident though, is it?'

'Nothing is,' said Dad. 'That's impossible. Anyway, the boy needs a good bike. Give him some street cred.'

'Street cred? He doesn't want street cred. He wants common sense.'

Next night they were back arguing and I was ear up to the door again.

Dad was saying I needed some top billing. Skinny getting all the spotlight wasn't good for me.

Good move, Dad. Make Mum feel guilty. Get me the bike as compo.

'If he feels we're ignoring him,' Dad was saying, 'he might go off the rails and run after the wrong sort of attention.'

Wrong sort of attention?

Mum was all ears. What did that mean? Wrong sort of attention?

Bad move, Dad.

'Well!' He hesitated. 'You know . . . girls. That sort of thing. The slappers that hang around Gants.'

'They're not all slappers, as you call them,' said Mum. 'And, anyway, what's wrong with girls? It's bound to happen sooner or later. He's old enough, isn't he?'

Yeah, yeah. I nodded like I was milkshaking my brain.

'Well, he'd improve his chances with a new bike.'

'Girls aren't interested in bikes,' said Mum.

'The right sort are.'

'The right sort?' said Mum, her voice rising. 'Well, the sort that go after bikes dress in leathers and wear studs in their noses.'

'And what's wrong with studs and leather?' said Dad.

I groaned. I could see my new bike disappearing in a Mum-versus-Dad mud splash.

'What's wrong with them? I'll tell you what's wrong with them. People like that have the morals of alley cats and live on that Feck estate.' Mum was worked up now. 'I'm not having any son of mine,' she snapped, 'going out with someone with studs in their nose. It's not healthy for a start. It's disgusting.'

Then followed a long silence. I knew Dad was letting things cool down.

I thought of Alison. She had a stud in her nose, but it was only small. Some of them looked like pop-gun rivets. Not hers. It was more like a jewel; a silver asterisk, a distant star.

Was she a 'right sort' of girl? According to Jigger there were only two sorts: yesses and noes, tarts and pigtails. But he's a Feck brain. Alison had class. She was the right sort through and through. Not for my mum, maybe. But she'd change once she'd met Alison and seen just how right she was.

Then, a voice behind me said, 'What you doing?'

'Never you mind, Skinny.'

'I'll tell if you don't say,' she said. 'You were listening, weren't you? It's rude to listen into other people's private conversations.'

'Get lost, Skinny. Go back to bed.' I really wanted to see if Mum and Dad would get back to bike business.

'I'll scream,' said Skinny, 'if you don't tell.'

'I'm going to get a new bike.'

'Why?'

'Cos I am, that's what.'

'Well, if you get one, I'm going to have one as well.'

'Look!' I turned to Skinny. She was frowning and clutching Rabbit to her chest. 'If you don't shut up they'll hear us.'

'I don't care,' she said. 'I'm going to scream anyway.'

'You're just jealous about my bike, you are.'

Skinny shook her head and then opened her mouth.

I clamped a hand over half her face.

'OK. OK,' I hissed. 'Just wait a bit. Then I'll take you in. I'll say you had a bad dream.' This was one of Skinny's scams. Pretend bad dreams so she could snuggle up on the sofa and watch adult telly.

She agreed.

I withdrew my hand.

'Tell them it was a nightmare,' she said. 'Tell them a big snake tried to eat me up. Tell them it was those Ju Ju thingies.'

Skinny really knew how to stir it.

Suddenly Mum was speaking. 'He's got to chance his arm sometime, I suppose. Find himself.'

I smiled. Find myself? I could just see Dad's face. Find yourself? What a load of cobblers, he'd be thinking.

For him, life wasn't about finding. It was about cred. And not losing it.

'I just hope,' Mum continued, 'he keeps away from that Jigger boy. Finds himself some new friends, some-body else.'

'I dunno,' Dad said. 'Jigger's OK. Lad's a bit rough but he can hold his corner. That's what Lee's gotta learn. Fight his own corner. No one else will do it for him. Real kids kick ass.'

'No need to be coarse,' said Mum.

As for that Jigger boy, he stank, she said, of chip fat and she wasn't having that in her house.

No surprise there. Our house has shop-window rooms. No mess. Like everything's arranged. I suppose you could say that's where my mum's 'found herself' –

reflected in the shining brass stuff and the ping-clean surfaces all over.

There was another pause. 'If he rides it outside I want him wearing a helmet,' she said.

Thanks, Mum! Thanks a million. Who do you think I am? Skinny B?

'Course he's going to ride it outside. What else do you do with a bike?' said Dad.

A pukey helmet!

Mum!

She was always keeping me tie-straight, a shirt-in kind of kid. A helmet! Jig would kill himself laughing.

Still, the main thing was – the bike was mine.

I pushed into the living room carrying Skinny.

'Big snake's back,' I said.

Two months later I got my Saracen Assault, an all-terrain bike. Twenty-seven gears, flexi-arm suspension, Yamuchi gear shift, clam-bite brakes, the whole works.

Ace.

Soon as Jigger saw it he wanted a try, but I said no, he'd rally and ram-wall it one. He had this old tank he called Wrecker. Weighed a ton, no suspenders, could crunch a battleship. Down The Swamp when we played Mayhem he was always doing burns with it and trying to sideswipe me. He could be a maniac, could Jigger.

'Duel to the death,' he said. 'Wrecker versus Assault.'

'Get lost,' I said.

'Mud Bath then?'

Mud Bath was where we belted down this slope in the Swamp and blasted through a patch of right squelch. Mum

20

would go mental if I came home mud up to the armpits.

Put my Assault through that? No way! It would wreck the shift.

'Ju Ju then?' he said.

'Nah.'

Jigger said he still saw them down The Swamp. Just occasionally. I think they've got inside him without him knowing. Maybe he's turning into one of them. Soon he'll disappear and join their shadow world, a soul lost for ever. All his marrow gone. A phantom.

Juju-ed.

'Yer right, Lee. Load of crap, Ju Ju,' he said.

I agreed.

But in the back of my mind too they were still there, lurking in the brain goo. I don't think I'll ever shake off the Ju Ju.

We still walked to school together, Jig and I, but he didn't call at my house now like when we were at primary. 'Your mum doesn't like me,' he said. 'She thinks I'm Feck rubbish.'

'No,' I said. 'Course she doesn't, Jig. No way.'

Thing was, Jig did seem to be getting spots and blackheads and things and often looked a bit sick. Sometimes he smelt too, like he hadn't washed, like he had dried doo doo in his kecks.

Anyway, I explained to him about how Skinny B made a career about being sick and how my mum cotton-woolled her and how she hated germs and stuff.

I told him how Skinny was conning us all playing sick when it suited her, when she wanted a new top or some other kiddie gear. I told him how they were running a right family scam the two of them – Mum dashing off down town pretending it would do Skinny good, cheer her up to have another drawer full of pink T-shirts and Pollyanna tights. And when my dad complained, I told Jig how she could slab him with one of her looks. What did he know about sick kids when he was out all hours cruising up and down Gants looking for rides?

'Kelli's the same,' said Jig. 'Right skeffin ballet shoes.'

We were standing on Gants Road looking down at The Feck estate. Jigger spat. 'You're all the same,' he said suddenly. 'You posh-uns. You think if we come from The Feck we must have something.'

I shrugged.

It wasn't just The Feck and Assault that Jigger and I didn't agree on.

There was Alison; Alison Libidowicz.

Jigger thought she was a right washboard. Nothing up front, he said.

Well, I thought, she's not that flat. She fills out her bra enough to notice. And she's OK about being flattish. It must be hard for girls like that especially when you've got slapper Garrett showing off her upsies, as Jigger calls them, like she's stuffed a pair of full-blown water wings down her top. I told Gran about Liz Garrett. She was from The Feck as well and Gran knew her. 'Like a wardrobe, that one,' she said. 'Back to the wall. All front and no drawers.'

We turned into Canterbury Way.

I knew Jigger fancied Garrett. 'A juicy tart,' he called

her. 'Got a right pair on her, that one,' he said. 'They say she's down The Shed every Friday and Saturday and she's always up for it. We should go, Lee. You and me. It'd be a right laugh. My uncle's a bouncer there. He'd get us in. What you say?'

'The Shed?'

'Yeah! You know. The club, top end of Gants.'

I knew. Dad had said. Full of pissheads and tarts. That was right off my map.

'How come she gets in? She's not old enough.'

Jigger rolled his eyes. Made out I was a right bozo. 'They want tarts, Lee. They don't care. All they want is tarts. That's what it's all about. A shed load of tarts. Anyway, when she gets slapped up she looks twenty gone.' He paused. 'And that girl you fancy, Libidotits. She's started going there. All The Feck tarts go.'

'You mean she lives on The Feck?'

Jigger nodded and then dashed across the road to join some of his scalphead mates.

Since the time Mum had sounded off about leathers and studs and stuff, I'd played it cool with Alison. Kept a distant eye on her as it were.

If Mum ever found out Ali came from The Feck, it would be goodbye, Libi, hello, lonely hearts.

Thing was, I hadn't really tried it on with Alison, asked her out or anything. So far it was all drool and dreams. She was mostly in my head right up there alongside Ju Ju and Jigger and Skinny Big Snake. Maybe that's where I should keep her.

*

Jig often disappeared from school at lunchtime and I would walk home on my own. Not that I minded.

The thing was I didn't really want Alison seeing me around with a bozo like him. I knew what she thought about brick brains. I mean, I do still like Jigger. He'll always be a mate. But not when A. Libidowicz is around he won't. And living on The Feck didn't make her a tart, whatever Jigger said. And going to The Shed place didn't either, whatever Dad said about it. No way.

We lived in Far Pastures Close, on the edge of The Feck estate, not in it, but too near for Mum's comfort, too near to Gants Lane for starters. It was OK for Dad, he'd lived there all his life; one of the Gants Lane originals. But Mum was from the other side of town and, though she was OK at first, once Skinny B was born she wanted to get right away. I think she felt Feck air would make Skinny sick, infect her, like. From then on she hadn't got a good word to say about it.

Mum and Dad used to row about 'the F place'. Dad's words. Mum said she hated the people there. Common as muck that lot, she said. Dad said she could think what she liked, it was that lot kept us going. Most of his fares were to and from The Feck. The more muck, the more brass he'd say. Mum went quiet and tight then. She wanted a front garden bigger that a tea cloth she said, big enough to grow flowers and where flowers got time to grow before they were pulled out by vandals from places like The Feck. Well, said Dad, the best flowers grow where's there's most muck. He nodded at Mum like she was his best flower, like she was too.

Row over.

I moaned to Gran about how Mum felt – after all, if Gran lived there The Feck couldn't be all bad. She sighed. 'No, but it's hard for a mum, having a frail child, Lee. You're too young to understand, but she feels bad about it; feels it's her fault. It's all too much for one person to bear, so it's good to have The Feck around to take some of the blame. That's what places like The Feck are for, Lee, to take the blame. Make it easy for someone else. Crime up, blame The Feck. Schools bad, blame The Feck. Feck's everybody's kickarse.'

Mum's included.

You get the best view of The Feck from Gants. You can see it all laid out from up there. On the edge, where Gran lived, it didn't look much different to round our Close; the houses still had gardens and fancy iron railings and criss-cross windows and lacy curtains, like tart's knickers as my dad said when Mum bought some for our front room.

But once you were right in The Feck the gardens disappeared, the houses turned grey, trees vanished. And if you wanted a kick around it was the Co-op car park or front of the lock-ups. The Feck wasn't like Far Pastures. It didn't have a park and nothing like The Swamp either. It was a right dump.

And Gants stretched all the way round it, the longest road in the neighbourhood. Dad called it The Runway because at weekends kids OD on speed and hot wheel it so fast they take off and land up in the back of an ambulance.

In the distance, you can see The Flats, big bozo blocks they are. Fawlty Towers we called them, right in the middle of The Feck. They found a dead baby in the bin there one time.

Later, I discovered there are things in The Feck far worse. Worse than Juju-ed babies and dog gobs like Garrett.

Much worse.

Like, for instance, Hoodz 5.

I didn't realize it then but they were going to turn my life upside down. Ju Ju me big time.

Them and Skaz Dutton together.

3

Skaz

Skaz isn't from round here. No one really knows where he came from. Some kids say he's a gypsy, lives in a camp somewhere. They could be right about the gypsy bit, cos Skaz is definitely a traveller. He kind of comes and goes. One minute he's there in Cropper's class, next you don't see him for a week.

He's off doing a 'bit of biz' as he calls it.

He just disappears and always comes back with a doctor's note. No one ever twigs they're forged. For a quid he'll do one for you. He got Jigger once with a right cracker. Wrote him a note saying he'd caught something called the clap and his mum went mental down at the surgery till she found out it was one of Skaz Dutton's scams. Threatened to go to the school and expose his lucky number till, according to Jigger, Skaz offered to prescribe her some little white powders of his own any time she needed.

When other kids skive off, they bozo out listening to boy band tracks on CD all day or spend the time down the shopping mall dodging the anti-bunk squad. Not Skaz. He'll be down Swanwick's Amusements doing his business – odd-job boy, rodeo-riding the dodgems, freeing up the jams, swinging from the conductor pole like a monkey, grabbing the wheel, grinning with the screaming girls and broadsiding everyone in sight, bouncing through head-ons and side-swipes.

In fact, Skaz lives in The Feck. Makes his way doing a bit of this, a bit of that. And he's one of the few kids I know not brown-baggy scared of people like Hoodz 5. Nothing scares him. It's not that he's a tank or anything. In fact he's not much bigger than me.

It's just that he looks you over sometimes, like you're not there, and you feel like you don't exist, like you've had the lights punched out of you.

Yeah, it's all in the eyes with Skaz Dutton.

Nothing blinks him. Sledge him with a jackhammer and he'd stay dead cool. Like nothing had happened. Then turn your back and he'd smack you like he was slabbing concrete.

Thing is this, that . . . well, soon as you think he's your mate he goes and shreds you behind your back, gives your life a right good kicking. A one-day mate is Skaz Dutton, the sort you'd like but daren't really have.

And that was our problem, Skaz and me. We acted like mates, wanted to be mates, but never quite made it.

We sort of first met after what happened in one of Cropper's lessons.

Cropper was our Science teacher and a right psycho. He had this funny eye. The right one. Get him mad and it went bulgy. Gobby. He'd fix you with it and you felt hypnotized, like it was casting a spell all over you. Girls were terrified of him. So, no one messed in his class, not even Skaz. Boys he called vermin, and girls, tarts, but we didn't complain. We didn't dare in case we got the Eye.

First day back Cropper asked names.

'Yours?' He pointed at Alison.

'Libidowicz.'

'Spell that.'

She did, very slowly, her head bobbing to the sound of each letter. From where I was sitting I could see the pale hairs on the back of her neck shake with every bob. When her hair was tied up like this you could see how long her neck was and how she had dead little ears. They looked like a pair of prawn crackers; the sort Dad has with his Chinese.

Cropper had moved on.

'What's yours, boy?' He pointed to a little kid we called Worm. Worm was asthmatic and sounded like he was breathing out bees most of the time.

'Come on, I haven't got all day,' snapped Cropper.

Under pressure, Worm went repetitive. He stuttered and each syllable stuck like a cod bone in his gullet. He was forever gagging on words.

'B-b-b-b-b,' he bee-d.

Cropper's eye began to bulge.

It wasn't fair, we all thought. Worm couldn't help it.

'Give me patience,' shouted Cropper. 'What are you jibbering about? Now get it out.'

'His name's Beverley, sir.'

We all turned to see who'd dared chip in to support Worm.

Cropper swung round. 'Who asked you?'

'No one, sir. It's just that when you're asthmatic words can be absolute b-b-b-bs.'

'That's enough,' snapped Cropper. His eyes narrowed. 'And just who are you?'

'Skaz.'

'Real name.'

'Skaz.'

Cropper shot up. There was silence, pin-drop loud. He liked it that way.

Out of the corner of my eye I could see Skaz sitting very still, a pencil lightly tapping his lips. He was staring at a wall chart about human evolution straight ahead of him. He looked like everybody's picture of a boy brain and not the least scare-eyed. Typical Skaz – while the rest of us are sat here like a load of battery-dead bunnies, he's there playing the IQ king.

Suddenly Cropper spoke.

'Don't mess with me, boy. This isn't a TV quiz show. Now, who are you?'

'Name's Skaz, and I live in The Feck.'

Cropper stood up and his eyes widened till the whites started to show. We knew what was going to happen. 'Kaiser' Cropper, the Fuehrer with the Whopper, was going to teach a bit of Feck vermin a lesson he wouldn't forget in a hurry.

'Come here, boy.'

Skaz walked slowly up to the front.

Cropper forced him round so he faced us and then placed his hand on Skaz's shoulder like he was being buddy.

'Now, class, what do we call someone who doesn't even know his own name?'

Silence.

'Thick,' Cropper shouted.

Slowly he ran his eye over us. Then he pointed at a kid in the first row. 'You,' he rattled. 'What do you call someone who doesn't know his own name?'

'Thick,' said the kid.

'Right.'

'And you?' he said, pointing at the next kid.

'Thick, sir.'

And so on round the class he went.

'You?'

'Thick, sir.'

'You?'

'Thick, sir.'

I watched Skaz. His face was expressionless. It was like he was blanking us all, like he was saying: 'Look at yer, you may be bum-sweating bozos, but me, I'm not going to noddy and knuckle down to a right little Hitler like Cropper.'

Thing was, anybody called Skaz thick outside he'd have lathered them. Normally no one would have dared. Now here we were all slagging him off. All of us doing the dirt on him. He'd never done me any favours but, well, that didn't mean we had to help Cropper make him eat doo doo. In fact, I suddenly realized Cropper was making us all eat doo doo. Making us do a real bozo thing splitting on a mate cos we were all wet-keck scared.

Suddenly, I froze.

Cropper was pointing at me.

'You?'

I swallowed. Hesitated.

'Lost your tongue?'

Then I saw Alison Libidowicz looking at me. Her eyes blue and beautiful.

Stuff Cropper.

'You?'

'Yes, sir.'

'Answer the question.'

'No, sir.'

Cropper's eyes popped.

Next thing I knew, I was standing beside Skaz and Cropper was shouting: 'What do we call someone who doesn't even know the question?'

'Thick,' the whole class mumbled.

'Again,' shouted Cropper.

'Thick.' It was much louder this time.

'Again.'

'Thick. Thick. Thick.'

They were shouting now, really going for it.

'Again,' ordered Cropper, his eyes bulging.

'Thick. Thick. Thick,' everyone screamed and screamed. It was like they were on the terraces and wellying the away fans.

Then the tune changed, got sharper, louder. All of a sudden it seemed as though the class had a mind of its own and didn't need Cropper any more. The roaring swelled and swelled cut through with shrill girl calls and booming with the dark drumming of desk tops and stamping feet.

I started to step back. Skaz grabbed my arm. 'Don't

move,' he said. 'Just look straight ahead. Don't let on you're scared, yer wuss.'

But I couldn't not stare, because I'd just caught sight of her – Alison Libidowicz. She was crashing her fists like she was pounding Skaz and me to pulp. She was right there, at the front, her face flushed, white cat teeth edged round her red mouth.

I was gobsmacked. She'd gone mad. They all had. They were like animals: muzzles crimped, eyes full beamed, canines hanging ready to score flesh, razor bone.

'Look at them,' I heard Skaz sneer. 'Skeffin bozos, the lot of them.'

I nodded, too numb to speak.

Suddenly Cropper raised his hand. The class quietened instantly. Dog obedient. They were puppies in his hands.

'Sshh,' he said. 'After that bit of basic instinct let's get down to being civilized, shall we?' He pointed us back to our places.

As I walked back behind Skaz, I caught Alison's eye. She was smiling.

I was too gobbed to smile back.

I sat down.

Stuff me.

One minute she and the pack were ready to tear us to pieces, next they were smiling all over us.

What was going on?

Did she really smile?

At me?

I sat down.

Slowly my heart-thud quietened.

Or was it Skaz she was smiling at?

I went warm and cold at the same time.

I grabbed a breath and for something to do I opened my textbook. *The Story of Life. Intermediate Level.*

I looked across at Skaz.

He was sitting there all casual-like as if he'd just got a gold star and a swank certificate. He was taking out his stuff dead slow – pen, ruler, exercise book – and arranging them on the desktop like he was laying the table. Then he folded his arms and slowly dropped his head, pretend obedient.

Cropper probably saw the whole thing as a successful bit of rodent control, thought he'd well and truly smacked down just another pair of lippy louts from The Feck but, if Cropper had got to me and the rest of us, we knew he hadn't touched Skaz, not inside. He hadn't hurt him in the head where it really matters.

'Right,' said Cropper. 'That's today's first lesson – the strong rule, the weak face the music. The crowd survives the individual. Exercise books out. Textbooks out.'

We rummaged for our gear.

I scrambled around in my bag. Got books but no pukey pen. Bag was empty. Not a sign of a pen, pencil, biro, felt tip. Nothing.

Cropper would kill me. Set the wolves on me. I could feel the sick surging.

'Hands up those who've forgotten books.'

I gulped.

Not a single hand rose.

'Hands out those who haven't got a pen.'

I closed my eyes. I was about to die.

Slowly I put my hand out.

I looked around.

I was the only one. The only one in the whole class. I swallowed hard.

Suddenly someone spoke. It was Skaz. 'It's OK, sir. I've got his pen. He lent it to me last lesson, sir. It's here.'

And before Cropper could say anything he got up, put a thick blue pen on my desk and went back to his place.

I gave him a slight nervous nod and waited for Cropper, holding my breath and hardly daring to move. If I stayed dead still he might not notice me.

He wasn't moving either. He was like some scaly predator slowly turning its head this way and that, his green eyes darting, tongue flicking and sipping the air, trying to pick up the terror of boy.

Wait any longer and my heart'll stop.

'We've wasted enough time,' he said suddenly. 'Let's start.' He pointed to the wall chart. 'This term we're studying the theory of evolution. That's all about how we changed from being apes to being men. How we grew from being wild animals to civilized human beings.' He paused. 'Though judging from today's performance here it looks like civilization is just the sheep's fleece covering the wolf beneath.' Then he murmured, 'Are you cubs or kids, I wonder?'

He came from behind his desk.

'Civilization didn't just happen overnight, it took a

long time, millions of years, in fact, before *homo sapiens* appeared on Earth. That's us, *homo sapiens*, wiseman. Once we were savages, now we have mobile phones and vacuum-packed bacon.'

Cropper looked round the class. 'The whole business of human development has not been easy. We still have people who think they're monkeys. They start off monkeys, grow up like monkeys, behave like monkeys and live like monkeys.'

He looked hard at Skaz.

'Maybe we should mount an expedition to darkest Feck,' he said, 'and see them first-hand. What do you think?' He fixed his gobby eye on Skaz.

Skaz shrugged his shoulders. He couldn't care a monkeys.

Nothing from him.

The class held its breath again.

Dutton, say something, say something, I was thinking.

Cropper moved towards Skaz's desk.

Skaz waited till he was next to him then said: 'The Feck's a monkey-free zone, sir. The only one we've got is Jungle Jim, the Big Gorilla ride at Swanwick's.'

Cropper seemed amused by this. He walked back to the front of the class.

'Well, as far as I'm concerned, Three B, you've started like monkeys but I'm going to civilize you. We're going to pack five million years of evolution into ten weeks. It's called education and it's what makes us different from the animals, right?'

Skaz nodded vigorously, chattered his teeth and giving a big grin.

'Uhhmm,' said Cropper. 'So you're going to change. That's what evolution says it's all about – change. Those who change survive, those who don't die. Simple. Get with the flow or you go to the wall, that's evolution for you. Wimps don't win. It's the law of nature. And you can't argue with that.'

He paused.

'So, how did we grow to be go-go girls and not gorillas? Well, it's all about the environment, genetics and sex. Yes, sex, boys and girls. Genetics is the strategy, sex the tactics. Sex is what stirs the genetic pot. That's how nature does it, just stirs us up. Now turn to page a hundred and fifty of *The Story of Life*. Read and summarize. Start now. The evolutionary race has begun.'

Twenty minutes later I'd finished the chapter about Darwin and fossils and heredity and stuff. I opened my exercise book, took up Skaz's biro and pressed the stud to push the ball point out. Click. Nothing. No ball point, no ink, no anything. I tapped it on the edge of the desktop as quiet as I could, because in the silence of the room even the smallest sound shouted. Skaz, the pukey thing's empty.

I shook it and squeezed hard as though juicing it would do it some good.

Then suddenly it started to whine like a mobile going off.

I stiffened.

And then it stopped, just as suddenly.

Cropper was looking around, alert. Suspicious my head down, got in with Darwin and *The Be

hoped Cropper was too full of eating kids to want to crunch another morsel.

Nothing happened. He didn't move, everyone else had heads down and I began to wonder if I'd imagined the whole thing.

I looked at the pen's fat blue barrel like you'd look at a failed firework you daren't touch. For all I knew it could be smouldering and ready to explode again.

And, as I stared at it, I saw a line of white writing printed on the casing. 'Krazy Krackers,' it read. 'Tricks and Novelties.'

Skaz had given me a krazy pen. A bozo biro. Probably nicked it from the giant gorilla at Swanwick's or one of the crap stalls they have down there.

I looked over to where he sat. Like everyone else he had his head down. It was only me in the firing line.

I just hoped Cropper wouldn't start doing a round, checking out work. If he did I'd had it.

Then I had another puke-up thought. What if he saw I wasn't writing? He'd want to know why. In my mind's eye I could see Cropper's reptile eyes on me, his tongue flicking and sniffing the air like I was a scrap of road-kill.

I shifted position so I was mostly hidden by the kid in front of me.

Time passed.

I decided that, if I was going to get Croppered, I could be cool too like Skaz. I'd show them. I'd show Alison. Skaz wasn't the only hard head around.

The blue pen sat on the desk. I didn't dare touch it. To me it ticked silently and I was sure it would go off again at any minute. I was sweating cobs.

Still ten minutes to the bell. Christmas! Was I going to give Skaz Dutton some when we got out.

I was just thinking what I was going to say when Cropper got up. He stretched and then started to walk down the aisle furthest from ours. I cursed Skaz and his joke biro. I cursed his lippy cool, Swanwick's, The Feck, the lot.

I could hear the squeak of Cropper's shoes as he approached my desk. When I judged he was nearly alongside I turned over to a fresh page of the exercise book as if I'd just filled the previous one and was thinking of what to write next. Yeah, I sat surrounded by deep thought like I was there with Mr Darwin himself, puzzling over the mysteries of Galapagos turtles.

In fact, I was sweating kecks and wondering how I could alter the evolutionary destiny of Skaz Dutton for ever.

4

Bunny Soft and Plum Bruised

Cropper passed by.

At break I looked for Skaz. I found him in the lower playground standing by the steps with a bunch of girls, one of whom was holding his hand and examining the palm like she was reading his future. Even from this distance I could tell by her long straight blonde hair it was Alison bending over and giving Skaz a chance to take a good look down her blouse.

Skaz Dutton, a right monkey.

I hurried over.

Skaz looked up, took his hand away from Alison and grinned.

'Soz, mate. Forgot it was one of them funny pens. Soz.' And he put his arm round my shoulders like we were brothers or like I'd just laid a goal on for him.

I could have put one on him, as Jigger would say but, well, he had said soz.

'You looked right scared in Cropper's class,' said Alison to me.

I frowned. Had she forgotten why I was up there in the first place?

'What'd you expect?' I said. 'While you were all wagging tails for Cropper, Skaz and I were up there facing the aggro. Right animals you turned into.'

'Yah! Come on, Lee. It's just a game. Teacher frothing.'

'It's ritual behaviour,' said Worm, hardly humming. 'Or the herd instinct, one or the other, I'm not sure.' Worm could be a right boffin.

'Ooh, ahh, hark at him,' said Garrett. 'Personally I like a bit of herd instinct.'

'Herd instinct?' asked Alison, looking at Worm. 'What's that?' She was serious. She liked to get Worm a bit of attention. She felt sorry for him. It was no fun being a wheezy wuss.

'It's where everyone behaves like a . . . where everyone behaves like everyone else.'

Skaz spat. 'Heard about the nerd instinct?' he said.

'I was only trying to be . . . you know what,' said Alison. She stuck her tongue out at Dutton. 'Not everybody's a big super hero like you.'

Skaz shrugged. 'Not everybody's got to be a nerd. Isn't that right, Matthews,' he said, turning to me. 'We start nerds, doesn't mean we gotta stay that way.'

I wasn't sure if he was implying I was or wasn't a nerd.

'Yeah,' I said. 'No, I mean.'

In the afternoon we had PE with Buzz Milburn. 'Buzz' because he looked like Buzz Lightyear. He had big shoulders and a jaw line a bucket'd be proud of. Buzz was great and he ran the Tae Kwon Do club at the community centre. Today PE was mixed baseball and I was on second base. It was Alison's turn to bat.

She stood there in her short skirt and white top, her hair tied back and the bat resting on the floor, the handle leaning against her thigh. Somehow the ball had gone missing and everyone was just hanging around.

Once Buzz had it back, he lobbed Alison a doddle. She smacked it into the outfield and started to run. She was past first base before one of our side fielded and hurled the ball to me. I could easily have run her out, but instead I decided to give her a chance and deliberately fumbled so she could get home. I tossed the ball to Buzz and went back to base and stood next to Alison. She was breathing hard and a faint perfume seemed to drift off her. I gave her a wink, kind of letting her know I'd done her a favour. She scowled. 'I'd have got in anyway,' she said. 'So, no thanks for you.'

Girls!

Skaz was frowning. Buzz had made him captain and he didn't like to see his team go down. We had five mins left and but for my fumble we could be on to a winning.

We weren't and we lost.

'Soz, Skaz,' I said as we changed.

He shrugged. Did he care? 'It's only a poncy game,' he said. Then he eyed me. 'If you fancy Libidowicz you'll need to hold on to yer balls.'

I frowned.

Just what did that mean?

He winked and left.

*

I walked home with Jigger.

'What's up, Jig?' I said.

He shrugged. His mum was back ill and he had to do the Co-op shop.

'Chicken clucking nuggets again.'

'Oh!'

My mum wouldn't let nuggets in the house. 'Riddled with chemicals and hormones,' she said. If I didn't know Mum would go mental I'd have invited Jig home for tea.

'You know those nugget things are full of chemicals, don't you?' I said.

He stopped and scowled at me. 'Yeah. So?'

'So, they're bad for you.'

'Oh, you a food expert, suddenly?'

'No. You?'

'No.'

'Well then.'

We walked on in silence. You can't talk to some people.

We had come to Pratchetts Hill. This was where Jigger went down into The Feck and I went up to Far Pastures.

Suddenly he grabbed my arm. 'Look.'

He was pointing across the road to where a group of girls had gathered. One of them was Alison.

Had she seen us? I needed to dump Jigger.

'Gotta go,' I said suddenly. 'Got to get home for Skinny.'

I turned but I'd hardly moved a step when I heard a voice shouting across the road. 'Gonna drop yer balls for me, Matthews?'

It was gobmouth Garrett. Slag! And behind her was Skaz Dutton, laughing all over his face.

They were all laughing. Hee haw, donkey jawing all of them. Reminded me of Cropper's class that morning.

At first, I just stood there staring.

A right prat.

What was so funny?

Then I gave Garrett the finger.

She gave me two. 'Go home to mummy.'

'Slag!'

Everyone went 'Ooohhh!' Shock horror time.

Cars whizzed past.

Garrett tried to cross the road but was pulled back before she was road kill.

Shame!

'Up yours, Matthews!' Garrett again.

Then I noticed Alison standing to one side licking a lolly. She waved it at me like a wagging finger, like she was warning me or something. Then she gave it a long slow lick. Like she was sort of teasing, like she was saying I've got it and you haven't.

I watched her bright-orange tongue slide back into her mouth.

Then she turned and joined arms with Garrett and the others and a line of them went swinging off, chanting down the road into The Feck.

Watch your tongue, Ali. Get frostbite that way.

By now Jigger had started down the hill. I watched him. He had his cap reversed, head down, the strap of his backpack hanging loose like a bartender's braces, as my dad would have said.

*

Just before you turn into our road there's this massive hoarding. It's like you get in a wide-screen cinema. Today it was showing a field of golden corn and this couple were running through it, hair flying and laughing as they came rushing towards Far Pastures.

I stopped and looked at the woman. Same hair as Alison, blonde and free. Her mouth was laughing and her lips were orangey from the falling sun, just like Alison's from lolly licking. She had this floating dress and I felt the guy was trying to catch her and that every time he got near she slipped away. I knew he'd never get her. Not unless she wanted him to. And she didn't. She was having too much fun running.

That could be me and Alison, I thought. The grasses hushing aside for us as we run, the breeze sifting her golden hair, the sunlight, evening-soft, haloeing us both.

I turned into our road.

Suddenly I could see Skaz Dutton's laughing face in my mind's eye, see him standing behind Garrett. The two of them together. And then I remembered his crack in Buzz's PE class about Alison and dropping balls.

Garret had said the same thing just now.

Something very cold began stirring in my stomach.

I knew it. Dutton and Garrett had been gobbing together about me. That's what they were all laughing about back at Pratchetts. The more I thought about it the more I knew I was right. I remembered them leaving the changing rooms together, cracking on and giving me the look. Skaz was probably mad at me fumbling and losing the game and Garrett was always gobbing someone.

45

I hadn't thought anything about it then.

I did now.

I could see them together giggling and sniggling. The slag pack. All of them shredding me. Behind my back. Alison probably heard it all. She goes with that crowd – Garrett, The Pole, tall and thin as pencil lead, and that little kid, Suzie something, the one they all call Mouse.

Suddenly my face felt dead warm, cheeks, forehead itchy hot.

I closed my eyes.

What a bozo!

She probably thought I was a right loser, Alison.

Skaz Dutton again!

He'd given me heart stop with that prankster pen in Cropper's class.

Now he was shredding me with Alison Libidowicz.

But Alison wouldn't gob me. She's not the sort. Perhaps that's why she was waving the lolly, trying to say it was OK with her, like it wasn't her idea, that she really quite liked me, that she didn't think I was a loser at all.

Ahead, I could see Dad's taxi parked in the road. 'Fight your corner,' he had said.

OK, Dad. OK, Skaz. OK, Alison.

Gotta show you I'm not a serial nerd, a bozo like Jigger.

Jigger.

Well, at least he was a mate you could rely on. He wouldn't ditch you. He'd been bozo-ed by his dad and by his mum, but at least he didn't shred you behind your back.

Soon as I kick open the back door, Mum's in the kitchen shushing me like mad. The Big Hush is on. Skinny's feeling tired. It's tiptoe time.

She's in bed already and if she's up to school tomorrow I'm going to have to take her, see she's OK.

Well, kiss my kecks, can't she find her own way? What if I bump into Garrett and her mob? I'll look a right pretty. I can see them all, line of girls, Alison at the end, arms linked, dancing down Gants to the tune of ''Ere we go, 'ere we go'. Except it won't be ''Ere we go, 'ere we go'. It'll be: 'Nanny Lee, nanny Lee, nanny Lee. Where's yer nappy, where's yer nappy, where's yer nappy?'

Next thing, Mum has me in the front room, slippers on, doing the homework shift. Table's set: coke, biscuit, dictionary. I feel like Sammy the hamster.

I sit down and stare at the clock purring quietly on the mantelpiece. I try and see if the minute hand is moving.

No sign. Time's stopped. No more tomorrows.

I open an exercise book. It's Geography. We've got to draw a map of our area, show what it's like, the good as well as the bad. I'd asked Miss Bunce what she meant, 'good' and 'bad'. She said in the old days if people didn't like a place they filled the map with monsters and giants and things. Good, I thought. I'll fill The Feck with witches like Garrett and draw it all black and smoky like

47

Hell. And in The Swamp I'll put the Ju Ju men, only this time I'll show them up to their waists in mud so they can't escape.

And I'll put our house in, big as a mansion, with Skinny asleep, Dad's taxi, Mum's flowers and me on Assault.

In the sky, like an angel, I'll put Alison. I'll give her black hair so no one will know it's her.

Then I realize this isn't a map of where I live, our neighbourhood. It's a map of what's in my head. It's a map of me, my life. How I feel. How I see things.

Mum comes in. Wants to know why I'm doing Art homework. I explain it's for Miss Bunce. It's a map of our area where we live.

Mum wants to know where the roads are and the buildings like the primary school round the back where she works.

I tell her I've got to make the map from memory and I've got to include how I feel about different places around here.

'Well, that's not much of a map. What's the point if it doesn't get you from A to B?'

I shrug.

'It's more like a map of me,' I say.

Mum frowns. 'What's the use of that?'

She walks round the table. 'What you should be doing, Lee, is reading more, not doodling. Reading builds up your vocabulary. I don't want you like one of those kids from The Feck.'

Yes, Mum.

'Books are your best chance.'

Sure, Mum. Get your head in a book at school and they think you're a swot, snobbing everyone.

I think about Jigger. I think I'll draw him in riding Wrecker, smashing through The Feck, the unstoppable Ju Ju slayer, his tattooed skin lid shining through the smoky debris.

On my way up to bed I sneak up to Skinny's door and edge it open.

'You OK, Skinny?'

No reply.

I look in. Her little pink Dumbo bedside lamp is glowing.

She's asleep but she's squirming about like she's trying to escape from the bedclothes. Occasionally her arm flops up and down on the pillow like she's trying to squash it out of the way because it's stopping her getting free.

I back out.

I'm just wondering whether to get Mum when she comes up the stairs behind me.

'What are you doing, Lee? Come on out. I don't want her disturbed.'

She puts her head round Skinny's door.

'Now look what you've done. She's awake.'

I can hear Skinny mewing.

She's hot and she wants some water and I'm in the way.

Typical. You try and help and it's no thanks, Lee, goodnight and go to bed.

*

I decide to redraw my map. I'll put me in the dog kennel, Skinny in The Swamp with the Ju Ju, and Mum on the roof with a tall black hat and a broom.

Next morning I'm back-up team, big brother, ready to baby-walk Skinny to school. Now I'm in Year 9 things are different, I'm told. I've got to start growing up, according to Mum. Start being a big person. I've worked out that this means doing things adults don't like doing themselves. Like walking seven-year-olds to school.

Basically I'm just a stand-in adult. Bit of a kickarse really.

'Nursey, me,' I said to Jigger, first time I took Skinny. 'Everyone'll think I'm a right blouse if they see me walking her down Gants.'

'Skeffin nightmare!' said Jig. He knew. For years he'd been handholding his little sister, Kelli, all the way to Gants Road Primary. 'Rather take a dog for a walk,' he said.

This particular morning Skinny was loading up. Yellow plastic lunch box, panda back pack, blue allsorts case, goodie bag with seeds and nuts for Harry the class hamster and the bird table, stuff for Harvest Festival, and her pink petal umbrella. One-girl luggage train was Skinny B. The car-boot kid.

'Help her,' said Mum. 'Come on. And remember she's not one of your mates. She's your little sister and needs proper looking after.'

We walked down Canterbury to avoid Gants, me with Skinny's Harvest bag and Harry's fodder.

Skinny held on tight; on to my pinkie.

Stop her toppling over.

'You don't like holding hands,' she said.

I said nothing. I was keeping an eye out for Garrett or Skaz or Alison and walking close to the wall.

Suddenly Skinny stopped and pulled her hand away.

'What's up?'

'You don't like me, do you?' she said.

'Course I do, Skinny. Now come on.'

'No you don't. If someone likes you, really likes you, you can tell. They hold your hand nice and bunny soft.'

I shrugged. Bunny soft? Was she serious?

She didn't move. 'And don't call me that stupid name. You wouldn't say it if Mum was here.'

'Well, she's not, so move it.'

'Sharn't.'

I hard-stared her. She stared back. No blink. Not for ages. Skinny could do that. She toughs you out. You have to blink to escape.

I blinked.

Next thing she'd be crying. She could turn tears on any time. I didn't want her bawling in the street and everybody gawping at us.

'I feel tired,' she said suddenly. 'I'm going home.'

'No you're not,' I said.

If I had to walk her back I'd be late for registration and Cropper would have me out front looking like a right bozo. That was the last thing I needed.

I grabbed Skinny's arm and pulled her.

51

'That hurts. Get off.'

'Just move it.' I gave her another tug.

'Hurts!' She dropped her umbrella and lunch box and they clattered about on the pavement. 'I'll tell Mum,' she said, holding her arm like she'd taken a Ju Ju hit. 'I'm going to tell. You hurt me and you're a bully. And I'll tell at school.'

I let her go.

'OK. Please. Come on, B. You're going to make me late. Please.'

She hung her head down like she was a soft toy short on stuffing.

'Look, I'll carry all your stuff if you want.'

Just then someone came racing round the corner and nearly sideswiped us both. It was Jigger.

'Soz, mate.'

Evidently, some kids from The Feck had hot-wheeled a car the night before and rallied it through the Co-op's front window. Jigger was doing action replay.

'Glass everywhere,' he said. 'Ace.'

I turned to Skinny B.

She'd gone!

There was just her lunch box and umbrella still spilled on the pavement.

'Hell, Jigger! What's she done?'

'Who?'

Thud! Thud!

Just my heart head-banging to get out. Any time now I could hear the squeal of tyres, the sick bang of little girl hitting tarmac, blood and squelch.

Mum would kill me.

Oh, no, no, no, no.

It was Jigger caught her and brought her back.

'What'd you do that for?' I shouted.

She backed away. 'I want to go home.'

'Well, you can't.' I took hold of her shoulders. My heart was still bungeeing about a bit. 'You could have got yourself killed and then where would you be?'

'Dead,' she said.

I stared at her.

She looked down.

'I'll be good if you hold my hand,' she said quietly. She raised her arm, hand dangling, like I was supposed to kiss it or something like they do if you're the queen. 'Bunny soft, remember,' she said. 'Bunny soft.'

Jigger heard her and started hooting.

'Bunny soft! Bunny soft!'

Shut it, Jigger.

I grabbed the hand.

He was still chanting and hopping about after we dropped Skinny off and raced back to school. 'Bunny soft. Bunny soft. Bunny soft.'

That's what happens when you knock around with bozos.

That evening when I got home from school, I got a double earful.

'You do this?' said Mum as I walked in the kitchen.

Skinny was sitting on a stool with just her kecks and white vest on and Mum was holding her arm up and pointing.

'This?' she repeated.

I stared at two dark marks on her skin.

'No. What are they?'

'Bruises, Lee. She says you've been hitting her.'

'No way,' I said.

Skinny B was nodding.

'Well, these bruises say you have.' Mum came round the table and I tried to back off but too late. She got me by both shoulders. 'She says you grabbed her and she dropped her lunch box and you pushed and pulled her all the way to school. Now is that true? Did you grab her?'

'Well . . . I . . .'

She started shaking me. 'How dare you? Look what you've done. She's only a kid. She's your sister. What were you thinking of?'

'She just stopped,' I said. 'Wanted to come home. Wouldn't move.'

'That's no reason to drag her about like a sack of potatoes. If she wanted to come home then you should have brought her home.'

'But she was making me late for school.'

'You're so stupid and thoughtless, Lee. You know she's not been well lately.'

She let go my shoulders and glared at me, shaking her head. 'Sometimes, Lee, I don't believe you're real.'

I could see she was trembling.

'She's sick, Lee. Don't you understand? When are you going to start growing up and get it into that thick head of yours. She's sick.'

Behind, I could see Skinny nodding.

Then I blew it.

'No she's not,' I shouted. 'She's play-sick.' I edged away towards the door. 'And I'm not thick. It's everybody round her who's thick. Can't you see she's having you on, pretending half the time.'

'You call this pretending,' Mum shouted back pointing again to Skinny's bruises. 'Now get to your room. Wait till your father comes home and don't show your face down here until he does.'

I slammed the door, stormed upstairs and sat hunched on my bed, staring at the floor.

I didn't grab her that hard. Probably one of her teachers did it.

I looked out of the window towards The Swamp. Get the Ju Ju to chew, chew Skinny. They wouldn't be interested, not in skin and bone. They like plump children.

Why am I always the kickarse round here?

Dad was so late in, we were all in bed.

I lay awake a long time.

He'd kill me.

I sweated hot. I sweated cold.

Lather me.

Maybe Skinny wasn't just conning us. Maybe she was sort of delicate. Maybe she had plum flesh and bruised dead easy.

Maybe it ran in the family.
Maybe I bruised easy.
Come morning I was going to find out.
One way or another.

5

Tae Kwon Doo Doo

Next thing, I was being shaken awake.

It was Dad.

'You. Out.'

He was unshaved. Looked hard, cop-mean.

'What's this your mum tells me? You hit Skinny?'

'No way,' I mumbled.

'You dragged her down the street, admit it.'

'I never, Dad, honest.' I tried to pull away but he had me by the arm, clam tight.

'Well, we'll soon prove it.'

He dragged me on to the landing and down the stairs.

Skinny was sitting in the kitchen, mouth full of Krispies. She gave me a watch-out-you've-had-it-and-serves-you-right sort of look.

Dad rolled up her jama sleeve.

I stared at her arm. Just above the elbow, looking like smudges, were these four purple marks.

Bruises big time.

Faint yellows haloed each one. They looked like the pansies Mum grew in her window box, only blurred.

I shook my head. 'That's not right,' I said.

'Too bloody right it's not right,' said Dad.

'No, listen, Dad,' I said, trying to break out of his grip. 'Last night there were only two.'

'What do you mean?'

Skinny rolled up her other sleeve. Held up her thin arm.

She had bruises there also.

Two.

'You mean those?' said Dad, swinging me round to face him. 'That's more of your handiwork, that.'

On both arms? What was going on?

Dad grabbed my hand, forced the fingers apart and stretched them round Skinny's arm till they matched the marks.

As soon as I touched her, Skinny pulled her arm away.

'Ow,' she said slowly, like a cat does sometimes.

'Christ, Lee. What were you trying to do?'

I was gobsmacked. I'd only grabbed the one arm. I was sure. I couldn't have done both. No way.

I tried to explain. 'Tell, B,' I said, frowning at Skinny. 'I didn't drag you down the road, did I? I didn't shake you about. Not to hurt you.'

She scowled.

'No, but you frightened me. I'm not big like you. I was tired. I didn't want to go to school. And you made me.'

I looked at Dad.

'Mum said I had to take her,' I said.

He wasn't sure now.

'Maybe someone's hitting her in the playground. Or one of the teachers,' I said.

'Don't be stupid.' Dad's eyes were wide and angry. 'And don't try and blame someone else.' He rested his fist against my chest. 'Don't you ever, ever lay a finger on her again.' He pushed me against the kitchen door. 'Or I'll knock the living daylight out of you. Do you hear me?'

I nodded.

A lot.

Slowly he withdrew his hand and uncurled the fingers.

I grabbed a bowl of cereal, backed out and scrambled upstairs.

I sat on the edge of the bed, the spoon dithering in my unsteady hand, the milk slopping on my chin.

I couldn't understand it. Both arms? It just didn't make sense.

I looked out of my window and over our back garden. At the end was a fence and a mass of bushes and the path that went all the way round the rim of The Swamp.

Maybe the Ju Ju had got Skinny after all. Tried to drag her out of her dreams and rush her down into the lair of their evil ruler.

Then I remembered the map. I'd put Skinny in The Swamp. Got her in real trouble. I had to get her out.

I grabbed my rucksack. Found the Geog homework, found my eraser. I rubbed her out of The Swamp and drew her very carefully lying fast asleep in bed.

Not a bruise in sight.

And I put Mum back in the garden.

Mum didn't really get it either.

She was going in with Skinny to see if the school knew anything.

59

'Maybe it's just one of those things,' I said as I picked up my rucksack.

She gave me that dead-dog look of hers like she still had a bit of left-over anger, like I was still the family kickarse.

After school today it's Gran's for tea then Tae Kwon Do with Buzz in the Gants Lane Community Centre. Alison'll be there. I hope. Buzz says she's a natural at TKD. He says she's got ki, in spades. Ki is spirit. It lives in the deep well of self, says Buzz.

Yes, Buzz.

But he's right. About Alison. She always looks ace with her hair tied up, bouncing on her feet, ready to do her moves: *leaping salmon, tail of the tiger*. She's a green belt. Green because she's a fresh shoot emerging, opening to the air ready to blossom, says Buzz. Me, I'm still a yellow, a seed, not yet ready to surface, he says, but getting there.

Suzie, the kid they call Mouse, was talking about Alison giving up TKD.

Can't be.

Could be.

Because Mouse is one of Alison's best mates. She should know. She comes from The Feck too. Mouse has a face like a kitten and dead small. She has curved-up lips, a thumb nose and green eyes that go all whisker wrinkles when she laughs. She's not bad when you look hard. Not sure she's my type. She does her hair in plaits that criss-cross over the top of her head. Sort of old-fashioned little girl look.

She makes me think of something in a pop-up book. All you have to do is pull a pigtail and she'll unfold into a princess or swan or something.

We were in the library.

'Why's Alison giving up?' I whispered. 'Tell me.'

'Well, lick my lolly. How do I know? Ask her yourself,' said Mouse. She wrinkled her nose at me like she'd spit me one in the eye if I'd said get lost.

They're all the same that lot, Alison's lot – Mouse, Garrett, The Pole. Stick together, back you off. Right secret society girls can be.

As I wandered home, I thought if this really was Ali's last time I had to be there. Had to be. Then I thought: she couldn't give up TKD, it was the path to enlightenment, the way to all knowledge, Buzz said. You couldn't just jack it in like that, not the path, not enlightenment.

When I got to Gran's she was in the kitchen.

'Eggs, beans, chips,' she said. 'No arguing.'

I asked if she heard anything about Skinny B.

No answer.

She plonked the plate down in front of me. I said nothing. When Gran rattled the crockery you kept your head down.

She began making herself a cup of tea.

'Waste of time this life. Trust us to have the bad-luck genie sitting on our backs.'

I forked up some beans.

'You OK, Gran?' She looked kind of tired bent over the cooker.

'Yep.' She straightened up and turned to face me. 'You'd better get praying, Lee,' she said, banging the pot on the table so the lid bounced. 'Because God can be right forgetful of little uns. And he needs reminding of his duty.'

I knew she was thinking of Skinny B.

'What the school say?'

Gran shrugged. 'Nothing much. But I think something's going on.'

I can't say I was much into praying, even though Gran was keen. It was OK for her. She went to church. Don't get me wrong. I used to be OK praying – to Jesus at primary. According to Miss Toker, our class teacher, he was one who sorted out lepers; cured them.

Leprosy appealed to Jigger. The idea of skin and fingers falling off cracked him up. He wanted to give the Ju Ju a dose of it, kill them slowly.

Waste of time, I told him.

They always come back.

Then, sometime when I was growing up, Jesus took off and, while my back was turned, changed into God. Jesus was like a mate. If he turned up in the playground he'd be playing footie before you could say Man U. I couldn't see God doing that sort of thing. He was like an absent dad who turned up at weekends to check we were OK. Whenever he was around we didn't really know what to say. Nor did he. So we gave up talking. Just sort of pretended he wasn't there.

As Jigger said, for somebody who was supposed to be all over, it was really hard to spot him about.

Yeah, I said, but if you blank someone for years you can't expect them to stick around, do you favours.

It's like with Jigger's old man.

According to what Jigger says now, his dad calls and takes him to McDonald's, then they walk in the park, then he goes home. They get to Gants and he goes one way, his dad the other.

That's how it is with God and me. He's gone one way. I've gone another.

Gran is staring into space.

I prong another chip.

I suddenly remember what Cropper said about us once being monkeys. I suppose back then God was a big monkey – Jungle Jim himself, The Big Monkey.

'It's genes that really decide if we survive, not God,' I said to Gran. She gave me one of her looks. 'Cropper says,' I said quickly.

She frowned. 'Well, go to my back door! And who's this Cropper thinks he knows everything?'

'My Science teacher.'

'Well, he can keep this gene stuff,' she snapped. 'In my book it's God decides and he'd better pull his finger out for Bea and quick.' She stirred her tea. 'Yer poor mum.'

I suddenly noticed the time. Hey, I was going to be late for the bus.

'Slow down, Lee,' Gran said. 'That's a fork not a shovel. What's the hurry?'

'TKD tonight.'

'You got plenty of time.'

She sounded disappointed and I panicked for a sec wondering if she was going to ask me to stay. Mum said Gran never got lonely because she had the bingo and the church and Tig, her Jack Russell.

Didn't sound much to me. I'd be lonely if all I had was Two Fat Ladies, Hymns of Praise and a dopey dog like Tig.

'Don't know what you see in that stuff,' she said, dead grumpy. 'Kicking and violence. I'm surprised you don't do yourself an injury. Does that Jigger kid still go with you?'

I shook my head.

TKD had been a shock to Jig. Buzz told him it was about your life's journey from innocence to understanding.

Jigger thought it was about kicking the hell out of each other.

After just one session, he wanted to be punching out walls with his fist and flying through the air like Bruce Lee on a double dose of E. Thirty minutes of bone opening and of *leaping salmon* stretches, he'd had enough. 'Tae Kwon doo doo,' he said. 'Pukey PE in pyjamas.'

'Watch out for that one,' said Gran. 'He's getting into bad company. Load of riff-raff in The Feck, gangs and stuff. You keep out of it, Lee.'

'Course.'

'No, I mean it. I know you. Open yer gob before yer eyes, you do. Just keep out of trouble, you hear.'

I nodded, wondering why Gran was all of a sudden sounding warnings.

'I know what goes on round here, believe me.'

I kept quiet.

She pointed to her sideboard. On one of the shelves was the photo of me getting my yellow belt.

'Should have been a proper prize,' she said, 'like a silver cup or shield like you get for swimming and gymnastics and things.'

I could see she was getting into a bit of a strop, so I tried to explain. 'You see, Gran, Tae Kwon Do trains the mind and the body,' I said. 'It's a way of life. It's not about prizes and winning things and kicking yer opponent's head in.' That's what Buzz told us first lesson.

'You are now entering the way,' he said, 'followed by the great Korean masters of the past, the path to enlightenment and self-knowledge.'

'Self waffle, if you ask me,' said Gran.

Out in the hall, she gave me a big, quick hard hug as I left. I didn't know whether she was wanting to hurt me or hold me. It was like she was trying to squeeze something bad out of me.

She looked me hard in the face. 'It's Bea's birthday in a bit, Lee. Why don't you get her a really nice present this time.'

'I always do,' I protested.

Gran ignored that. 'She's not good right now and I know your mum would like it. And your dad. Will you do that for me? Get her a special one?'

Course, Gran, I nodded.

I ran down the path. I was probably going to miss the bus now.

I felt real peeved Gran thought I never did good pressies. It's a right headache with Skinny cos she has everything, drawers and drawers full of stuff. And she never uses most of it.

And another thing, I'm not made of money. I have to earn it and doing freebie papers for Jamil wouldn't buy monkeys peanuts.

All this because of a few pukey bruises.

I ran into the Centre car park, weaving through the cars like the waft of a tiger's tail, heart pumping and thinking of Alison Libidowicz.

The class had started.

Buzz says we should lay out our sparring gear real neat before putting it on; jacket with arms flat and folded, trousers and soft shoes. It's a ritual, he says. It shows you got respect. It's a way of preparing yourself. Putting on the gear is like putting on the new self, clean and bright, he says. That's why you have to have dead-white gear. Dead white except for the belt. Never wash the belt, says Buzz.

I tell Mum that. I tell her every time – don't wash the belt. She doesn't take a nick of notice.

I tell her it's supposed to get dirty. She looks at me like I'm mental or something. She doesn't understand dirt. To her it's like germs, it has to be washed away, till everything gleams and sparkles. Clean shirt, clean mind, she says.

But Buzz says: dirt isn't just dirt full stop. It's life. It's the mess we go through every day. If this belt is clean it means life hasn't touched you. Dirt is what life throws at you.

Life's thrown a bit at me lately, I think. Like Skaz shredding me with Alison, like Garrett bad-mouthing me, like Skinny getting sick, like Alison leaving TKD.

I pull off my shirt.

You've got to learn to handle the mess, is what Buzz says. If life doesn't leave its mark on you, you've learnt nothing, he says. So, get stuck in, he says and slaps you on your back.

I pull on my sock.

He's like that, Buzz. Comes out with this cool rap stuff. Like 'Muck maketh the man' and 'Dirt is God's thumbprint'. According to him this is what the Great Masters of the East say.

I told Mum that one day when she was ramming the washing machine with all sorts like she was stuffing a turkey. 'Dirt is God's thumbprint,' I said.

She gave me her dead-dog look.

'It's the wisdom of the East,' I said. 'Buzz says so, Mr Milburn I mean.'

'Sounds like the ignorance of the East to me. If they had more washing machines they'd change their religion quick enough, wash God out with the dirt.'

I nodded. 'True,' I said, not really knowing what Mum was about.

Then I told her: 'Mr Cropper says that dirt's an evolutionary necessity. Helps us build up resistance to disease. Otherwise humans would get too healthy and die out. And that's biology.'

'Learn what you like, Lee. You can't have too much health. One day you'll understand that, when it comes to necessities, a bar of soap's better than Mr Buzz's Eastern promise.'

I reach into the bag for my belt, draw it out.

Well, kiss my kecks! It is mum-washed and fluffy-chick yellow.

Not a speck of dirt, not a sign of life.

I reach down behind the changing bench to where the hot water pipes run. I brush my hand along one of them and draw it out, furred with dust. I stroke the belt, run it through my fingers till it is smudged and grey. I put it on and stand in front of the mirror.

I am wearing the belt of experience tied into the hard knot of life, as Buzz would say.

I thrust my right foot forward, my hands raised in the attack position. Then I turn and shoot my leg into one of the mesh partitions. A right *yop chagi*.

The whole panel rattles.

Watch out, Skaz Dutton. That could be you rattling.

6

Chucking the Whole Dobok

They were still doing the warm-up when I entered the gym and joined in, stretching my back like *a turning salmon,* as Buzz put it.

I looked around. Alison was in front of me, bending low, *sowing rice,* her blonde hair tumbling and touching the floor. *Willow weeping,* I thought. Suddenly she snapped up, twisted, caught me looking and gave a wink.

Eye of the chameleon.

Then Buzz had us in pairs doing *sogi* – stances. Me and this big kid had to do *choon bi,* the ready stance. The idea was that he started and I had to copy exactly his every move. This way I got the balance right, stayed within the lines, held the *in* and the *yo* right there. This copy kid stuff is the best way, says Buzz. You see the pattern outside you and then you take it in.

Indeed!

Thing was, the kid was bigger than me by a mile and a green belt so he knew the *sogi* in and out, you might say.

We bowed and he took up the stance. I copied, mirror

image me. Then every time I got copy perfect he'd move, throw me like he was playing a game.

'What's this about?' I said. 'I thought you knew *choo bi*.'

'*Choonbi*, man, and watch your mouth.' He looked around, saw Buzz was busy with some kid, turned on his heel and wopped me a right *chirugi* side of my head. I staggered back.

'What's that for?' I said.

'Tae Kwon Do kid keep his eyes open and his mouth shut,' he hissed. 'Or I'll break your skeffin legs.'

I took a deep breath. Time for *yo* control. I looked into his eyes. No go. They were black and unblinking. Bullet-hole eyes. I bowed low and backed away like I was leaving the presence of his imperial highness.

'Bastard,' I mouthed when I was out of *chirugi* range.

He read my lips and started forward.

Just then, Buzz called a halt.

Bullet-eyes stopped and gave me the finger. Then he sliced his hand across his throat.

Get stuffed, I thought. I got a *chirugi* too, and one day I'll Bruce Lee you. I'll land you one right up your jacksie, a reverse turning back kick with double flip and noodle. And that'll larn yer, as my dad would say. And he's a darts champ, top ockey, could bullseye you before you had time to *choo bi* or not *choo bi*.

Then I realized Buzz had Alison doing a demo. He was slowly pushing her leg forward.

'That's more like it. You're getting sloppy,' he said to her. 'Focus the mind. Find the *ki*. Feel the flow.'

As he turned away I saw her give him the finger. *Showing the fang.*

Bad sign.

'OK,' he said to the rest of us. 'Seek your space, feel the centre.'

Then he had us thrusting right feet forward doing spear fingers and shouting. 'Punching with your voice' Buzz called it. He wanted to waken the dragon of life in us, fire us up.

We punched and shouted, punched and shouted till we were exhausted.

'Stop!' shouted Buzz. 'Now you've burned out all the day's dead and dross, the mean and the mess in your lives. Out of these ashes new shoots can grow. Go, walk the way.'

'Who's that?' I asked Alison afterwards pointing to the kid in the hoodie walking ahead of us. I'd got changed dead quick after the session and waited for her by the Coke machine, ready to shove in a coin as she approached so it wouldn't look like I was hanging around for her like some bozo dog tied up outside the Co-op or something.

She shrugged. 'Seen him around. Hoodz Five probably.'

We were walking towards the bus stop.

Hoodz 5! Not good news.

'They're street scum,' she said. 'Pushers, twockers, retards. You know about them?'

'Yeah, I know. Of course, sort of.' I took a quick look behind. 'What's he doing here?'

'Sharpening his moves so he can chop a few kids probably. Why?'

'He *chirugied* me. Tried to drop me.'

'Then watch out.' She swigged her Coke. 'You must have pissed him off.'

I hadn't. I was sure.

I said nothing. She might have asked if he'd hurt me!

Alison looked me one. 'Get on the piss side of H Five, as my dad says, and you're in trouble. They do facials and not-so-nice body adjustments. They scare people. And people pay them not to scare them.'

Then I remembered what Jigger used to say about the Hoodz. They were the Feck wild life, he said, scary like lions. Scary in your head anyway. You can handle a scare like lions when they're in zoos or boxed up on telly. You only get brown baggy scared if the bars disappear and they escape from your head and come growling round your tent. Somehow I felt Hoodz were off the safari run now, out of the cage and closing in on my life.

Soon we'd reached the bus stop and I was wondering whether to follow her.

'Walk me home, if you like,' she said suddenly. 'If that's what you want.' She paused. 'Unless you'd prefer to catch your bus.'

'Oh, no, no.' I said. 'I can get a taxi.'

'Oh, who's posh,' she said.

'Soz about that baseball stunt,' I said.

'Oh, that.' And she shrugged. 'It's no big deal.'

We walked in silence. I didn't really know what to say. I was alone with Alison Libidowicz, and suddenly I didn't know what to say. How crap is that? All the times I chatted her up in my head, running through the floating wheat fields, and now in the happening world I couldn't think of a single syllable. Dumbo or what!

She strode along and every now and again I had to skip to keep up with her.

'You looked good tonight,' I said at last.

'Thanks. So you like my hair.' She seemed surprised. 'Donna at Karin's streaked it.' She smoothed it down with her hand.

A spring breeze passing through new grasses.

That's how Tae Kwon Do disciples walk though life, says the Grand Master, moving others, not marking them.

I watched her pulling at the strands as we walked.

'Well, er, no, not exactly. I mean, yes, the hair looks great. But I really meant your *sogi* looked good.'

'Oh, ta ta,' she said groaning. 'Anyway, what do I care? I'm giving it up. *Sogi,* the lot. It's getting just boring.'

Giving it up? So it was true. I panicked.

'Just cos Buzz slagged you off back there tonight it's no reason to jack it in.'

She stopped.

'Milburn's a big puffer who likes dressing up in white baggies! Anyway, there was nothing wrong with my *shogi*. He's just scared of girls.'

'No,' I said. 'No way. He's a black belt, third dan. I mean, OK, he shouldn't have slagged you in front of everybody, but –'

'Too right, he shouldn't.'

She walked on ahead.

I caught up. 'You can't give up now, Ali.'

'Yes, I can. And don't call me that. It's Alison to you.'

'OK. OK. But you just can't.'

'Can't?' She stopped and frowned at me.

'You've got to get your blue belt.'

'Who says I got to?'

'Well, it's what you do after green.'

'Well, it's not what I do,' she snapped. 'If I say it's boring, it's boring, right? And that's it. I'd rather go down The Shed Thursdays. I've had it with crappy gear and all this mumbo-jumbo about *ki* and *shin* and Buzz banging on about the way of the spirit and fish leaping. He can jump in the river with the salmon as far as I'm concerned.' She leaned towards me. I could smell the soft odour of her body; *dawn breath,* as Buzz would say.

'Got it?' She slammed the words in my face.

I nodded, gob-mouthed at her sudden anger.

She strode ahead.

She was burning with the mean from her life all right.

'But it's all about new shoots,' I called after her. 'And life. What about God's thumbprint? You can't just walk out like this.'

'Watch me,' she shouted back. Then she turned to face me, hands on hips, legs apart. The Feck *shogi.* 'You can shove it, Lee. There's more to life than poncing about in white baggies and bum belows. From now on my life's about having a good time. I ain't under anybody's thumb. And you can stuff all that new shoot crap right up your *shogi*, Lee. So bye-bye, baby.'

As she walked away, so cool, heels clicking, I felt

74

suddenly chill inside. I'd taken another *chirug*i, this time to the heart. She'd door-slammed me. She made it sound as though it was all my fault.

Why? What had I done? What was she on at me for?

I tried to call her name but nothing much came out, just a bit of a squeak, baby style.

Alison. Alison.

I wiped my hand across my mouth like it was bleeding or something.

I was just so sick. One minute I was walking her home, next I was standing like a wuss, middle of the night, slabbed.

It wasn't my fault she'd gone right off Buzz and lost her pukey *ki*.

I stood watching her fade in the dark between the nearest two street lamps and reappear for a brief bright moment in the pooling light of the next.

Then she'd stopped about fifty metres away.

I thought she was going to look to see if I was still here, if I was OK. Maybe even come back and say she didn't mean it about slagging me off and about chucking Tae Kwon Do. She was probably going to apologize, say I could walk her all the way to her house.

But she didn't.

All she did was put the bag down, yank out a bundle of stuff and throw it over the hedge into someone's front garden.

All her sparring gear, the whole *dobok*!

Before I could shout stop, she'd disappeared without even a look back.

I stood there like a bozo just shaking my head. I couldn't believe it.

Next to me was a lamp post. I gave it a right kicking. One *chirugi* after another.

She'd regret it, I told myself. I knew she would. She'd wake up in the morning mad with herself and want her gear back.

I would.

I'd arsekick myself if I'd dumped thirty quid's worth of stuff. I know girls have wobblies and impulses at times, but this was something else. Impulse without discipline is like an egg without a shell, says Buzz.

I ran down the road towards the garden.

As I walked back to the bus stop with Alison's stuff under my arm, I kept looking behind. No sign. I began to hope helplessly that she'd suddenly jump out of the dark, all smiles and we'd swing round the lamp post till the light and the swirl made us dizzy.

But she didn't and all I'd got was the image of her in the lamplight.

I sucked on that picture all the way back like a kid with a lolly.

I got off the bus at Gants and decided to go home through The Swamp instead of taking the longer way round by the road. I didn't want Mum banging on about Tae Kwon Do and stuff, not just yet. I just wasn't in the mood.

To get down to The Swamp you had to enter a ginnel, a narrow, fence-lined pathway that led into the hollow.

Once past the gardens, the path dipped down into shadow and then the deeper darkness below.

I walked to the end of the ginnel and checked for Ju Ju.

Around the rim of the hollow, strung like a huge circle of lanterns, glowed the lights of a hundred houses. One of them was mine.

In the moonlight I could just make out the dark shapes of a few unlit homes. These dark few were vacant for a reason. Once, they were the Bone Huts where Ju Ju men went to die after Jigger and I had wounded them and where they turned to dust in less than an hour.

Now is now and I entered the edge of the scrub picking my way along the winding track, past the reed beds and finally into a clearing, the heart of The Swamp.

I stood still.

There was no one around. No kids doing last-min wheelies.

Nothing was moving.

Beyond the rim, I could just hear the hum of traffic and sometimes, nearer, the hush-hushing of tyres along Gants.

Suddenly I felt chill. I pulled Alison's bundle closer to my chest. I took a deep breath.

And for the first time caught the smell of her.

I took another.

Yes.

I could see her now motionless, right foot forward, arms up, fists clenched, the perfect *choon bi*.

Hardly an hour ago she'd been wearing this very

jacket. It had pressed itself to her soft skin, wound itself round her lovely body. I hugged it to me breathing in yet again the faint perfume of her. I felt I had in my hands the last trace of her being, her *ki*.

I buried my face in the warm folds of the cloth.

Into Alison.

For some time, we swayed together, she and I, at one, under the moon.

Then I froze.

There was someone there. Watching maybe.

I jammed Alison's stuff under my arm.

Then, close by, a rustling.

I looked across the clearing. The sound stopped.

Then I saw him, staring straight at me, his eyes green in the moonlight, his ears pricked.

A fox.

Neither of us moved. Just stood, trapped in each other's stare.

Then I heard a faint squealing.

I started.

Something was wriggling in his mouth.

Rat?

Still alive?

Fox jaws tightened.

A long tail fell out of his mouth and hung limp.

I felt sick rising and bit on the back of my hand to quell the surge.

The fox turned, gave me a can't-be-arsed-with-you look and disappeared into the bushes.

I took a deep pull on the cool night air.

Then I walked carefully across the clearing to where the fox had stood.

The whole place stank of him. Fox doo doo. Old pee and sour vomit.

I stuffed Alison's jacket over my nose to stifle the stink. And the smell of her mingled with the odour of fox. Strong and animal.

I sniffed the cloth again.

Alison, but different from before. Now the smell of her was heavier. Full of body. It was sweat and scent together, sour under the sweet.

I took a few steps sideways into fresher air.

As I climbed up the path home I decided that when I got back I'd put her gear in the machine with mine, give them a double dose of softener, lavender-scented, and let them spin and hot wash together.

I'd do it as soon as I got in because she'd want her stuff for tomorrow. I knew she would.

Later, in bed, like on a fairground ride, Alison came Big Wheeling through my head. Round and round, with Skinny and Gran and the big kid with bullet-hole eyes.

I watched the moon.

It kind of slowed me down.

It was pale and sick-looking like Skinny.

I hated her being sick. It made us all bad – Dad, Mum, me, the house, everything. And it was worse if she'd been OK for some time, and then got sick.

Mum went manic.

Got the bleach out. As soon as you opened the front door you knew she'd been at it, the smell was that strong. She'd cleaned like mad. Bleached everything like it was the house's fault, like she was giving it a right chemo, like Mr Muscle was medication that might somehow rub off on Skinny and flush her clean too.

Sure, Mum! Wrap her up, wrap us all up and put us back in a germ-free box!

Except, for me, the more she scrubbed and scrubbed and the more she disinfected floors and worktops, the more the air inside was like chemicals and a poison that hung over us all.

I suppose for Mum it was something to do.

And whenever Skinny was unwell we turned the volume down on the TV and closed doors slowly. It was like the house went dead quiet too, lying there like a sick animal waiting and hardly breathing.

When I was young and it happened I was glad to get out down The Swamp with Jigger.

Now?

Well, now it's different. I just don't want the hassle. I can't help it if Skinny B's gets bad. I've got stuff to sort out too, you know. It's no joke being slagged off by slappers like Garrett behind your back. No fun blowing yer chances with a girl like Alison Libidowicz.

I glanced through the open curtains. Over The Swamp the moon floated like a hot-air balloon. A few shreds of cloud hung to it like frayed ropes, and they gave the impression that a great gas-filled bag was floating aimlessly into space and oblivion.

I thought of Alison again. It wasn't really fair of Buzz to slag her off, not so we could all hear, not in front of everyone.

I watched the moon drift.

Maybe he was testing her, see if she could take a slagging. The strong bow down to chastisement, the weak run away. That's what Buzz says, that's what the Master says.

What Alison says is: wimps bow down to slagging, the strong piss off.

I decided to iron Alison's stuff, so it was dead neat, no creases, skin-smooth.

She'd like that.

All folded, sleeves crossed.

She'd bow when I gave it to her. 'Thank you, Grey Warrior of the Northern Winds.'

'The honour is mine, Lady of the Magnolia Moonlight.'

Then I remembered what she'd said about going down The Shed. I couldn't see it myself. Lady Magnolia with Garrett gobbings and Jigger lads and loads-a-tarts.

Alison wasn't like that really.

The moon had drifted out of sight.

I knew Mum would go mental if I used her iron so I'd have leave extra early for school and go to Gran's. She had a steam iron. She wouldn't mind.

*

Gran was still in her dressing gown when she opened the back door. She wasn't too surprised. After my paper round I sometimes dropped in for a chat and a packet of crisps.

'What's wrong with your own iron?' she said.

'Steamer bust,' I said, placing Alison's trousers on the board.

'Better let me do that, Lee.'

I looked up, shook my head. I didn't want anyone else touching her stuff.

'Tae Kwon Do disciples prepare their own gear,' I said. 'It's part of the training. Doing the humble tasks of life.'

'Training? What rubbish. Look at those shoes. When did they last get a bit of humble polish?'

I shrugged and began pressing the iron along one of the legs starting from the ankle and slowly moving up towards the thigh, sensing the coarse material soften and yield under its steamy palm.

'You're better doing it on the other side in case you burn it,' said Gran.

I pulled the legs inside out. Started again.

'Thought these were yours,' said Gran, nodding at the trousers.

'Yeah,' I said.

'Then why's it got *Alison L* written here across the back?'

I looked dead gobbed.

'Must have picked them up by mistake after Tae Kwon Do.'

'Oh, in the girls' changing room, I suppose.'

'No. No way. By the Coke machine. We always have a Coke afterwards.'

'She someone you're soft on?'

'No. Me? No way.'

'So why you ironing this lot? Can't she do her own?'

'Well ... er ...'

'You are soft on her, aren't you?' She nudged me out of the way, flipped over the trousers and rammed the iron up and down them.

'I suppose.'

'She know about this?'

I shook my head.

'You're daft, you are, Lee. She'll think you're off your end washing her stuff.'

'No, she won't.'

'Well, if you ask me, you're wasting your energy chasing after some flighty little madam like a dopey servant.' Gran stopped. 'She's not a Feck girl, is she?'

'Well ... er ... just on the edge. And she's not flighty.'

'Huh, says who? She's a Feck girl, isn't she?'

'Yeah but ...'

'Thought you were holding something back.'

She ran the iron up and down. I listened to the steam shushing and gasping and wondered when she was going to start sounding off about Feck girls.

'They're not all like that Garrett,' I said.

'Well, if you ask me, you're better off doing your homework and helping your mum.'

She finished and folded the trousers and top together.

'Don't blame me if she smacks you one.'

'She won't. In Tae Kwon Do we believe in non-violence and the power of the *ki*. Alison would never hit anyone.'

Gran pulled a face. 'Grow up, Lee. She'll smack you for this. You watch. And what will your mother think? A Feck girl!'

7

Cluck Cluck

'Heard you got a belting last night, Matthews.'

I was walking down Canterbury when Skaz came alongside.

'A Hoodz Five head slap, eh!'

'Who said that then?'

'Saw it myself. Up on the roof. You lot pratting about all in yer Bruce Lee baggies.'

'What you doing on the roof?'

'Prat-watching.'

I stopped.

'Yeah. And monkeying around above the girls' room, yer perv,' said Jigger, joining us.

Skaz grinned. 'Nice turf down there,' he said and gave me an elbow. 'Jealous, Lee. Lee a bit jealous, eh? Little Lee jealous?'

He chucked me under the chin. I pulled away.

'You stick with yer baggy boys, Lee.'

'Too right,' said Jigger, wandering off.

'You're some smart-arse, aren't you, Dutton? What do you know about the Tae Kwon Do?'

'Gnat all, Lee. So show me.'

'Eh?'

'Show me.'

'You don't just do it in the middle of the street. It's not a stunt. It's a way of life.'

'Oohh! And there was I thinking it was just posh for judo.'

'You can laugh,' I said. 'What do you know?'

Skaz went very still. Then he came right up to me face on face.

'If it was just you and me,' he said quietly, 'you wouldn't stand a chance, mate. I'd smack yer pocky face stupid before you had time to jump in yer kick boots.'

'I bet,' I said. 'Anyway, it's not just about combat. It's about inner strength. If you've got it you can do anything.'

He stopped and eyed me.

'You got it, Lee?' he said quietly. 'You really got it?'

'Yeah,' I said, not too sure, but I was fed up with Dutton trying to put one over me. 'Yeah, I got *shin*, good *shin*,' I said, looking him straight in the eye.

'*Shin*?'

'Mind.'

Suddenly he put his arm round my shoulders.

'Save it for the Hoodz boys, Lee. You'll need it then. And forget Jigger. He's a smack head.'

We walked on a bit, Skaz with his arms still round my shoulders like he was being brother and giving big-bro advice.

'Tell you what, Lee,' he was saying, 'let's check out this *shin* stuff.'

He looked round at the kids drifting towards school. 'Look at them. Losers the lot,' he said. 'It's easy when there's ten of yer. It's on yer own it counts.'

We turned down The Drive.

'You know The Water Tower, down by the railway, the big monster on stilts?'

I nodded.

'Let's bomb it,' he said. 'Tonight. Just you and me.'

'Bomb it?'

'Yeah.' He took his arm away. 'You and me.' He fisted my shoulder. 'Be there. Five-ish, after school. You'll need a load of *shin* for this one, Lee. See ya.'

And he was off, back towards Gants and away from school.

'And bring some tins,' he shouted.

'What's bombing?' I shouted back.

No answer.

Alison wasn't in for registration so I waited for everyone to leave for the first lesson and then slipped the gear into her desk. I put a note on the top. 'See you at TKD next week,' it said. And I signed it: 'Dark Warrior'.

She wasn't in Cropper's lesson either. He wanted to know if anyone had seen Libidowicz or Dutton. I said nothing. Nor did Garrett. Nobody did. We'd all had seen him, of course. On The Drive, down Gants, in The Feck. He was everywhere and nowhere.

But Alison came in later. And she threw a right wobbly with me at end of school in the classroom.

*

The bell had just gone and I was dashing out. 'What you call this?' she said, standing across the aisle and blocking my way. Some of her mates – The Pole, Mouse, Garrett, Becky Smith and a few others – had closed in round me.

She flung the jacket and trousers in my face.

'You're a sicko, you,' she said. 'Going round nicking girl's stuff.'

'I didn't nick it,' I said. 'You threw it away. I just thought –'

'Oh, yeah.' It was The Pole sneering. She was a right drink of water. 'You just thought. Only a weirdo like you'd do stuff like this.'

'I'm not a weirdo.'

'Oh, no?'

'No.'

Alison stared at me like she was sizing me up, not too sure what to say. I could see her tie was loose and the top buttons of her blouse undone.

'You've no right to interfere like this. I've told you, I decide what I do and don't do. So just leave me alone, OK? Get out of my life.'

I nodded dumbly.

At least she hadn't tried to smack me one. Wrong there, Gran, I thought.

'Yeah, yer tosser, what you staring at?' said Garrett. 'Leave her alone.'

Alison pointed to her stuff sprawled on the floor. 'I'll have that back.'

'Yeah, pick it up. She wants it back,' said Garrett. 'Before some other wanker gets hold of it.'

I reached down for the jacket and trousers, handed them over.

No one spoke.

'Let's go,' said Alison at last.

Only Garrett stayed back.

'What you want?' I said.

'It's saddos like you give girls a bad name,' she said. 'You start waving Ali's stuff around and all those tossers in Three B will think she's nothing but a tart and want a bit.'

'Like you, yer mean?'

'Yer snotty little knicker sniffer,' she shouted.

That was it. I'd had enough of Garrett and her dirty gob.

My *chirugi* caught her right across the mouth. She staggered back, hand to face, blood leaking through the fingers.

She pulled her hand away, stared at the blood.

'You ... you ... bast– You've knocked my teeth out.' She wiped her hand on her blouse and put the tips of her shaking fingers into her mouth. I could see the lip was split, the teeth glossy scarlet.

Suddenly she collapsed on to a desk, tears pouring; nose, chin and white blouse smeared with red. Then she was up and running for the door and screaming, screaming her head off.

I grabbed my bag and started to walk out, all pretend calm and trying to stop my hands from shaking.

Stuff Garrett, I had a paper round to do.

'You shouldn't go round hitting girls,' said a voice.

I stopped. It was Mouse. She was standing in the doorway.

'What?'

'You heard me,' she said. 'Girls are not for hitting, kicking, slapping, slagging off.'

'Well, she asked for it, didn't she? Garrett's a right gob mouth.'

'Even so.'

'You a mate of hers?'

She stuck her tongue out in puke mode. 'Get lost. She's a tart. You should see her down The Shed. Or hanging out with that gang lot. She's a slag queen.'

'Gang lot?' I said uneasily.

'Yeah, Hoodz Five. She goes out with one of them.'

I froze.

My throat closed. I could smell lion.

Hoodz 5!

I'd jammed one of their tarts. I could be in it up to my neck and over.

'Anyway, you can see for yourself,' said Mouse. 'Alison's having her party at The Shed.'

I stared at Mouse. 'Party?'

'Oh, right. I see,' she said. 'You've not had an invite.'

'And I'm not likely to get one now, am I?' I said. 'Not after this.' I nodded at a smear of blood on one of the desks.

'Dodgy, especially after you made Ali look stupid in front of her mates. What do you expect?'

I didn't say anything.

'She didn't mean it,' said Mouse. 'She's just a bit pissed off, that's all.'

Sure, Mouse. Wait till she hears I've just sledged one of her mates. I'll get a right shredding. Hoodz 5 first. Then Alison Libidowicz.

My life wouldn't be worth getting up for.

'Fancy her, do you?'

I didn't answer. I wasn't so sure any more. Maybe she was a bit of a slapper like Gran said. A load of trouble.

What a mess it all was now.

She was pissed off? What about *me*? I didn't need a slap down in front of her mates either.

'So you do?' she said.

'Do what?'

'Fancy her?'

'Uhhmm.'

'Thought so,' she said brightly. 'I suppose you'd like me to get you a party invite. Right?'

I hesitated.

'Well, don't say thanks or anything.'

'Thanks or anything.'

'I'll sort Ali out, you watch.' Mouse smiled. 'Now you owe me.'

Sure, Mouse. I owe lots all of a sudden.

'Look, I gotta go. Paper round. See's ya.'

'Sure,' said Mouse. 'Any time.'

All the way to Jamil's paper shop my mind was whirring. Did Alison really mean I was out of her life? Would I get an invite to her party? If I did I'd need a pressie. That put me between a pinch and a slap, as Gran says. I'd promised one for Skinny. Now one for Alison. I didn't have the money. Not for two. Not unless I did another round for Jamil or something.

Then I thought of Garrett gobbing blood. Alison would go mental. Bye-bye, party. Bye-bye, Ali.

Still, maybe Mouse could sort it.

Maybe.

I hurried. If you're late for Jamil you lose it. It was 10p for every five papers so I couldn't afford to miss out, especially now.

Then I realized.

I was supposed to meet Skaz about five.

No way could I do it for Jamil *and* do The Water Tower with Skaz Dutton.

Was I in it now!

What a shed load of *shin* I was going to need tomorrow in the playground for when he and I met up. All I got now was prat with chicken written all over it. He'd shred me for this. I knew it. I just knew it.

When I got to Checkers News shop, Jamil was waiting. He's the owner and always wears one of those Afghan hats. But he's OK is Jamil.

'Where you been, boy?'

I told him an old lady had fallen in the road and I had to help her to safety.

Jamil was happy with that. He is one of these Muslim people and they like to hear about kindness and helping. Dad said they make such a big thing of it in their religion because they get precious little of it in real life.

Yeah, Jamil was OK.

He asked me if I wanted to 'make some quid' because

the kid doing The Feck was thinking of jacking it in. The Feck, I thought. Yes, why not, I needed the money. But I didn't want to seem overeager. Jamil might pull the quid if he thought I was grabbing for it. I decided to play for sympathy. Maybe, I said to him. I'd think about it. My sister was sick, dead sick and that made it difficult.

'Dead and sick? She be real bad?' he said.

'Yeah, dying,' I said.

'Oh, Lee. Sorry too. No, no *Advertiser*.' He waved me out of the shop.

I shook my head. 'No no, Jamil,' I said. 'She could still pull through. I'll get the *Ad.* done. People rely on me.'

It was true. I'd never missed a round in two years.

'You a good kid, Lee,' he said. 'Wait there.' And he turned to the sweet display.

'What's sister name?'

'Skinny B.'

He pulled at my arm. 'Give Shinny from Jamil, do please.' And he put something in the palm of my hand. It was a pink and green packet of Refreshers. 'How old?'

'Seven.'

'Oh! Little, little girl.'

I said yes she was and it was dead kind of him about the Refreshers. He said he was sorry but if I ever wanted I could do The Feck route and get double what I earned now doing the posh side of Gants. Then, he said, I could afford to get Shinny a big, big present.

Outside, I took a deep breath. I felt dead bad. Cracking on about old ladies falling and sisters dying. Kidding people like Jamil, OK, people, wasn't really on, I know. But sometimes the path of life gets a bit rough, as Buzz would say. So what's wrong with a few little fibs ironing it smoother?

When I got home Mum was busy busy in the kitchen polishing pans and stuff like we were short of mirrors, so I knew something was up. Skinny had eaten and was in bed tired out again. I ate slow and quiet and thought of telling Mum about jam-facing Garrett in case her dad came round complaining.

Or Hoodz 5!

In the end I decided to save it and see what happened at school next day.

Dad came in late and after I'd gone to bed, I could hear them talking in the kitchen. I crept halfway down the stairs to listen.

Good news. No more bruises on Skinny.

School not much use. Mrs Worrall, the head teacher, asked a lot of questions. Wanted to know how long Skinny had been bruised. Had it happened before? Had she been to the doctor? Did she have a good relationship with her brother? Had they always been OK together?

OK? Mum had asked. What did that mean?

Dad was all for going down to the school and giving the Worrall woman a few answers of his own.

Mum tried to be calm. 'If she gets one more,' she said, 'we're straight down to Dr Manning.'

'Lee started all this, you know. He's too rough-handed that kid,' I heard Dad say. 'Let's hope she's over the worst,' he added.

Rough-handed? It just wasn't fair. It wasn't my fault.

*

Next day in Cropper's lesson Garrett was missing.

No sign of Skaz. Good!

I tried to catch Alison's eye, see if she was mad cos I'd wopped her mate but she was head down doing the worksheet on aeons and eras and fossils and stuff.

Cropper finished the lesson as usual, waving his hands about like he was Gandalf on magic moos moos.

'Remember,' he said finally. 'Modern man's been on the Earth about thirty thousand years. Compared with the age of the planet, that's less than a blink of the eye. Our average lifespan today is about eighty years. Compared with the planet's age that's about a thousandth of a second. You've been here for thirteen years. Compared with the age of the planet you don't even register on the evolutionary scale, not even a blip. In fact, on a time scale of one to a million you don't get past zero, any of you.'

Cropper grinned. He seemed dead chuffed he'd reduced everyone in the class to one big nought.

After dinner Jigger and I were in the library. Me cos I wanted to keep out of Skaz Dutton's way – he often wandered in p.m. after a morning on the market or down Swanwick's – Jigger cos he was sussing out how to nick the fines box Lu Lu the librarian kept behind the counter.

He'd got out a book thick as a brick and it lay opened on the table in front of him. He looked wrecked.

'What's up, Jig?'

'Snotty cold, mate.' And he started sneezing. Marathon stuff. And it went on so long I never heard someone

95

come up behind us till a pair of hands clamped over my eyes.

'What you doing in this sin bin? You right pair of saddos.'

I recognized Skaz Dutton's voice. His hands smelled of oil and perfume.

'Just leaving,' said Jigger.

'What's this chicken shit yer reading, Matthews? *Photography Weekly*? Yer dirty little git.'

'Look, Skaz. I couldn't make it to The Water Tower, right. Forgot I had paper round.'

'Yeah, sure, clucky.' He grinned. 'See ya in PE. Don't forget. Be there, chicken balls.'

And he left.

There was something in his voice that said 'watch out'.

We had PE last period that day. Buzz time. Dutton had obviously planned something for me and it wasn't going to be all-day freebies at Swanwick's with hot dogs and ketchup on top.

Was there anyone I hadn't screwed up with?

Double Art was first.

I was making this dog in clay, sort of tribute to Banger, once our family pet and like all our pets a bozo and a dachshund, a German sausage dog. Dad called him Banger cos his favourite was sausage and mash. Banger lasted a week. He ran under a bus. No Banger, just mash.

Which sort of explained why I was mashing the clay again. I just couldn't get the shape right. It looked more pig than dog. And 'Creep' Harris, our lechy art teacher, who looked like some deadbeat pop star from the Ice Age, straggly hair and face so wrinkled it looked like it had collapsed, wasn't interested in boys or dog sculpture. The peak of art for him was the female form, he said.

Especially the forms of all-over slags like Garrett and Millie Sumners, we all thought. He'd take a peek over them any time if they gave him the chance. But even Mill and Liz drew the line at scrawn like Harris.

The other reason I was knuckling Banger to pulp was I just couldn't focus, as Buzz used to say. Truth was I was sweating kecks waiting for PE.

I stepped back from the table to try and get a different angle on the dog lump lying there. The legs were bent under and the earless head twisted oddly. Contents: Min dog, max clay.

Harris came over.

'Supposed to be a dachshund, sir.'

He took Banger in his hands, squeezed here, twisted there, pulled a bit, pushed a bit, added a leg, pinched two ears. Born-again Banger all but barking. Freak to dog in thirty secs. Brill. Dad would be dead proud. He liked Banger.

'Ta, sir.'

'Your dog?'

I nodded. 'Got run over, sir.'

'Well, we'll biscuit-fire him. Give him that tough, live-longer look. Then you can take him home,' said Harris.

He wandered off. I watched him stop and lean over Millie Sumners.

Lech!

A sudden thump startled me.

I turned round.

On the tabletop, Banger lay squashed, his legs splayed out like he'd dropped out of the sky and landed on concrete.

Someone had fisted him flat.

I looked up.

It was Alison.

'That was for my dad,' I said.

'And that was for Liz Garrett.' She held up her fist: the red clay from Banger had coloured her knuckles.

'She was slagging me off. Deserved it.'

'No girl deserves a smack in the mouth. That's violence against women.'

'No boy deserves to be called a knicker sniffer.'

'Serves you right.' She paused. 'Is that what she said?'

I nodded.

'Are you?'

'Get lost.'

'Smacking's not very TKD, is it?' she said. 'Not exactly the Buzz way to enlightenment.'

I shook my head. She was right, of course. Buzz would brain me if he found out.

'I think you should apologize.'

'No way. After what she called me?'

Alison went silent for a moment. 'You want to come to my party?'

Sure I did.

'Then you apologize.'

'What? Really?'

'And,' she said, 'I want an extra-big pressie. OK?'

I sort of nodded.

'Good,' she said. 'Now let's manipulate the dog.'

She picked up the clay that was Banger. She was almost as good as Harris. 'Should have him walking next to no time.' She gave him a final twist. 'There, back to normal.'

She smiled. 'By the way,' she said. 'Watch out at PE. I think Dutton's going to try something.'

Then the bell rang and she was off.

Thanks, Ali.

So, I was right. Dutton was planning something. So what! I was sorted with Alison Libidowicz. That was the main news.

I dashed down the corridor towards the changing rooms.

As soon I saw the door of the boys' changing room close I knew it was Skaz time, like Ali said.

Suddenly, I heard giggling behind me and felt myself being pushed inside the room. Before I knew what was happening I was grabbed, had something shoved over my head and my jacket torn off. I kicked and squirmed, but it was no good. They mashed and mashed me and I was down to kecks in no time.

I ripped the bag off my head.

They were all standing round me in a big circle, most of the class, squawking and jumping up and down and doing chicken-wicked elbows in and out like they had whoopee cushions up their armpits.

'Clurck, cluck, cluck, cluck. Clurk, cluck, cluck, cluck.'

One kid, Snot Simmonds, jumped out the circle and

started doing the chicken dance right under my nose. Before he knew it I gave him a right *chirugi*. Sent him fluttering back on his jacksie.

Next thing, it was a brawl-for-all.

I freaked. I was Tae Kwon Do kid all over, kicking and skipping and chopping. I was hot. I was burning it.

Smack. Slap. Thump.

Suddenly, everything went hush and someone grabbed me by the neck.

A big hand.

It was Buzz.

He let go. We all stood still.

Then he raised the palm of his hand and slowly lowered it.

'Calm. Calm. Calm,' he said. 'Now who started this?'

Everyone looked at me.

I'd lost my kecks in the fight. I was standing there clay naked, Banger on two legs.

8

Bombing

Eventually Buzz worked out it was all about Skaz and me and he had us sin-binned for the first ten mins of the class sitting right inside the goalie nets.

At first, Skaz said nothing. I sat cross-legged chewing a stalk of grass.

Then I heard him chuckling.

He sat on his haunches in front of me and stuck his hand out. 'Soz about the chicken stuff,' he said. 'I was just pissed off with you. Mind, we saw more than a bit of your *shin* there. Didn't they get the whole fronty monty! Right widgy winkie you got, Lee.' He did a few pretend *shogi*. 'Girls got a right eyeful.'

'Girls?' I said horrified. 'How come?'

'Video cam,' he said. 'Top of the lockers. Got it off the market. Super zoom. Palm size. Hide it anywhere.'

'You videoed it?' I choked. 'Me, in the nod? In the buff? They'll be able to see . . . everything?'

Skaz nodded in pretend horror. 'Right down to the last tidgy widgy winkie. Full screen. Real blow-up job.'

Stuff me! They'd all see it. Millie, The Pole, Mouse,

101

Garrett. And worst of all, Alison, blonde and beautiful, Libidowicz.

I stared at him, gobbed.

'And if you're thinking of shopping me to Buzz, forget it. Unless you want yer willie on prick of the month in *Playground* mag.'

'You're a bastard, Dutton. You really are.'

'Now, don't wet yer willy, Lee. You're OK. No one gets to see today's stunt. It's on ice, honest. But –' he paused – 'if you step out of line, well then that's different.'

'Yer a skeffin criminal,' I said. Then a thought struck me. I stared at him. 'That time, at TKD, you were on the roof.'

He grinned. 'Told you. Girls chuff naked. Got the lot.'

'All of them?' I said slowly.

He grinned.

'Alison Libidowicz?'

'Wouldn't you like to know. Give you a peep one day. When yer a big boy.'

'You're a sicko, Dutton. A right perv.'

'We're all pervs underneath, Lee. Pervs and peepers. Look at you. You've had her in yer head. Libidowicz. In the buff, you and her. Peeping at her in yer head. Perv yerself, Lee. Dying for a looksie, aren't you, now you know about the piccies? Too wuss to say so. Go on admit it. Go on.' He nudged me in the ribs.

'Get lost,' I spluttered. I'd never thought of Ali like that. Suddenly I had this image of her half girl, half salmon sluicing through the water bubbles, silvering her skin and streaming over her breasts. Then the big picture near our house came into my head. She and I racing through the corn, the sunlight streaming over the waving field – she naked, me standing, just watching. Yeah, like Skaz said, she was in my head. But not tarty like he made out, not tarty at all. Not me and Ali.

'What if she finds out you've been peeping on her?' I said, looking up the field to where distant figures were hacking at a ball.

'But she won't, will she?' Skaz looked hard at me. 'Will she?' he repeated.

I shook my head. No, I wasn't going to tell her. I knew if I did I just might find myself piccied full frontal in the school playground. And anyway, keep on the right side of Dutton and I might get a peepsie.

I fell silent.

Why did I always get on the wrong end with him? I stood up. The chill from the grass had given me bum-numb.

I was getting tired of being Skaz's favourite bozo. I needed to show him, and a few others, I wasn't some kind of wonk. Dad had me down as a baby basher, Alison probably thought I was a prize prat now, Gran thought I was top dumbo.

Then I said, or something real bozo inside me said, 'We'll do it tonight.'

Dutton knew I was on about The Water Tower.

'Bomb like you said. Tonight.'

He eyed me for a moment, weighing up the offer. Making me wonder was I worth the effort.

'Fivish.'

'Fivish.'

We shook hands.

'Don't forget yer cans.'

When I got home I told Mum I had to do extra for Jamil because one kid had gone sick and couldn't do his round.

She shook her head. 'If it's down that Feck place, no way, Lee.'

We were in the dining room and Mum was laying the table.

'It's not,' I said. 'It's this side of Gants.'

She frowned. It looked like a NO. I had to think of something.

'I need the money for B,' I blurted.

Mum looked up, frowning slightly.

'For a pressie,' I added quickly. 'It's her birthday in a bit, isn't it?'

'Yes, but not just yet.'

'Well, I'll get her something cos she's not been well. Because of those bruises and all.'

'She's often not been well, Lee, and you've never got her anything before.'

'No, well ... I, er ... just thought this time ... it was ...'

Mum's face softened. 'It's a kind thought, Lee. That's the main thing. '

She put a plate on the table. 'I suppose your gran put you up to it.'

'No,' I protested, hurt she didn't believe me. 'It was my idea.'

'Good, I'm so pleased.' She started on the cutlery. 'She'll be so happy you gave her something.' She half smiled. 'At last, you are beginning to –' She searched my face. 'Well, you know what I mean. Let's be honest, Lee –' she waved a fork at me – 'being brotherly hasn't ever really been a top priority for you, has it?'

No, I thought. But, well, now I'd given myself no choice. I had to play big brother or it was no deal with Skaz and the bombing.

No go to Skaz and I'd be chicken for life.

No bro to Skinny and I'd be dead meat at home.

'What shall I get her?' I said. 'What would she like?'

'Look better if you choose yourself, Lee, don't you think? Shows you care. That's the important thing.'

I nodded. Maybe Gran would have some ideas.

'So I can go to Jamil's?'

'Course,' she said. 'Hurry, or you'll be late.'

I was out.

Then I was back in. 'How is Skinny today?'

'OK. Bit tired. No more bruises, thank goodness.'

'She getting better then?'

Mum didn't answer that one. 'Off you go,' she said. She gave me a smile in a hurry, as Gran would say; the sort that shooed you out so she could get back to serious worrying on her own,

I slipped out of the lounge and sneaked into the kitchen fridge for two of Dad's beers. Boddies. He has them for Sky Sport when we watch United.

If Skaz said 'cans', then Boddies were the boys.

The Water Tower is this mega metal bin on top of five giant concrete pillars. They're linked to each other with criss-cross rods thick as drainpipes.

I walked slowly down the path next to the railway sidings like Skaz had said and found the gap in the fencing he told me to crawl through.

Once on the tracks, I had to follow the outside rail. It led directly to The Tower.

I picked my way through the grass clumps and claggy plants between rails and finally got there.

No sign of Skaz.

About a hundred metres away stood a hut. I moved on to the dark side of one of the leg columns and watched the red scalp of the sun poking up from a bandaging of cloud. I was wondering what the hell had happened to Dutton.

'Hey, is that you, Lee?'

I looked round, up the rails, down towards the hut.

No Skaz.

'Up here.'

I stepped out into the dusk and looked upwards.

Five metres or so above me was Skaz, standing on the rung of a metal ladder that seemed to rise above him all the way to the top of The Tower. It looked a million miles up. It wasn't just high. There was altitude up there, Everest almost.

'Come on.'

'You mean climb up there?'

'Course. What else?'

So this was bombing. Shinning up some mega climbing frame. Good one, Skaz.

I started.

The lowest rung was about head height and I had

to haul myself up hand over hand, rung to rung, until I could get a foot on the first and catch breaths.

By then I felt wrecked. I held on to the side rails hoovering in air, blinking rust particles out of my eyes and shaking them out my hair.

I looked around. I could see the whole sun now blister raw in the smokey autumn light. Suddenly my legs began to shake.

'Hey, Lee. What yer doing?'

I wrapped my arms round the ladder and tried straightening up. Bit by bit, the shakes went.

'It's OK,' I said in loud whisper.

Truth was, I was in panic mode. I'm not good on heights, but I'd never been like this before.

It felt like I was suspended, nothing above, nothing below. I felt disconnected. The plug had been pulled and everything – Gants, The Swamp, Jigger, Mum and Dad, Skinny, Cropper, Alison, The Feck, Tae Kwon Do – had all whooshed away into space and left me in utter darkness, drifting no-wheres, man-overboard, clinging to a rusted ladder.

Any moment now it would disappear rung by rung until there was just the one left.

And then, just as that last one dissolved and I began to tumble into the void, Skaz caught me, grabbed my hand, so to speak.

'Come on, Lee. Get yer arse up here.'

I opened my eyes, shook my head, felt a rung of iron branding my cheek cold.

Skaz! Thank God you're here.

'What you doing? Gone clucky on me? Let's go.'

I looked up.

He was there, chuckling, little black monkey crawling up his ladder.

I smiled. I was saved. I could see smoke rising from houses and hear the drone of a distant plane. It was OK now. It was all back together, reconnected, rungs to ladder, ladder to tower, tower to rail, rail to Gants, Gants to home.

I started to climb.

At the top of the column where it joins the water drum itself was a walkway. Skaz was waiting for me.

'You can see the whole town from up here,' I said after a bit.

'Let's go,' said Skaz.

'You mean we go higher?'

'No. We do it here.'

'I thought we'd done it?'

'Done it? What you on about?'

'Done the climb. Bombed The Tower.'

'Prat. We're not swinging monkeys. We're sprayers.'

'Sprayers? How do you mean?'

'Like in holding cans and pressing buttons spraying.'

'We're going to spray this lot. I thought –'

'Yeah. You're a right plod, Matthews. We're talking graffiti here, Lee. Not mountaineering. Now wake up, bozo brain.'

I did, double quick. I could feel the weight of the tinnies against my thigh. Skaz was expecting a canful of racing red and I had a pocket full of best Boddies.

He took some stuff from inside his jacket. 'Got yer cans like I said?'

I looked at him.

'Well?'

'Yeah, but –'

'Get 'em out. I'll show you.'

Slowly I got out the Boddies. Held them up for him to see.

He looked hard at them for a moment. I thought he was going to go mental. Instead he started laughing quietly, sort of gurgling, like he had a neckful of best bitter down him. 'You dumb tosser,' he spluttered. 'Here take this.'

He shoved a paint can in my hand.

The plan was for Skaz to sketch the shapes and for me to fill them in. So at first I just watched as he stood on the outer rail of the walkway and reached up two metres or so to do the outlines. His arm moved quickly, easily, in great hissing confident arcs. And each time he stretched to the limit, I wondered if the railing would take the strain. All the time he moved backwards and forwards it creaked and twanged and the sounds came back from within the great metal drum we were working on like deep painful groans.

I guessed it was letters we were doing but, because the outlines were so cramped and nestled together, it was difficult to make out what the real picture was. And, anyway, we were too close to the thing. We could only step back about a metre from the drum wall because that's how wide the walkway was.

'What we bombing here, Skaz?' I asked.

'Work of art, Lee. Work of art.'

OK, Skaz, play mysterious. It's one big bomb. One big blow-up. Skaz and Lee hitting The Water Tower.

Once the outlines were done I started spraying the fill-in, but, because it was such a still evening, it got so thick with gagging chemicals, I had to lean over the outer railing to get some fresh air every so often.

And each time the whole walkway creaked.

Skaz was unaffected by the spray because he had a scarf for his mouth and nose, and gloves so he didn't get any back spray all over his hands.

We worked in silence and fast.

Skaz says you don't hang around when yer bombing case you get caught. And that's always on the cards cos the best places to bomb – bridges, shelters and stuff – are right up there in the public eye. As Skaz says, ain't no point unless you get the art seen. If you want invisibility, do cave walls. You'll just have to wait 30,000 years to get discovered.

That's what Skaz says.

Time to go.

'We'll see it tomorrow.'

We started to descend, Skaz first, chuckling again over some private joke, and sliding down the ladder like he was on a fireman's pole.

Me, I waited for his head to disappear into the dark, and began to lower myself, dead slow like I was getting into ice-cold water. I clung to the rails, flattened myself to the ladder and, stretching my right leg down, bit by bit began feeling about for the next rung.

And each time I reached down, the ladder twanged – bad vibes from Skaz scrambling and sliding below. I held on, sensing in my fingers the tremors in the metal. It was as if flickers of electricity were shocking through both hands, trying to unsteady me and loosen my grip.

'Slow down, Skaz, you'll have me off,' I hissed.

I heard him below. He was doing chicken. 'Clurck, cluck, cluck.'

Skeffin bastard. He'd shaken it deliberately. I knew it.

Then the ladder stilled and I guessed he'd dropped off the bottom to the ground.

I relaxed a puff.

Deep breathe, says Buzz, deep breathe and you can do anything, walk on water, run on air, lose some gravity.

Sure, Buzz. Ten metres up a rusted ladder, wobble-legged, mouth dry as a bag of biscuits, you don't lose gravity. Gravity loses you, dumps you dead or veggies you for life.

I blew out some oxygen and sagged against the ladder.

Then I began to back down again, foot stretching for each rung, never convinced it was going to be there, fingers still gripping the rails like they were welded on. With each step it was like I had to prise my hand free because inside there was this shit-scared bozo wanting to bike-lock himself to a rusty ladder.

Skaz knew it. And he wanted the chicken to cluck.

About halfway down it did.

*

I'd gone a few rungs and was beginning to think I could actually make it.

I imagined Skaz at the bottom watching out for me. He could probably see me hunched to the ladder like some little mechanical toy, a black tin beetle, crawling slowly down, click, click, click.

I took a rest and glanced left and right. I could see the shadow lines of the railtrack below running into a scatter of dark station buildings lumped alongside the station car park. On the other side, the sidings narrowed into a single track that passed under a bridge and disappeared into a blind gulley beyond.

Standing there, hands holding the side rail at shoulder height, I could niff the petrol smell of the spray from my fingers. It was probably all over my skeffin clothes. I'd have to get cleaned up at Gran's. If Mum got a sniff of it she'd go mental.

If I could have waved my hands about, wafted the claggy stuff away, I would have, but I was too scared of leaving go the ladder and falling. You can ride a bike one-handed and wave at yer mates, but ten metres up the vertical you don't trapeze about like Spiderman.

I needed to get going again before I stiffened up and got clumsy.

I began to lower my left foot. But before I could reach the next rung something stopped me, froze me mid step.

Oh, God!

The ladder was moving.

Wasn't it? Didn't it?

I waited. Not breathing.

I could hear Skaz calling, hissing from below, 'Shift it, Lee, before someone comes. What's wrong with yer?'

'Ladder's moving,' I called, not daring to look up or down.

'Crap. Stop being a wuss.'

Then it did move. No question.

It twanged, then shuddered.

Skeffin hell!

Something went whizzing past my head, landed with a thud below.

I ducked my head under the rung above, twisted my neck and looked up.

I could see the bulk of The Tower rising high above me.

Had a bolt rusted through? Bit of walkway grating?

I squeezed metal.

'What the hell?' I heard Skaz shout.

Then it seemed everything, me and the ladder, were all slowly juddering like the world was cranking into some crazy new arrangement, diagonal and disastrous.

I screamed and groped through the rungs, grasping at the concrete pillar. My nails could only graze it.

I was trembling, breathing quick, hiss breaths.

'Skaz!' I squealed. 'Ladder's coming off. Help me!'

I reached through the rungs again. Could just touch the pillar. A metre away, maybe more.

'Skaz! Skaz!'

'Get down quick.'

'Can't. I'll fall off.'

'Just get down before someone sees yer, yer prat.'

I was going to fall, I knew it. I knew it. I was hanging out in space. Any minute the whole lot would go. I'd fall. I was going to fall.

Oh, God!

'Come on, Lee. Don't be so poxy chicken. Come on, now.'

Dad. Dad. Help me! Help!

Why don't chickens fly? Why don't chickens fly? I kept thinking.

'It's OK,' Skaz was calling. 'It's come away above you. Now just take it easy. You can get down. It's only a bit of a drop. Just slide.'

I said nothing. Mouth was stuffed with chicken-scare.

Slide? Could I?

'Lee, you OK?'

I could hear a bit of chicken in his voice too.

'Lee, answer. Answer will you, you stupid prat!'

I didn't.

'Lee. Lee. Get down. Come on. Come on.'

He was clucking now.

'I'll knock yer off.'

Just try, Skaz, and I'll land us both in cabbage land, pronto.

I took a deep breath. Somehow the cluck in Skaz's voice made me feel better.

Birds of a feather together, Skaz, you and me.

How cool is that?

I looked up.

Skaz was right.

I could see that a full seven metres of ladder had

come away and was tilting out into space. Train track to nowhere.

At its fullest extent it had swung about three metres from the upright and I was stuck halfway down, arms wrapped round the rails, hands clasped together in a hopeful hug.

I felt wrecked and rested my forehead against one of the rungs. What with the spray up my nose I felt as bombed as the scabby Tower.

I began to inch down, neck craned upwards, watching the floating length of ladder above for any sign of movement. And all the time Skaz was skeffin me on for being a wuss and a prat and a tosser and getting me so stonking mad I forgot I was downing a vertical high enough to fall off and flat-pack myself.

By the time I reached the point where the ladder was still fixed to the concrete, I had to rest. My arms were aching, my legs felt limp as warm spaghetti, my hands were numb, my fingers so stiff they could have been mummied in bandages for all I could feel of them.

But I was almost safe. I'd done the worst.

'How far to go?' I called down.

No answer.

'Skaz?' I hissed. 'You there?'

No answer.

Skeffin bozo. Where was he?

I waited. Listened. Only the murmur of distant traffic.

'Skaz!'

Nothing.

The bastard had gone, left me. Vanished.

I got to the ladder end about two metres short of the concrete platform where The Tower legs rested.

From here I had to lower myself and, hanging from the last rung, drop the short distance to the ground.

I was halfway through this move, feet braced against the pillar, hands on the last but one rung when I heard a noise behind.

Before I could turn, I was grabbed by the legs and pulled down into someone's arms.

9

Hoodz 5

'OK, Skaz, now let go, yer prat,' I whispered savagely.

'Hey, boy. Yous going nowheres.'

I stiffened.

Then I was turned round and dumped against the pillar. A dark figure stepped back.

I could see there three of them, hoodies up, faces hidden.

'What yous up to, boy, trespassing on railway property?'

Rap boy. A real joker, I thought.

'Maybe yous got something for us poor boys.' The figure motioned one of the others forward and he began searching my pockets.

I could smell his breath. Gas and vomit.

Thank you, Skaz.

The kid stepped back, holding up a can of Boddies. He hadn't bothered with the paint spray.

The leader examined it, then tossed it to the third figure still lurking behind him.

'Now. That's bad, boy. Likes of yous taking to drink before yours time.' He stepped back. 'Well, my friend, since yous donating us a drink seems only right and kindly we give yous a receipt for yer charity.'

Still rap-boy speak.

He laughed.

Receipt?

I froze.

I knew who they were now. Hoodz 5. Skeffin hell!

'Little stamp of autority we calls it. My artist boy here, Miz, calls it scalp art. Head graffiti yous could say.'

Two of them came forward.

They were going to bomb me.

I reached inside my back pocket, drew out the sprayer and let them both have it right in the eyes.

Then I darted back under The Tower and 999ed out on to the single track and dashed up the line way I'd come in to meet Skaz.

I could hear them behind me, cursing and running.

By now I was out in the open. Somewhere on my left was the path, but where was the gap?

I looked over my shoulder as I stumbled along, slipping and sliding on the sleepers and gravel.

They weren't far behind. And my heart was pounding, running on the spot.

If they got me I was in for a right whacking.

Suddenly a figure leapt out of the darkness, grabbed my arm and dragged me aside into a clump of claggy bushes.

Skaz.

We raced and smashed our way through the dark like a pair of run-amok robots. Skaz seemed to know a way. He never stopped, never faltered. Kept his head down, kept us both going.

Before I knew it we were on the path and heading towards Gants. We burst into a side street, legged it a few metres till Skaz did a sudden right turn down someone's ginnel and into a back garden.

A dog yacked but we were out through the end fence and over another before anyone could turn down the telly and check for burglars.

Suddenly Skaz stopped.

'Time to split,' he said hoarsely. 'You that way. Me this. Don't stop till yer get home to mummy.'

Then he was gone.

When I got to Gants I slowed down. Start running there and you soon get a race after you.

Soon as I turned into Far Pastures I knew something was up. Parked outside our house was a strange car.

I checked my watch.

Six thirty.

I went round the side and let myself in the back door.

The three of them were sitting at the kitchen table – Mum, Dad and the visitor, a tall thin woman, all staring at me like I was off of the moon or something.

'Where the hell have you been?' said Dad. 'We've been one hour waiting.'

The woman stood up as if to quieten things down. 'This is Lee?'

Mum said 'yes' dead quiet. 'Lee, this is Miss Andrews,' she added.

'What's up?' I said.

'I'm part of the County Child Protection Team,' said the woman. 'My name's Maureen.'

'Protection Team?' I said. 'I don't need protection.'

'This isn't just about you, Lee. It's about your sister,' said the woman.

'But she's dead ill. And she's going to get better, isn't she? What's she need you for?'

'I'm not a doctor, Lee. Now sit down. I'd like us to have a little talk.'

Dad pulled out the other chair and I sat opposite the woman.

She stared at me for a moment. 'Now, tell me,' she said. 'How do you get on with your sister? You do argue with her, fight with her?'

'No,' I said. The woman was stupid. I looked at Mum. At Dad. He was dead dogging me. He had bullet-hole eyes on me. 'What's going on?' I said. 'What's she on about, Mum? What is this?'

Mum looked wiped. 'She's only trying to help,' she said quietly.

'Help? How, when she's not a doctor?'

'Lee, you don't understand,' said Miss Andrews. 'We've had a complaint. From the school.'

'I knew we shouldn't have gone to that bloody school,' said Dad.

I saw the woman give him a hard look.

And then it dawned on me. What a bozo I was. The school had told them about me and Garrett, and me doffing her one. That's what this was about. Skeffin hell!

Mum and Dad would go mental. No wonder Dad was dead bricking me.

'Look, she asked for it,' I said. 'She was gobbing me.'

'Gobbing?' said Mum. She looked horrified. Dad stood up.

'You mean you did hit her?' he said, his face crowded with anger and puzzlement.

'Just the once. I wasn't thinking. Honest!'

Mum had her head in her hands.

'Now let's all calm down here,' said Miss Andrews. 'Let's get at the facts first.' She lowered her voice, spoke softly. 'First, you say you don't fight with her, now you're actually telling me you hit your sister? Bruised her so badly she's going to end up in hospital?'

'No!' I shouted. 'I'd never hit Skinny. She's too little.'

There was silence. Mum had her eyes closed. She let out a long slow sigh.

'I meant someone at school. A girl,' I said. 'She was slagging me off.'

'A girl? You hit a girl?' said Dad.

The woman put an arm out to block him.

I slowly nodded. The way Dad said 'hit' made it sound real, bad, blood bad. Garrett's screams suddenly filled my head and the glitter of her red teeth.

I felt sick.

'This you'll have to resolve between yourselves,' said the woman. 'My concern is about your daughter, Beatrice. I'd like to see her if you don't mind.'

'Well, we do mind,' said Dad. 'She's not well and she's sleeping.'

'That's not going to help the situation, Mr Matthews, I'm afraid. If you're going to be uncooperative I'll have to –'

Mum interrupted. 'She is ill. She has a high temperature. I don't want her disturbed.'

Miss Andrews was silenced. Something about Mum's tone of voice seemed to convince her.

'She's not ill because of me,' I said. 'I never touched her, honest.'

'But you do lose your temper. And we do seem to have a history here by the sound of it,' said Miss Andrews. I think she was glad to get back on the attack.

'History?' I said.

'Of . . . er . . . strong feelings and aggression. Maybe we need some anger management here.'

I thought of the Ju Ju and how Jig and I spent a whole year spearing and chopping and stabbing them.

'Aggression?' I heard Dad growl. 'What are you suggesting, Miss Andrews?'

'I see a lot of domestic violence in my job, Mr Matthews. So I have to be careful. I'm sorry this is causing you embarrassment. But some things are better out in the open. My priority is the safety of vulnerable children. This is only a preliminary inquiry. We are legally bound to follow up any complaint, any complaint whatever.'

'Preliminary?' said Mum. 'Follow up? You mean you could be back again?' She looked horrified.

Miss Andrews ignored Mum's question.

'I don't believe this,' said Dad. 'You come into our house, our home, and you more or less accuse us of . . .

of abusing our kids.' He leaned forward. 'You're sick, you are. Sick!' He spat the words out.

Miss Andrews took them smack on the chin without flinching. 'And we see a lot of verbal violence in our job too,' she said coldly. 'Words can be so hurtful, especially when directed at impressionable young children unable to defend themselves.'

I shut my eyes. I could see Dad exploding, doffing her one and punching the lights out of our future as nice, respectable people.

'That's enough, Derek,' said Mum to Dad, suddenly taking charge. 'I've heard enough.' She turned to the woman. 'Miss Andrews. My daughter sleeping upstairs is a child loved beyond measure. And so is this one.' She pointed to me. 'Hitting someone,' she went on, 'is inexcusable. But a kid losing his temper doesn't amount to domestic violence and child abuse. Now, if you'd kindly leave we can get on with being an ordinary family again and sort out our little differences for ourselves.'

'Without any more nose-poking do-gooders,' said Dad.

Mum gave him smack-in-the-eye look for that.

The woman got up.

'I'll have report this to the Protection Team,' she said. 'I have to say I didn't expect such hostility and lack of co-operation.'

'And we didn't expect such insinuation and insensitivity,' said Mum.

'You know I could call in Social Services,' the woman answered.

'And threatening behaviour,' Mum added. 'Did

anyone ever accuse you of abusing innocent families?'

The woman stood up. 'Don't think this is the end of the matter. And if the child's as ill as you say she is, I suggest you take her to the doctor, because on the evidence of what I've been told we're going to have get the professionals in anyway. The sooner she gets a proper assessment the better.'

'Get out,' said Mum, 'and take your nasty suspicious ways with you.'

After Miss Andrews had left, Mum turned to me. 'What a thing to do,' she said. 'Hit a girl.'

Soz, Mum. Soz a million.

'What were you thinking of? Why, Lee, why?'

'She slagged me off.'

'I beg your pardon? She what?'

'She insulted me. Said I was a er . . . a . . .'

'What?' said Dad sharply.

'A wanker.'

'And you hit her for that?' he said. 'I've a got a good mind to –' He raised his hand and then saw Mum start.

Soz, Dad. Honest.

But I knew he wouldn't hit me. Not in front of Mum. I knew too, that like me, he'd have slapped Garrett. Slap people like that, he'd say, or they gob all over you. Law of life, mate, he'd say. Get in there first. Just make sure you're not found out, he'd say. Keep it quiet.

I wasn't so sure about that now. Smacking just got me a load of trouble.

*

Then Mum spoke very slowly, very quietly, each word hurting like a hot slap across the cheek. 'Never again do I want to hear about a son of mine hitting a girl. Do you hear?'

I nodded dumbly. Then Dad got his act together.

'Yeah, and you've put us right in it with that Andrews woman,' he said. 'Why couldn't you just keep your big mouth shut?'

'This'll get out,' said Mum. 'We'll have to leave. I won't be able to show my face. I won't.'

'Ahh!' said Dad, suddenly lightening. 'It'll blow over.' The only way he could cope with Mum having a wobbly was to pretend everything was really OK. Now he was in calm-it-down, smooth-it-over mode. Bit like Buzz really. 'The woman will come to her senses,' he went on. 'She'll realize soon enough we're not the sort of family knocks kids about.'

Mum didn't look convinced. 'It's so shaming,' she said. 'To think she could think that of us. Oh, my little Bea,' she said, beginning to cry.

Dad looked at me. I looked at Dad.

'I'll get some tea on,' he said. Tears just weren't his thing.

I edged towards Mum and, bit by bit, put my arms round her shoulders. She wasn't shaking or heaving. She was hard and stiff as wood and the tears were being forced out against her will.

She pushed me away slowly. 'I've got to see Bea. See she's OK.' She squeezed my hand. 'We'll talk in the morning.'

Suddenly she started sniffing. 'What's that smell? It's

like petrol.' She turned to me. 'Lee, it's you. What's going on? And look at your hands. They're half white.'

Dad was peering into a cupboard and not really listening.

'It was in Art,' I said, thinking fast and wishing I'd never heard of bombing and water towers and break-away ladders. 'Yes, Art . . . and . . . er . . . we did spraying – aerosol art with Mr Harris.'

Mum frowned.

I blathered on about how Harris said art wasn't just for paintings on walls. How he said we had to work on a bigger canvas. Art was about scale and ambition. The whole environment was ours to aerosol and scrawl on and scribble over. We had to muralize the street, titian the town hall. Paint it red and black and blue and bright orange, he said.

Mum looked suspicious. Aerosols were flammable, didn't I know? To be safe you needed protective clothing. Art and chemicals didn't mix.

'Art is chemicals mixed,' said Dad suddenly.

We both stared at him

'Just make my herbal,' said Mum.

It was then I realized what I suppose I'd kind of known for some time, that it was Mum not Dad who was the stronger of the two of them. Dad made all the waves, but Mum was the real force, not just about Skinny B but about everything really.

And in front of Miss Andrews she'd called Dad 'Derek'. I'd never heard her say that before. It seemed dead freaky, like she was talking to a stranger, different

126

from my dad. Somehow he didn't seem so . . . so Dad-like now, just more . . . ordinary, I suppose.

I thought back to all the other times Skinny was ill. Dad didn't know what to do with himself. He'd prowl about from room to room like he'd lost something. Then he'd go very quiet till someone stepped out of line or the phone rang or something. Then he'd leap up like he'd been jump-started. Mum would close her book with a clap and say, 'Why not go to the pub?' And Dad would be off like all he was doing was waiting for her permission. He'd go down to The Yeoman, smacking a few lamp posts on the way, and there he'd shoot darts like he was trying to javelin them through the board and out the other side.

Then he'd come back late, slump on the settee and fall into a snore in front of yawn-time telly.

By then Mum was asleep a long time.

In bed that night I prayed. Jesus first. Told him a miracle was due. Skinny needed it. Mum needed it. Dad needed it.

It was up to him.

I thought of sick kids on telly where they show them in trolley beds all wired up with tubes and masks, and I thought that's Skinny there, that's going to happen to her.

Jesus had to do it for her. Do it for Skinny.

Maybe the Ju Ju had got her at last!

I thought of the Chicken Fight, The Tower and Hoodz 5. I thought of Garrett, face all blood-sprayed.

If they found out about me going up The Tower and

me and Skaz doing the bombing I'd be over my head in it.

Now we had Child Protection on our backs. All because of me really, me smacking some girl.

Gran says Keep out of trouble. Fat chance, I was neck in it and rising. A thirteen-year-old boy trying to get my stance, my *chogi*, right, get my *chirugi* up with the best, and show Alison Libidowicz I was the sort of kid could bomb water towers any time she asked. It wasn't much to ask.

I lay wide awake staring at the curtains. Through a gap I could see two distant eyes peering at me. They were light years away, fox glint from some distant galaxy.

Skinny's in bed all Saturday. According to Mum she's eating OK, which is OK, but is sleeping overmuch, which isn't so OK. I have to babysit all morning while she does the shops. I'm not to go in her room, I'm not to turn up the TV, I'm not to have my stereo on, I'm not to have any mates round. Unlikely that last one, Mum. They're all from The Feck, don't fall out of bed till after the cartoons. Nothing else to get up for, says Gran. Except to get lathered down the boozer, says Dad. Sshh, says Mum. She doesn't like the word 'boozer'.

Sunday night things go bad. Skinny's hurting and cries a lot. She wakes me up. I lie there listening. Mum I can hear humming Skinny to sleep. Dad's banging doors in the kitchen. I can hear the kettle whistle so he must be making more tea.

All goes quiet. I hear Skinny's door shush on the

carpet. I hear Mum going back to her room. I hear the door click.

Outside: frost crazing the window, the low-volt twinkle of the stars, and then the sudden call of Skinny, mewing.

I put fingers in my ears and listen to the hidden hum of myself, brain traffic, my head congested with scares and worries and thin stalk arms blued and blotched and going bad and blood lick and Dracula kisses.

I wake suddenly. School again. I'm late. Dad's in the bathroom so I run down to the kitchen. Mum's there still in dressing gown. She looks wrecked. She's not going to work.

I stuff some cornflakes in and she picks up the phone. Calls the doctor.

While she's ringing I sneak up to Skinny's room and nudge the door open.

She's lying on her back, eyes closed, wheezing a little with each breath.

I look at her curly curls and her pale face on the pink pillow and one-eye-awake bunny beside her.

Suddenly I feel dead bad. I'm wussing on about water towers and she's wheezing like it's a bee fest.

I tiptoe over to the bed and take her hand in mine and hold it bunny soft. It's hot and a bit damp on the palm and heavier than I expect, like it's just come out of the bath.

Slowly I roll up her sleeve.

Jesus!

She's black and blue and red and yellow.

All round her arm she's got these dark blotches. I count up to ten. They've grown like dark blood bursts.

'How you feel, B?' I whisper.

She opens her eyes. 'OK, Leelee.' Her voice is croaky. She's not OK.

'Leelee' is what she called me when she was dead little.

'I want a drink.'

'Coke?' Blood of the Cola Bird!

'On the table.' She indicates with her eyes. They're big and bright and her lamplight glitters in them like star points. I know they're following me round the bed.

Skinny big eyes, all I can do is give you drink. The rest is up to Jesus.

I go and get the glass. It's orange. I try and get her to sit up, but she's too tired. I put the orange down so I can use both my arms to lift her but she's gone asleep again.

Probably best. I might bruise her more if I try and pull her up.

Just then Mum comes in and sounds off about me disturbing B. I say I was only trying to help and Mum suddenly gives me a big hug, biggest for ages.

She's trembling and she's making me tremble and suddenly I'm shaking and crying and I don't know why and I wonder if I've got something too.

Crying! What a wuss!

It was sunny on the way to school and I felt better for being out of the house. Suddenly the traffic and the lorry fumes and the graffiti and the bird splat all seemed ordinary and easy. Not like home any more.

I could get on with my life for a few hours. Forget Skinny for a bit.

Then I saw Jigger ahead. I slowed down. But he suddenly turned and stopped, obviously waiting for me to catch up.

We talked money. I told him about Jamil and the paper round in The Feck. 'Got to buy my sister something, Jig. I need the money.'

'So, you going down The Feck?'

'Yeah. Tomorrow. Got to.'

'On yer bike?'

I shrugged, 'Maybe. Maybe not. Why?'

Jigger shrugged. 'Watch out for Hoodz Five, that's all.'

'What you know about them?' I said, not really wanting to hear any more than Alison had told me.

'This is what I know,' he said. He bent forward and flipped over the hair on the back of his head. 'That's Hoodz Five. Bastards.'

At the back of his skull a patch had been cut out leaving a large square of grey skin. In the centre of the square were some letters.

'You got yourself tattooed, you prat?'

Jigger spat.

'What's it say?'

'Skeffin H Five, that's what.'

'They did it?'

'Course they skeffin did.'

'Why?'

Jigger shrugged. 'They were hassling me so I told them to get stuffed. Got me next day, back of the Co-op.

Dropped me with one.' He pointed to a bruise high up on his cheekbone. 'Then they did the skeffin tattoo. They do it all the time. Half the kids on The Feck are H Five. We'll get a skeffin bar code next.'

Like a chill hand suddenly on your back, I shivered. That could have happened to me under The Tower if I hadn't managed to escape.

'Why were they after you?'

'It's since my dad left,' he said, shaking his head as if he still couldn't believe it. 'My mum needs the stuff. It's bad now. Keeps her going, she says. Calls it her medicine. It's just till she gets over my dad. Till she can get back on her feet, she says. Believe me, she says. That's why she works all hours at Kwick Pax. Needs the stuff.'

'I know what you mean, Jig. About medicine. Mine's the same.'

'Yeah?'

'Whenever my sister gets sick she's dead depressed again and takes this stuff for it.'

'Gets it from Aunty too, does she?'

'No. Goes down Boots. Who's Aunty?'

Jigger stopped, held me still, looked me up and down and shook his head. 'Bozo brain,' he said. 'We're not talking aspirin, Lee. We're talking the business. Biz. Uppers. Benzies. Pinks. You don't get them on the sick. No way. Aunty provides. Aunty looks after yer.'

Now it dawned. Biz was, well ... er ... biz, drugs, loot, bender-boy.

'Who's this Aunty, Jig?' I said, a bit brain-smacked about Jigger's mum and him saying she was a druggie. 'What stuff?' I said.

132

'Sod it, Lee. You know nothing, do yer.'

A car screamed past

'Well, how is your mum now?' I said at last. 'Does it make her better?'

'Same,' he said. 'Skeffin, skeffin same.'

'Pills no good?'

'What you know about them?' he said, stopping and suddenly looking mad eyes at me.

'You told me just now, Jig. About yer dad and stuff, remember?'

'Yeah, well, we're all sick, aren't we? Everybody.'

'Not me,' I said.

He turned. 'Oh, no? So smacking girls' teeth out ain't sick?'

And he started off down the road.

What the hell was up with him? He had a right one on him, as Gran would say.

He probably still fancied Garrett, all tarted up down The Shed. And didn't like it cos I'd smacked her.

I thought of Alison. If she had bad-mouthed me would I have cracked her one?

Hit Alison? No way. I'd be mad. Maybe I doffed Garrett cos I didn't like her. Simple as that. She was a slag. Down with slags.

Talk of the devil and there was Skaz waiting by the school gates.

'Get home OK?' he said, walking across the play-ground with me.

'Yeah. You?'

He didn't answer.

'Why'd you run away, Skaz? Leave me stuck up the spout like?'

He looked at me hard-eyed. 'Saved yer, didn't I? Wanna survive, Lee, use yer head. What you got brains for?'

'Right. I still could have got a scalp tattoo like Jigger.'

'Could but didn't. So don't complain.' He kicked at a stone. 'You seen what you done?'

'Done? What?'

'On The Tower.'

'No.'

'Take a look sometime!'

The way he said it I knew something was up.

10

Sex, Sex, Sex

Cropper was banging on about evolution again, genes and rabbits and stuff. I wasn't listening too hard cos I was thinking about Alison. Me, the only bunny in the class not got his ears up.

'. . . and it's sex, sex, sex. Yes, yes, yes,' said Cropper, thumping the desk with his fist. 'Rabbits or humans, it's no different, it's what gets life going and evolution up and running.'

He looked around the class.

'Thought that would wake you up, Matthews,' he said, fixing me with his gob eyes. 'Come here. I'm going to show you how it works.'

Someone giggled.

'Now, Matthews. Move.'

I walked slowly down to the front. He turned me round to face the class.

What was he up to? All eyes were on me. Garrett, Mouse, Alison, Skaz, the lot.

I felt like I was naked, skinned. Some kind of exhibit, me.

'Well, what have we here? Boyo erectus. Brown hair,

blue eyes, thin nose, two legs, two arms. Bog-standard model. Eats junk food, goes to school, watches telly. No extras. Perfectly adapted to his environment. Grows and grows.'

He stopped.

'And where did all these features come from? Flexible limbs. Internal heating. Scalp mat. All-round vision? Big brain? From genes, boys and girls, the small print of life. We owe it all to our genes. And that small print, DNA we call it, is transmitted to the next generation through sex. Why? So they can benefit from our success in the race to survive. Remember: features favour the future. Simple.'

He paused.

We all looked at him, rabbits staring at some dark horizon slashed with lightning and whirling with storms.

'Now, next big question. What's the most important thing about Lee Matthews?'

The rabbits looked puzzled.

'He's good at football.'

'He does Tae Kwon Do.'

'He's got nice legs.'

That was Alison.

Then Skaz spoke. 'He's got a little –' then he paused, long time – 'sister.'

'Wrong,' said Cropper. 'Wrong. Wrong. Wrong. The basic thing about Lee and everyone else here is that we're all different. Alison, you may think Lee's got nice legs, I may think he's got nice legs, but evolution ain't interested in legs. Just difference. Because if we're all different, or diverse, we stand a better chance of surviving.

Difference just means more options if things go wrong.'

Cropper lowered his voice and leaned forward like he had some terrible secret to tell. 'And things do go wrong.'

He stepped back.

'Take our Lee again, for example. We all know sex mixes up two people's DNA and produces kids with a difference. But what happens if nobody wants to mix their DNA with Lee? Bluntly put. What if no one fancies him? What's he going to do? Drop out of the great evolution race?'

Cropper motioned with his hands that he wanted suggestions.

'Put his stuff in a sperm bank, sir.'

'Wear silk nicks and attract the chicks,' said Skaz.

'And tight jeans.'

'Go The Shed, sir. He'd pull down there. Anyone can.'

'Get some muscles.'

'Hormone supplements.'

'Look like Brad Pitt.'

'Join a pop group.'

'Sunglasses.'

'Deodorant.'

'I know a good one, sir. It's got this chemical. It's like stuff that attracts bees. It has birds humming for it, it says on the bottle.'

'In yer dreams,' said Garrett.

'It's called Homme, sir,' said Worm.

'A big widger,' said Skaz.

Then, in the moment's silence that followed, a small voice said, 'But there must be someone who fancies Lee.'

It was Mouse.

The class 'oohed' big time.

Thanks, Mouse.

Cropper grinned.

'Well, boys and girls and Lee: sheds, hormones, birds and bees, that's what we call the Mating Game. Game, sex and match. Makes reproduction fun, gets a fresh mix of DNA every time, keeps the human race different every time.'

Again Cropper paused.

'But,' he said, 'what happens when something really big goes wrong? A major catastrophe? How do we cope then? Well, wait till next time when we're going to hear the story of Mr and Mrs Rabbit and their hairless son, Little Reggie.'

Class groan.

'Back to your desk now,' he said to me. 'From now on, Lee, it's silk undies and Boots Body Cream for you.'

I walked back to my place, feeling a right Little Reggie.

I sat down.

At least I had some pube fuzz. That was a start.

But stuff your fancy cream, Cropper. I had chest hairs, didn't I? Jigger and I counted them. He said some girls liked them, some girls didn't. He said he'd pull his out, and I could leave mine in and see who scored first down The Shed.

I think I best keep them. It's sort of natural. Means you're tough. Puts you on the mating list.

Or there again, maybe I should see Worm. Get some of that humm stuff. He seemed to know all about it.

*

Next, we were in the gym waiting for Buzz to get this video player to work.

'Going to Alison's party, big boy?'

Skaz came jogging over and put his arm round my shoulders. He never missed PE but he was always last out of the changing rooms.

'Going to the party of the year?'

'Maybe.'

'Got her something?'

'Like what?'

'Like what girls like. Silk undies or something. Use your imagination.' He winked. 'With Libidowicz, I do.'

'You're a right perv, Dutton.'

'Get her silk. Give her some, Lee.'

'But –'

'You fancy her, don't you? Go for it. It's party time.'

'I can't buy her that sort of thing.'

Skaz shrugged like I was bozo of the month.

'Got a catalogue if you want.' He wandered off.

Buzz blew his whistle.

What size should I get?

Did they have sizes?

I looked down the gym to where most of the girls were gathered. Barge-bum Garrett was there.

They had sizes all right.

After changing I looked out for Buzz. I found him blowing up footballs, sheltering in the bike shed.

'Want something, Lee?'

'I think I'm ready for my green belt, sir.'

Buzz stopped pumping.

'You think.'

'Yeah.'

'Well, I don't know about that, Lee.'

'Eh! But, sir. I've done all the moves.'

'It's not just about moves, Lee. You know that.'

I nodded uneasily. Yeah, yeah, yeah. It was about spirit, and discipline, and *ki* and stuff.

'It's about being in control. Control of our feelings, our body.'

I watched Buzz pick up the ball with one hand.

I nodded again. 'I know. I know, sir. But I am in control. I'm full of control, sir.'

'Not last week you weren't, fighting in the changing room. That wasn't control, Lee. That was mayhem. And mayhem ain't Irish for *chirugi*.'

'No, sir.'

'I was very disappointed with you there, Lee.'

'Yes, sir.'

'Most of Three B are chicken-brained. I thought you were different, that's all.'

'I am, sir. We're all different.'

He frowned.

Maybe he'd change his mind.

'You know why the belt's green, Lee?'

'No.' I did really but sometimes it's best to play bozo with Buzz. Let him talk.

'Represents growing, new shoots. Personally, Lee, I think you've got a bit of growing to do before you're ready for that belt.'

I sighed.

Buzz started pumping another ball.

'You should see this as a test. Remember the harder you have to strive, the higher you get. You're just a kid, Lee. You got plenty of time yet.'

'Right! See ya, sir.'

I walked into the rain – piddle on my parade.

'Kid'! That's what he'd said.

Me?

No way.

I've got chest hairs, Buzz. I've bombed The Water Tower. I'm going to Alison Libidowicz's party.

I'm some Kan Do kid.

DNA me.

Do Not Aggravate.

Outside the gym I bumped into Jigger. Today Jigger was all mate this and mate that. He seemed to have been following me everywhere. In the playground, dinner hall, round by the kickback wall on the D&T block.

Bozo on a lead.

'I hear you and that bog-brain, Skaz Dutton, did The Water Tower last night,' he said.

'Gonna show us?' said Worm, edging into the conversation.

'Yeah,' said Alison as she passed, bag slung over her shoulder. 'I heard it's something else.' She giggled. 'I warned you, Lee. I told you not to trust Skaz Dutton.'

I hurried off. What the hell had Dutton done this time?

Walking down the railway path you get to see bits of The Tower through trees and stuff, way before you can see the lot. But to get a full-on view you have stand on the single-line bridge.

When we reached it I helped Jig and Worm climb the metal side, which was about two metres high. It was wide enough to stand on. Once up, Jig reached down and gave me a hand.

'Skeffin hell, Lee!'

I stared at the side of The Tower, where Skaz and I had sprayed the night before.

The bit of broken ladder was still hanging down, and the walkway sagged just where we'd graffitied.

In huge letters, across the side, was one word. I stared at it, frowning. The letters seemed welded together and even at this distance it was difficult to separate one from another.

'What's it say?' said Jigger.

'I know,' said Worm.

Jigger was still screwing up his eyes, trying to sort out the smash-up of letters.

Then I got it.

Skaz, you bastard!

'First one's C,' said Worm.

He sounded out the rest: 'L . . . U . . . C . . . K . . . Y.'

'Spells CLUCKY,' said Jig. 'That you, Lee? Ace one.'

I just stared at The Tower. Last night it was all so quick and dark, so eyeball-close, no wonder I never realized what Skaz was up to.

That was my call sign he'd put up there, right under my nose. Everybody could see it. Skaz would make sure they did.

One day I'll do something dental to him, shove a few knuckles in his big mouth.

We walked back. 'You bozo, Lee. You could have got yerself killed up there,' said Jig. 'What you do it for?'

'A dare,' said Worm. 'Ritualized adolescent behaviour. A two-finger give. Get a buzz. Show he wasn't soft. Get the adrenalin surge. Right, Lee?'

Jig's mouth dropped open.

I wasn't sure.

'It's right,' said Worm, a wheeze beginning to creep into his voice. 'Why don't you believe me?' He blinked at Jigger. 'You're walking into the jungle now, you two. You ain't kids any more. If you gonna survive you gotta dare the tiger so you know how to escape when the big cat jumps.'

Jigger stopped and just stared at Worm like he might tiger jump him there and then. What the hell was the scrawny kid on about, I could see him thinking.

Thing was, cos Worm was all wheezed up like his lungs were claggy and couldn't do stuff like the rest of us, he read all these dodgy books. He was a right boffin brain. And I felt sorry for him. That's why I said he could ride Assault. Just one go, mind. I think that's why he follows me home sometimes.

Thing is, no one really took any notice of him. When you get a wonk amongst you it's hard not to want to get rid. So we pretended he wasn't there, ignored him. Like we kidded each other he was invisible. Mind, if you get to be invisible the tiger don't jump you! Maybe he'll survive us all.

'You should keep away from Dutton. I tell you, he's ment, psycho big time,' Jig was saying.

'Yeah,' said Worm. 'And he does stuff. Does business down The Feck.'

Suddenly in my head I heard the screech of metal, the clanging of wrenched bolts.

I stopped, shaky and chill.

Jigger looked back. 'You OK, Lee?'

'Yeah, I think.' Legs wobbled a sec but I was OK. Just an aftershock from that hanging ladder, the last tremor passing through me.

'You've gone dead white,' said Worm.

I smiled. 'I'm OK. Just a Ju Ju attack.'

Jigger punched my arm.

'Got some pills if you want,' said Worm.

Jig and I both stared at him like he was jungle Ju Ju.

He just shrugged and wandered off down the path.

On the way back I told Jig how we got to The Tower as the sun was dimming, how the walkway was dead shaky, how the ladder tore away while I was on it, how it flung me out into space like on The Orbiter at Swanwick's, and how I lowered myself to safety hand over bloodied hand and dropped straight into a Hoodz 5 handshake.

'You're right, Jig, I nearly died on there,' I said. 'And what did Skaz Dutton do? He chickened off as soon he saw the H boys.'

We walked along in silence for a bit.

'I don't get Dutton, Jig,' I said. 'One min he's on your side, next he's making you look a right prat. What's with him, you think?'

Jig didn't really know. 'Told you, he's a headcase.'

Ask a bozo question, get a bozo answer.

We got back on the road.

'Going to Alison Libidowicz's party?' he said suddenly.

I said yes, was he?

He shook his head. 'She doesn't rate me. Thinks I'm a bozo like all the others.'

'You're no bozo, Jig.' I told him I was sorry about Garrett. He seemed set on her.

'No way, mate. She's a slag. Deserved what you gave her.'

I thought back to Jig's remark about me smacking girls. Typical these days, I thought. Changes his mood, as Gran says, like a clock changes chimes. One minute he's all over mates, next he's shredding you. Don't make sense.

Then he was nudging me. 'This Alison. You in there, mate?'

'Dunno, Jig.'

'She asked you, didn't she?'

'She asked lots, probably.'

Jigger shook his head. 'Select party, few only,' he said. 'You're really are in there, Lee, you lucky sod. She's a cracker. And they got money. Mercs of it. Lotto loads. You wanna get her something nice.'

Yes, I thought. You're right, Jigger, mate. I'll get something really special. Try my luck.

'Ever bought girls' stuff, Jig?'

He looked at me, frowning.

'No, but I got some mags. Wanna see? Quid each to you.'

Then I remembered Skinny. And the doctor's.

'Look, Jig. Gotta go.'

'See ya tomorrow, down The Feck?'

I looked at him puzzled.

'You said you were doing yer papers, on yer bike.'

I didn't say anything. Thing was, I wasn't sure whether I was taking Assault. I had to persuade Dad to let me ride down The Feck. I reckoned if the Hoodz boys showed up I'd be fast enough to burn them, leave them standing like they were still living yesterday. Maybe Dad didn't know about H5, maybe he'd be OK about it. Me going. Maybe.

We'd walked a bit in silence.

Suddenly Jigger jumped in front, turned and blocked my way. 'Well,' he said, 'are you or aren't you?'

'Maybe. I said maybe, remember.'

'Yeah.' His eyes were gobby like Cropper's, hyper even. He grabbed my arm. 'I'll do it with yer. Give yer a hand.'

'No need, Jig.' I didn't want to go splits. I needed the money.

'Do it for free, for mates, Lee. It's your round.'

I didn't say anything.

'Go on. It'll be like old times. You and me, riding together, hunting Ju Ju.' He flung his arm in the air like he was throwing a doo doo bomb, like he was once again bits and piecing JJ men.

OK, Jig, you win, I thought. Let's go kill Ju Ju one last time.

I nodded. 'Just for mates then.'

'For mates,' he whooped. 'See you at Jamil's.'

*

All the way home I wondered why Jig was so keen to play mates. Probably stuffed with doing the Co-op shop for his mum and needed his life ju-juicing up.

I turned into Far Pastures.

Before I got to our front gate I knew something was up. Gran was round. I knew that because I could hear her dog Tig barking at the back. He wasn't allowed in the house. Mum hated dog hairs, especially in the front room, which we kept for posh and where Tig would nest on the settee and bask like a seal pup for hours on end if he got half a chance.

No, bad sign, Gran round in the afternoon.

Before I could get my key in the lock the porch light came on and the door swung open. Gran was standing there like she'd been waiting hours for me to arrive.

'That him?' I heard Dad's voice ask from inside.

I hesitated on the step, knowing I was walking into something not right. Dad doesn't normally sit in the front room. Usually between shifts he's legs up on the pouffe in the lounge watching telly.

'Move it, Lee, we don't want the neighbours nosing.'

Dad had his back to me.

'Dad?' I said. 'What's going on?'

He turned. 'Here, give me your bag, Lee. Now sit down, son.' He took a deep breath. 'I'll get you a Coke.'

'No. No. I can get my own. What is all this?'

'You'll be better if you have a Coke,' he insisted.

'Just tell him,' said Gran. 'And stop beating about the bush.'

'It's Bea,' said Dad. 'She's in hospital.'

'Hospital!' My heart sank. 'It's the bruises, isn't it?' I said.

Dad nodded. He seemed choked up.

I turned to Gran. 'It's bad, is it? Dead bad for Skinny, Gran?'

'Where you been?' she said. 'School finished ages ago. We've been waiting hours.'

'PE teacher kept us back. Girls had a fight. Now, tell me about Skinny. Please.'

'They think she's got leukaemia.' It was Dad's voice, struggling like the word was a lump in his throat.

'Leukaemia? What's that?'

'It's where your blood dies,' said Gran.

'You mean it just dries up or what?'

'Look, Lee. It's not a hundred per cent.' Dad seemed to have recovered himself. 'They've done some tests but the doctors need to do more before they know for certain. So we just have to hope and pray.'

'But she won't die or anything. Will she?'

'Don't be daft,' said Gran. I could see she was staring hard at Dad like she was examining him for cracks, or maybe warning him not to say too much.

'Can't they give her some new stuff, new blood? They can do transfusions, can't they?' I was gabbling a bit now because somewhere I'd heard about leukaemia and kids turning white because they hadn't got enough blood.

I suddenly wondered if I'd have to give Skinny some of mine. I knew about donors and stuff because Mum used to give hers regularly. She said they gave you tea afterwards. And a biscuit. The best bit was the biscuit. We could all donor for Skinny, I thought. Between us all we had a box of biscuits' worth. We could probably keep her going for ages.

'They've got medicines, drugs and stuff,' said Gran. 'These days they can cure anything.'

I nodded. But blood dying. I'd never heard of that before. And then I remembered what Cropper had once said about bruising. How dead blood pooled under the skin, the cells finished, dried out like fish carcasses in an emptied river.

I looked at Gran. She always knew what was what. Always sorted things out. 'But she is going to be all right?'

'Dunno, Lee. I just don't know. But you better do that praying like I said. Just in case.'

I looked at the fireplace. The brass fender was glittery gold in the light of the table lamp. Even I knew things were bad if you had to pray. Prayer was last-chance saloon. I didn't want to leave it up to prayer. I wanted Skinny fixed, sorted, now, so we could get back to normal.

'She may have to go on chemo,' Dad was saying.

'Chemo?' I said. 'Will that sort her?'

'She'll lose her hair,' said Gran, glaring at Dad like it was his fault, like 'chemo' itself was infectious, the sort of word you only had to breathe out and someone got sick.

'But she may have to go on it,' he repeated. 'It may be her only chance, a cocktail of drugs. We've got to be prepared for the worst.'

'Chemo?' muttered Gran. 'No need to scare people.'

The worst? Chemo's not the worst, Dad, I thought.

We've got Mr Leukaemia here, user and abuser of small girls. How bad is that?

Mum rang to say she was staying with Skinny, and Dad had to bring her pink Dumbo light and her princess book. Gran said she'd sleep over in case Dad had to be at the hospital all night.

'I can look after myself,' I said. I remembered Worm's stuff about living with the tiger. Well, there was a monster in our family now, something nasty out of the jungle. 'I can rough it,' I added.

Gran gave me one of her hard frowns, like I was a continuing mystery to her. 'I'm going to feed Tig,' she said. 'And you can have your tea and get yourself ready for bed.' She eyed me one. 'Now before you go up, tell me, you thought any more about getting that present for Bea? If she needs it at all she needs it now.'

'Like what?' I said, bit annoyed that Gran was arm-twisting me about Skinny.

Doing something someone else tells you to do is very different from doing something you've thought of yourself. When it's your idea it just gives it that red-ribbon feel. I wished I'd thought of the pressie thing first. Gran had beaten me to it and that pigged me off. It made me look as if I didn't care.

'Yeah. I've got an idea,' I said, 'and I'm getting the money.'

'You short?' she asked.

I knew she was going to offer me some. No way.

'Look, Gran. If I pay for it myself it's so much more worthwhile, don't you think?'

She nodded. 'Well, you better sort it out quick. That's all I can say.'

On my way to bed, I stopped outside Skinny's room. The no-boy area. 'She's growing up,' Mum used to say. 'She needs her privacy like everyone else.'

'And what about me?' I said. 'She's always coming in my room. Never knocks or anything. What about my privacy?'

'It's different for girls. They need a special space of their own.'

I pushed open the door, flicked on the light and stepped inside.

All her soft toys were there packed into a large plastic bag lying on the bed. The pillows had gone, and the pink pony set and the photos of Gran and Dad and Mum and me were all packed into a cardboard box.

On the floor was a pile of books, *The Little Ballerina* and kid stuff like that.

Looked like they were packing up Skinny B for good and taking her away.

Then I noticed a piece of paper on a chest of drawers. I picked it up.

'My Best Frend,' I read, 'is my big brother becoz he gets me Coke when I am tierd. And he holds my hands and takes me to skool. Yes. Bea Matthews.'

I felt a great gob in my throat.

I switched off the light and stood there in the dark.

Oh, please, please, Skinny. Get better. Please be better.

I lay awake for a long time in bed that night. I'd put her letter on the wall right next to my Beckham poster.

If Skinny was real bad and had to stay in hospital a long time Gran had said I'd have to come to her house. She had this scabby spare room full of junk, old electric fires and dusty shoes and bags of coat hangers.

I wasn't going, I said. It wasn't fair! Like I said, I was old enough to look after myself.

Why was I always dumped on? Skinny gets ill and suddenly I'm a refugee. Anyway, if he was back, I'd talk to Dad at breakfast.

I had something else too: I wanted to see if he'd let me take Assault to The Feck. I could do Jamil's round quicker that way. The Feck was a big no no land for fancy bikes but, as I say, I could outrun H5 if they showed and, well, I had some big bills coming up.

Cos now Skinny was real sick I couldn't skimp too much on her present. No. It would look so bad. And I couldn't not get Ali something dead good. As Jigger said, I could be in there and, anyway, as Gran says, penny pinching never makes friends.

Too right, Gran.

I began planning.

If Dad was still on the road or at the hospital I'd have to take the Assault without a yes. Big trouble if he found out. But he wouldn't. I'd only be there half an hour at most. Unless Jigger turned up on Wrecker and started doing burns and slams all over the round. I'd never get finished. It wasn't going to be like playing Mayhem down The Swamp, I knew that.

This was The Feck. Non-stop reality, 24/7.

I still wondered why Jig was dead keen to help all of a sudden. What was up? Was he pinning a freebie on me to set me up for a favour later? I hadn't a clue. I gave up.

I turned over and faced the wall. In the ghost light I could just make out one of my Man U posters, the Lord Becks curling in a trademark freebie just out of the flailing reach of the goalie.

No more benders now, eh, Becks?

I felt like that goalie, things curling just beyond my grasp.

For instance, where exactly was I going to find something for Alison? Jigger said he had a catalogue, but I didn't trust him any more.

Shame that. But he just wasn't the same as he used to be. There was still a bit of the old left but a new Jig seemed to be emerging out of the leftovers.

I saw this film once about body snatchers from outer space. They turned people into zombies, the living dead. But the thing was, you couldn't tell who was a zombie and who was not. Living and dead looked the same.

Dead scary.

Jig's like that now – zombie boy: mate on the outside, Ju Ju on the inside.

Maybe I was the same. Cluck on the outside. Skaz on the inside.

*

I began thinking about Buzz. Was he right about me not being up to the green belt? Maybe, like Cropper said, I was just standard bozo-grade boy.

Nothing special.

I don't think Mum thought I was special. I think she's scared of this special thing, the Skinny factor. Too much trouble. She wants me bog standard: a bozo buttoned-up blazer boy. No rocking the boat now.

The thing is, I've not got enough *ki*, that's what Buzz really thinks. *Ki* is mind, spirit, purpose. You don't get it in a bottle in Boots. It's there inside of you.

But the thing also about *ki*, is that it can hide away and you don't know you've got it. Or it can run off. You can have it one min, next it's gone. You've got to find it, but in your own way. No one else's way is any good.

Cats have great *ki*. The whole purpose and spirit of their life is to kill mice. That's their *ki*. And it's in every bit of their body. It runs in their blood. It's in every single hair of their fur. They have it in their claws, their eyes, their ears. Their whiskers quiver with it. Their tail sways with it. It's cat and *ki* in perfect harmony.

Be like the cat, says Buzz, find and hold the *ki*.

OK, Buzz, but answer me this. If the cat's *ki* is to kill mice, what's my *ki*?

What's the *ki* to my existence?

Eh, Buzz, Buzz?

No answer.

Of course! Bozo to ask. Someone else's answer is never yours, says Buzz.

154

Just keep looking.

And remember, he always says, Tae Kwon Do puts I Can Do back into your life.

11

Assault Goodbye

Gran was mumbling round the kitchen when I came down for breakfast.

'My dad not back, Gran?'

She shook her head. 'He's back tonight. They're both back.'

'How is B?'

Gran plonked a dish of porridge in front of me.

'As well as you can be when you got leukaemia.'

I looked at the porridge. I had no appetite.

'I don't eat that stuff, Gran.'

'You do today. It's two-coat cold out there and you need some warm inside.' She stood beside me, big wooden spoon raised in one hand. If I so much as blinked a protest she was ready to bring it cracking down on my head like it was an egg.

I took a few spoonfuls.

I bet if God hasn't sorted Skinny B out by tomorrow he's going to have Grannie Matthews storming down his aisle ready to wallop him one and then his knobbly knees'll be a-knockin' and his old teeth a-chatterin'.

'And keep your nose clean,' she said as I left. 'I know you. This isn't the time to go messing about.'

I went into the shed at the bottom of the garden and unlocked the Assault. I hadn't had it out since it was last cleaned and polished and, apart from the scratched saddle and a mark on one of the front forks Jigger made, it still looked shop-new.

A right cracker.

'What about yer helmet?' shouted Gran from the front door as I shot into Far Pastures.

Soz, Gran. Didn't hear you. Set my watch. Can't stop. Operation Pressie just took off.

I'd told her about the paper round and said I'd be back a bit later than usual. I didn't tell her I was going down The Feck. She'd let it out to Dad and he'd go mental.

First, I had to call in at Jamil's, check the Feck run was an OK.

He nodded. 'Go your bike?' he asked.

'Go my bike,' I shouted, sideswiping up towards Gants and school.

I winged it up The Drive, burning track, a thousand cc pumping through my legs. I could feel the murmur of wind in my ears, bike and me, bike and me, bike and me. I was skinning time.

I skidded into the playground.

Checked watch.

Nine mins, fifty-four secs.

New world record.

Lee Matthews does it again.

I decided that doing it for Skinny was like doing it for charity.

I swung the Assault into the bike racks and locked it.

I was cold, so I slipped into the library. Mouse was sitting next to the radiator doing the evolution homework.

'Hi, Lee. What's mutation?' she said.

'It's where you get a wonky individual who's born different from the rest.'

'But we're all born different.'

'A wonk is mega different. You have a wonk in the family and you've got trouble.'

'In my family that's me. I'm the odd one,' she said. 'Like my mum has black hair and is tall. My dad too and I'm . . . well . . . blonde and small.' She turned to me. 'You don't think I'm a wonk, do you?'

I looked at Mouse. She had changed. Her hair was up in a ponytail.

She was nodding like she wanted an answer quick.

'Course not,' I said. 'There are very few wonks around. Most of them play for City.'

She smiled ha ha and wrote 'wonk' on the answer sheet.

Then she started to gather up her books.

'By the way,' she said. 'I liked the thing you and Skaz did on The Tower. He told Alison it was your idea. That's just so cool. I didn't think you were like that.'

'No?'

'No, I thought you were a bit of a wuss. But you're not, are you? You're a sort of strong and silent type. I like that.'

So did I.

'I am?' I said. 'Thanks, Mouse.'

'Susie, remember!'

I nodded.

She thumbed me one and disappeared.

Strong and silent? Wuss?

She joking?

I played back her words in my head.

OK, Suze. 'Silent' maybe. But 'strong' I can live with. 'Cool', any time.

Someone thought I was cool.

Wow!

But why did Skaz tell Alison about The Tower? I wondered if she'd be as impressed as Mouse. I hoped so.

All day, no sign of Jigger. I avoided the playground and spent the breaks down the gym practising *chirugis*. Buzz didn't mind. He liked to see a bit of enthusiasm and kept a few spare trackie bottoms and tops around just in case anyone wanted a quick workout.

I was foot smacking the floor when I noticed someone watching from the doorway.

It was Dutton.

'Like the Tower job?'

I felt like smacking him one. 'That clucky thing was a shit trick,' I said.

He grinned. 'And you did it.'

'Why say it was my idea?'

'Well, you're such a wuss, thought you needed a bit of a leg up so to speak.'

'But why did you tell Alison Libidowicz?'

'Know what? It doesn't do me any good to be seen around with wusses. Let's say you needed a bit of promotion. That's what it's all about.'

By four I was at Jamil's.

No Jigger. Probably popping pills if you believed Skaz Dutton.

'How Skimpy?'

'Got bad blood, Jamil.'

'Blab bud? Here. This for her.'

He gave me a tube of Fizzies.

I held it in my hand like a firework, *Silver Fountain* or something, and felt bad. Yer right, Jamil, full of bad blab me.

Jamil, O kind person, leukaemia doesn't have much time for Fizzies. It's blood he's after. Count Leukaemia.

I slung the bag over my shoulders. I couldn't carry a full one. Too heavy on a bike. I'd have to come back for the rest.

I started top of the road where I'd walked Alison home that night she'd dumped her TKD stuff. I worked my way down criss-crossing right side, left till I reached a junction.

Now I was in The Feck proper and it was quicker cos most of the houses didn't have much of a front garden.

I zoomed in and out, dusting down paths, burn-marking kiss-close to front doors, slamming the paper through letter boxes or hurling it at windows so it fluttered down like a scattered bird crashing glass.

I had nearly finished the first bag and was halfway down this side road when I became aware of somebody behind me. I shot on to a path, skidded to a stop and peeped over the top of a hedge.

Five figures, hoodies up, walking abreast across the road.

Hoodz 5.

I was stuffed now. Too late to burn.

I looked around. A copy of *The Advertiser* was sticking out of the letter box like a handless arm. I shoved it right in and, holding the flap with my thumb, shouted through the opening.

'Anyone there. Help! Please. Anyone. Anyone there?'

'Empty house, boy.'

I shot round.

'Jus brimful of that great big empty feelin. Jus like you.'

Standing on the other side of the gate was a tall dark figure, hood up, face shadowed. I knew him, heard the voice, felt the eyes.

Big Hoodie from The Water Tower.

'No use shoutin to youself.'

The others I could see behind, dead still, standing in the road. Bad boy band strutting for a fashion shoot.

I turned round and gave the door a right kicking.

It didn't last long.

Someone grabbed me from behind and I was dragged into the road.

'I got news for yous, boy. Beating up on good people's front doors is jus for kiddie kicks.'

I scrambled to my feet.

All of them surrounded me.

No escape.

Big Hoodie started again.

'I'm thinking we goin to have to teach yous how to behave. I'm gonna give yous some fast learning, boy.'

Before I knew it, the news bag was jammed over my head and I was being marched down the road.

I don't know what I thought in those few scrambled metres. The bike! Dad! What they were going to do to me. Maybe they'd forgotten the bike. Maybe Assault was OK. Maybe I could get it later. Maybe they hadn't seen it.

Suddenly I was slammed against a wall or something and the bag pulled off.

We were in a garage, at the back. The up and over door was half down and a long wedge of lamplight brightened the concrete floor, its tip almost reaching my feet.

'Well, boy, yous ready for yous lesson? Lesson for today is taken from Hoodz Five, verse thirty-one. Thou shalt not tread on da property of da Hoodz no time o da day or da night. Unnerstand? Trespass is one big temptation and we don't allow temptation cross our path, boy. When it do we take our retribution. Law of da Hoodz.'

Someone pushed my head up and down.

'Yous damage our reputation, boy, then yous owe some confiscation. It's only right. Law of da land that. Second lesson, from da Hoodz book of hits, track twenty: no yid kid puts one on a Hoodz boy. Yous could have had ma frien's eye out with that can stuff. My frien could ha been one eye less. My frien's sight could ha been discontinued.'

Suddenly one of the Hoodz jammed the bag over me again. 'See what I mean, boy, bout being discontinuated. You end up in a bag.'

Silence.

I could hear my heart beat beating, feel it slamming in my chest.

Jesus, I was in for it now.

I felt sick like you do when you see something you can't stop coming your way like a giant wave it's too late to avoid.

Silence. Somewhere, a distant bell ringing.

More silence.

Had they gone? Was this it? Was it to shit-scare me?

I listened. Didn't hear them go.

I started to count. One ... ten ... thirty. They must have gone.

I ripped the hoodbag off.

They were still there, life-size cut-outs. All five, four dummies, one mouth and a bike.

A bike!

My heart sank.

They'd got Assault.

One of them was astride it, bent forward and gripping the handlebars like he was ready to take off.

'Nice commodity but it's ma duty take this for ma lawful booty. Because I tell yous what, boy. Since this yous first infringement of da Hoodz we be lenient with yous delinquent. Da bike comes with us, make up for da little dint in our reputation.'

'No,' I shouted. 'No. No.'

'Reparation is hard, boy, I know. Law is da law. Hoodz is da Hoodz. Tell yous what too, for yous own comfort, boy, that bike's an orphan from this now but we find him a good lovin home. Yous have my assurance on that.'

One of them lifted the bike and left.

'Give it back. Don't take Assault. Please. Please.' I struggled. But it was useless.

'I think yous mean "insult", boy. Good to see yous see the error of yous ways. A sniff of contrition is a welcome addition. Yous right, that spraying is one big insult stainin da Hoodz name. Well, down here, boy, it's an eye for an eye. Yous ready lose an eye? Yous ready to choose?'

I froze. Was he serious?

I pressed against the wall. Suddenly I could smell everything around, petrol, oil, sack-rot, damp.

'How do you mean, an eye?'

Silence.

'Look. I'm sorry,' I sniffed. 'Honest. I wasn't thinking. I just hit out. Self-preservation. Just ... er ...'

Big Hoodie stared at me.

'Well, seems nows our turn to learn da lesson, my friens. It seems self-preservation is da society to join. Members free to violate at liberty, eh, boy?'

I shook my head, my mouth dry of words.

'I think this preservation crap is desperation rap save yous skin, boy. I think yous need a little signature – from our dimension show yous in receipt of Hoodz boys' attention. That yous making a grateful contribution to their growing reputation.'

'No. No. No,' I blurted.

'Yes, boy.' He paused then snapped his fingers.

Two of the gang came forward, grabbed my arms and forced me to kneel. One of them shoved my head down and I heard a loud click like a blade flicking out. Then a hissing. Spray can!

They were going to graffiti me. Head bomb me. H5 me.

Dad. Help!

Silence.

A long pause. My heart pounding.

'Unless . . . yous wanna save that soft skin of yous and do a bit of biz with the Hoodz Five boys?' said Big Hoodie at last. 'We take yous on like an apprentice boy. What you say?'

'Biz?'

'Biziness. We needs a top delivery boy. You just the size we lookin for.'

Then I thought of Skinny bruised and wheezing in hospital.

'My little sister's in hospital. She's got leukaemia. I haven't got time to do deliveries.'

Big Hoodie whistled.

'My, I'm sobbing all over. So why yous on Hoodz turf and not weeping by that little girl's bedside?'

165

'Cos I need the money. To buy her stuff.'

'Stuff?'

'Pressies and things.'

'Oh, that stuff.' He went silent for a moment. 'Well, yous no head for biz, boy. You could earn yous pressie money here and save yous a skin print too. Bend him over boys.'

'No. No. I'll do it. I'll do it. Just give me Assault back and I'll do your . . . er . . . biz.'

Big Hoodie shook his head. 'In biz we take collateral. Rules of the game. It's only natural when we don't know ours boy yet. We need to build up trust here, so we keep the bike, not jus for reparation but guarantee of yous silence and co-operation.'

He reached inside his puffa and took something from a pocket. It was a handful of brown envelopes tied into a bundle. He held them up. The front one had a number written on it in bright red.

'Yous a Hoodz boy now. Welcome to da club. Jamil will tell you where to deliver yous Hoodz Five post.'

'What's in them?'

'Stuff. Top-spec happy stuff. Know what I mean, boy?'

I was beginning to. I remembered what Jigger said about uppers and benzies and dope and Aunty and his druggie mum.

Jesus!

They wanted me to carry the stuff.

'High fliers and hip hoppers for balloon heads, boy. Yous in it now.'

Big Hoodie was right about that.

'Get it from Aunty?' I said.

Big H turned on me, voice all hard. No rap riffs now. 'Another crack like that and I'll snap your arms off. Aunty's Osama round here, son. Skunk breath. Turd quality ganja. Got my drift? And don't let his name on our turf ever again. You hear.' He bawled down my ear. 'He's dog mess.'

I heard.

Then I was forced to the ground again.

Hoodie talk came back. 'That's right, boy, yous say yous prayers. Just take five mins while we leave. No peaking, mind, or we'll be back and muralize you, head to toe.'

One of them let off a long hiss of spray.

'Cos yous lucky. Yous lucky Hoodz ain't no bad feeling boys. Cos next time you hit one of Hoodz girls we take out your teeth so yous just good for spitting. Unnerstan?'

I nodded like a yessing machine.

'And bout this post, boy. Yous got just twenty-four hours to deliver. Everything first class for Hoodz boys.'

Then they went.

I staggered to my feet and stumbled out of the garage and into the street.

Empty as a sock in drawer as Gran would say. Holes of light, murk and fuzz everywhere else.

Where was Assault?

I scanned every drive in the street, checked hedges, dashed in and out of alleys and ginnels.

Not a skeffin sign of bike or Hoodz.

I raced all the way up to Gants hoping I'd catch sight of it.

It was nowhere.

Twocked.

Gone!

The biggest nowhere in the world.

A few cars swished past, careless and ignorant.

What did I expect? See it riding itself down Gants like some lost horse answering its master's whistle?

I stopped and leaned against a lamppost, heart sick.

Eventually I got to Jamil's. He was locking up.

He just stared at me. 'Where you been? You look bads jinni.'

'Geni? What geni?' I said, out of breath and verging on tears.

'Jinn is bads luck demon.'

'They took my bike, Jamil. My best, best bike. And yer bag.'

Jamil clapped his hands together and looked up towards the ceiling muttering.

'Feck full bads jinn.'

I got a quid out of him, no more. 'You sister bads, bike go bads. Me, bag go bads, paper bads. It bads always for me.'

I watched him get in his car.

Bads big time, Jamil. Bads big time for me too.

Then I remembered the envelopes. I had to get the addresses off Jamil.

Hell!

His car was halfway up the street.

I was stuck with them now. I had just twenty-four hours. I'd lost a bike for a crappy quid. Twenty-four hours!

And the clock was ticking.

12

Poison the Witch

Dad would go ment, psycho or what.

I decided to go to Gran's first.

I stood on the doorstep. 'They got Assault, Gran.'

And I burst out crying, blubbing like my chest would burst.

'Soz, Gran,' I blubbed.

And I gulped on about Hoodz 5 and Jamil till I ran out of snivel.

I didn't mention the envelopes.

She took my head and cradled it against her shoulder. 'I'll shaft the buggers,' she said.

'Thing is, Gran, what with Skinny B and all, Dad'll kill me.'

Gran raised her eyebrows. 'I'll tell them you were out getting her something, which is sort of true. That'll stop you getting red arsed. Maybe.'

She said she'd phone. 'And take this,' she said as I left.

It was a five-pound note.

Thanks, Gran.

Fifty more and I could buy another Assault.

Yeah and pigjinns would fly.

When I got in Mum was sitting at the kitchen table. 'On the worry', as Dad put it.

She got up and stared at me like I'd risen from the dead, like my face might have something vital missing.

'You all right, Lee? Gran just told me.'

'They got Assault.'

'I know. Dad will phone the police. And don't you worry. At this moment Bea is more important.'

I nodded. Of course she was. She was such bad news it made mine look a great big zero. Under all the worry the loss of Assault might just get forgotten. I began to feel better. And anyway Hoodz 5 were only borrowing Assault. Once I'd delivered the envelopes I'd get it back. No sweat.

'What's this?' said Mum. She'd taken my coat and was holding up Hoodz 5 bundle.

My heart skipped a beat.

'Just some stuff I gotta deliver for Jamil,' I said, trying to sound dead cool about it.

'No way,' she said. 'No more papers. That's it. You're not going near that place. You keep out of The Feck. Do you hear?'

I nodded dumbly. She was sounding just like Dad. I watched her slip the package into the bits-and-pieces drawer behind her.

'I know you did it for Bea,' she said, turning back to face me, 'so you could get her something nice, but that place is just too dangerous now.' She frowned. 'I don't know,' she said. 'It's this man thing. You've all got to go rushing about making mayhem, punching and shouting, roaring your engines and screaming your tyres, like you've got to be noticed. You're all the same. Even your dad. And it's rubbed off on you.' She sounded kind of sad as she said this.

'He'll kill me,' I said. I wasn't sure whether I meant Dad about the bike or Big Hoodie about the envelopes if it turned out I had to screw up his deliveries. 'He will, Mum. He'll lather me.' I wanted to lay it on a bit. Now she was feeling so non-violent. I wanted her to know I was seriously scared here. Get some commitment to peace.

'He'll go mental when he knows I was down The Feck with the bike.'

'Leave your father to me, Lee. I told you, don't you worry.'

I smiled. Thanks, Mum. A million.

I'll get her some flowers, I thought. I was beginning to see the point of this pressie stuff. A dozen, two dozen even, the whole hoggin florist's if she sorts Dad out.

I figured it was because she was well impressed with me over the pressie biz, she'd decided to persuade Dad not to ground me or whack me and otherwise trash my life. I hoped she would tell it so he didn't pin me to his dartboard and play bullseye with my buttocks. I hoped she'd tell it so I didn't get a forkful of humiliation down either ear. Hoodz 5 was one bad thing, but Dad could be turbo trouble.

From now on I was going to stay at home, keep out

of sight, stop rushing around like Mum said, keep out of trouble. Bin the Hoodz boys. Dad could sort them out. If he could sort out the bozos and the smack-heads on Saturday night he could sort out a few Feck yobs.

Then Mum told me about Skinny.

On Friday after school I was to come with her to see Bea. She was sure I'd want to and she was certain that Bea would love to see her brother. However, I was not to expect too much. It couldn't be a long visit because Bea was very ill and the drugs were exhausting her. All the time we were there she might not wake up at all. But I was not to worry. She was going to be all right. There were other kids in the ward who had leukaemia too and they were wandering about quite normal only without hair. And most kids like that recovered. Chemo was nasty but it cured. Only a few, a very few, didn't get better. And the consultant was very optimistic about Bea. And treatment was improving all the time. And new drugs were on the horizon, the nurses were saying.

Right, Mum.

She sat me down at the table. In our blood, she said, we all had these cells called corpuscles, white ones and red ones. The reds were good. So were the whites but sometimes, just once in a while for no obvious reason, they went off the rails, they went absolutely mad and started multiplying, doubling, quadrupling their numbers and overwhelming the reds.

The white plague.

I knew all about the body's defence mechanisms. We'd done blood in Biology with Cropper and I knew about

173

corpuscles and haemoglobin, the red stuff that carries oxygen, the breath of life, round the body.

No O, no life.

Whites 1 million – Reds zero, I thought.

Reds massacred. Disaster for Reds.

Poor Skinny.

Chemo wipes out whites, gives the reds time to recover. It's the white cell count that matters. That's what they check all the time. The Big White Cell Count. Tells you whether you're starting to live or starting to die.

Then I noticed Mum wasn't really looking at me any more. It was like she was talking to someone else, like she was getting it off her chest, washing all the blood and bad away with words, words, words.

The white blood cell count shoots up, she was saying, and if it goes on unchecked you die. She stared at the kitchen wall, her eyes wide as if she was looking straight at it, haunting herself with the idea of Skinny dying. Or was she making the monster come out of the dark, into the light where it just might wither and shrink into something that couldn't scare the shiver out of jelly.

Not to worry, said Mum.

Not to worry.

Mum's new mantra. Not to worry. Which meant of course she was worrying like crazy and putting a million little white worries inside me so my worry count was starting to rise high as hers.

Not to worry?

Skinny with colonies of whities blooming everywhere

inside her and we're not to worry. Mum, I wish you'd not told me all this.

Afterwards, in bed, I imagined myself and Big Hoodie, toe to toe, in TKD combat. Ya, Rap Boy, watch my leaping Bruce Lee action kick you into traction, so you're a permanent attraction at the NHS, a surgical mess, head in plaster, beaten by a master faster on his feet than you.

Then I heard the car door slam.

I waited.

No sound. No explosions from Dad downstairs.

Maybe she'd not told him about Assault.

I crept on to the landing.

I could hear voices in the kitchen.

Suddenly the door opened.

'Two hundred bloody quid that cost me,' I heard Dad shouting.

That all? I thought. I told Jigger three hundred.

'I'll have their balls for bullseyes.'

Dad was roaring now like he had a bolt through his brain.

I shuddered.

The door slammed shut.

I crept to the bottom of the stairs.

I could hear chairs scraping.

Mum was talking, about me, telling Dad to listen, telling him that shouting never solved anything. Telling him this was about Bea really, not a stupid bike. Telling him Bea was much more important than a bit of metal.

I nodded.

Stupid? Bit of metal?

No way. That's Assault you're talking about.

She told him about me buying Skinny a present. About how I was changing and developing. I wasn't a kid any more, she said. I was growing up. Getting responsible.

Dad grunted.

I guessed what he was thinking. Dad's Rule: no Feck, no bikes, no buts. And I'd taken not a gnat of notice of him.

Mum said I'd reached the running-the-gauntlet stage of adolescence. I needed risk in my life. That's why I'd gone into The Feck. Spice of danger. Like a do-it-your-self initiation test. An echo of primitive tribal behaviour patterns. He had to understand that.

Did he?

I doubt it.

He was probably thinking along the lines of giving me a primitive clout round the ear.

But Mum hadn't finished.

It was a male thing, she said. Puberty and all that. There was a blizzard of hormones whirling round in-side me. I was bubbling with chemicals, she said. I wasn't my own master. I was a slave, a victim of an over-enthusiastic biology.

Wow!

Well, kiss my kecks, I thought. Mum's a psychie all of a sudden.

Daft really. Mum expecting me to leap the chasm of growing up and up when it was she who had tried all the time to keep me home, a right white shirt with cuffs on.

*

Still, she'd stopped Dad's charge in its tracks.

Chairs scraped.

'I'll talk to him in the morning.'

I shot upstairs, hormones on full throttle.

I set the alarm for three. I needed to get the Hoodz package from the kitchen. Stash it under my bed. I just hoped Mum hadn't mentioned it to Dad. Otherwise I was dead meat squared.

Tomorrow I'd have a word with Jigger. Maybe we could work something out.

I stared at David Beckham.

Bad news, Becks.

Suddenly, I'm Hoodz for hire. Rap Boy's runner. Junkie post.

I wished they'd just head bombed me instead.

I lay down, not cold but shivering nonetheless. What happened if the police found out? What would happen if Big Hoodie shopped me? Maybe they were setting me up. Revenge for stiffing their girl Garrett. The door bell could ring at any moment.

It was hours before I fell asleep, and all night I seemed tumble and fall into one wild dream after another.

I never heard the alarm.

Next morning Dad eyed me over his newspaper.

We'd been sitting at the table for ages, slowly chewing cereal. Mum had gone round to Gran's so they could both go to hospital.

'You look half asleep. Something wrong?'

I shook my head. I was working out how to get the

Hoodz stuff out of the bits-and-pieces drawer without him seeing.

'I know about the bike,' Dad said after a while.

I nodded.

'Yer mum thinks it's to do with hormones.' He pushed his plate away. 'She should know, I suppose. She says you're upset about your sister. She says you're not in control.' He looked hard at me. 'And the way you ride that bloody bike I can see what she means.'

I nodded slowly.

Soz, Dad.

'And if you'd have done what I told you, that bike, that top spec, top wack bike, would be sitting there right now in the garden shed like per usual.'

He shook the paper. I felt the draught, bit of breeze before the storm. I didn't like the look of it.

'You can forget your bloody hormones.'

He was waving his spoon.

Bad sign.

'That's women's talk. It won't let you off the hook.' He leaned across the table. 'Two hundred quid down the drain. That's a week of my time, half of it driving under-age alkies and airheads down The Feck. And that's where you chose to spend your time. Down with the drop-outs and the dead-beats of this world.'

'I was only –'

He barged on past me.

'While your sister is fighting for her life. And no excuses, Lee. I don't want to hear a word. You don't know what your mum's going through. You don't know what your sister's going through. No, because you'd

178

rather be stunt biking and careering round the place like some doped up joyrider.'

Then I noticed bit by bit Dad was crumpling the paper, bit by bit his big fist was crumpling the news.

'Last night she had a temperature of one hundred and four, Lee. One hundred and stinking four. She was that hot she was burning, sweat just pouring off her, poor kid. It's just not fair. What are they doing? Nothing. Because there's nothing they can do. Absolutely nothing.'

I shook my head, more a shudder than a shake. I felt like when Cropper asked you a question you couldn't answer. I'd never seen Dad like this before.

'Doctors don't tell you anything. Don't know themselves.' He shook his head. His eyes were full of tears. I could see them even though he had turned sideways to me and was looking out of the window down the garden. 'Last night she was gasping. She was wheezing that much I thought she was going to choke.'

He seemed to be talking to himself now, not me.

'Thought she was going to ... Don't know what we were going to do if ...' His voice choked to a stop. I found myself holding my breath. It was like we were both standing together on the edge of a precipice, neither of us daring to look down into the drop.

'Soz, Dad. Soz.'

My dad, big as a barge, was shaking, shaking the table. It was freaking me out. I'd never seen him cry before. Not Dad. Not even when United lost the League. Never.

The paper was still caught in his grip, the pages splayed and pleated like feathers. Each time he moved they shivered.

The tremble of a dying bird.

I felt myself trembling too.

Dad crying!

It was like nothing was safe any more. It was like a crack in a wall opening up. Anyone could come in and get us: aliens, Indians, Ju Ju, the Creature from the Swamp. We were at their mercy. There was nothing between us and fear.

'Dad. Dad. You're spilling yer tea.'

'Tea? Eh! What you talking about? Soz did you say?' He squinted at me. 'Is that all you've got to say? Is that it? Soz? What does soz do? What did soz ever do?' He leaned towards me. 'Soz you, Lee. And I don't care what yer mum says,' he growled, 'from now on you're grounded.'

'Dad!'

'Grounded. Till I say otherwise.'

He stood up, caught the table. A cup toppled, fell and smashed on the floor.

'And you can clear that up. 'Bout time you did a bit of work round here. And if you think you're getting another bike, you can think again.'

And with that he was gone, banging his way out of the house.

Three days to Alison's party and I was grounded, left on the bench, sin-binned, put on hold, withdrawn from

180

circulation, quarantined, red-carded, put aside for later, suspended, kept temporarily out of use, held on remand!

I had to go. Alison wanted me to. I wanted to see her face when she opened her present. I wanted her to look at me, slow and deep into my eyes. I wanted her to come up to me, her face right up to mine. I wanted her lips to search for mine. I wanted her to kiss me. Not long enough for everyone to go oohh, but longer than just thank you. I wanted a not-quite-letting-go kind of kiss. A just-us kiss. A slow peel-away kiss that would surprise us both, where we pretend it hadn't happened but we both know it had and knew the other knew it had.

And, anyway, everyone else would be there. I wasn't going to be left out. No way. If I didn't go, Garrett for one, with her big mouth, would dummy suck me in front of the others: Mouse, the Pole, Alison, the whole bozo class if she got a chance. I could just hear her now, asking me if Mummy's little playmate wanted his nappy changing.

Stuff her!

Somehow I had to get Dad to change his mind.

Soon as he was gone I went over to the drawer. I was just taking it out when he came rushing back in.

'And don't you try and get round your mum. It won't work this time.' He stopped frowning.

'What's that you got there?'

'Charity envelopes. Got to take them back to school.'

'Charity? What you wasting time on that for? What charity?'

'For the new Drug Rehab Centre.'

'What you on about? Rehab? What do you know about drugs?'

'Me? Nothing,' I said. 'Honest. It's just our class voted to support it as part of our Community Link Scheme.'

'They would, wouldn't they. Half The Feck are in your form. Drugged up most of them. Bloody low life. They don't want rehab. They want R.A.K., a right arse kicking.'

Yes, Dad. Like Jigger trying to keep his mum together, like he has to do nursey with his sister, like he has to do all the Co-op shop crap.

'Oh, get to your lessons,' he said. 'And try and learn something proper.'

He left.

I let out a mega sigh. I could feel a cold ooze in my armpits.

Wow!

Dad had a right one on him. Was he on the down. Must be Skinny.

I picked out the packet and shoved it in my rucksack.

You want some of this stuff, Dad. Megawatt your mind. Put some woosh in your cab.

I needed to get hold of Jigger. I walked to school, my head all a-jumble and still trembling after all the heavy stuff with Dad in the kitchen.

Still, I had a smile for myself. I'd fooled him. Kept my cool, good *ki* as Buzz would say.

I didn't really notice Worm come alongside of me till he spoke.

'No bike. Lee?'

'No.'

'Can't have my ride then, can I?'

'No.'

'You OK, Lee?'

'No.'

'About the bike?'

'Yes. Got nicked.'

'No!'

'Yes.'

'Where?'

I told him the whole story.

'Hoodz Five are bad news,' he said. 'They run the streets round our way.'

'You live in The Feck?' I said.

Worm nodded. 'Told yer.' He shook his head. 'It'll be on The Santa Run by now.'

'The Santa Run?'

Worm explained.

The Santa Run was where the white vans from The Feck floor it to Sheffield up the M1 and offload loot like my bike to the wide boys, the scalp heads and bozos, the fly dealers, the hucksters, the conkers (cash only no questions asked) and the rest of the back alley low life there.

'How'd you know these things?' I said, amazed.

'Oh, I know lots,' he said.

'Yeah?'

'Yeah. Like you were set up with that bike and stuff.'

'Set up?' I stopped dead. 'What do you mean, "set up"?'

'Use yer brains. It's obvious. How come the Hoodz boys, all five of them, just happened to be in the same street as you? A dead-end street. Very convenient. Nobody around. No escape. And how come they just happened to have a couple of cans of bomber juice ready to do you a face job? Someone told them you were on your way. Happens all the time. They know what gear arrives. And where. And when. They just pick and choose. Your bike's van loot, Lee. Sorry about that. I fancied a ride. And you promised.'

I wasn't listening.

In the playground I left Worm. No sign of Jigger so I headed for the library. Everything in my head was fast-forwarding. I needed a bit of me on my own.

I logged on to one of the computers, tapped a few keys to jog its memory and left it doing screen savers.

Then I started thinking. Had I really been set up like Worm said? Who'd do a thing like that? Who knew I was going down The Feck with Assault? Skaz did, so did Jigger. And Worm. Half the school did. They'd seen me riding in first thing, riding out end of the day. But they were my mates. They wouldn't set me up with Hoodz 5. Would they?

Then for some reason I thought of Skinny. She'd been set up all right. By the white witch, the one who frightened Dad as he sat beside the bed listening to her, the blood eater, wheezing and gasping inside his child.

I typed in LEUKAEMIA.

Twenty thousand sites; one big white witch.

Abnormal white cells invade the blood. The whites and the reds die off. The body is no longer protected from infection. Unprotected it weakens and dies.

First the victim feels tired and feverish, suffers sweats and bruising. Without help the lungs collapse, the heart fails, coma and death follow.

Once she's taken up residence only poison kills the witch. Chemicals shot into the blood seek her out and attack her and her millions. But the witch fights back, tears out the victim's hair, shakes them like a rag doll, cramps their limbs, bends their bones.

It's a terrible battle.

'What's that?'

I shot round.

It was Mouse. 'Nothing,' I said and blanked the screen.

'Worm said that fancy bike of yours been nicked.'

I shrugged.

'Going on Saturday, to Alison's?'

'Dunno yet. My dad's grounded me after the bike biz and stuff.'

'I bet that Skaz Dutton had something to do with it.'

I looked at her sharply. 'Skaz? Why?'

'Cos he always has.'

'You don't like him, do you, Mouse?'

'Suze to you. Maybe I don't and maybe I couldn't care less.'

Thinking about it then I realized that I didn't know anyone who actually liked Skaz. Except Alison Libidowicz. She didn't seem to not like him. I suddenly remembered the scene in the playground after that Cropper lesson, him looking down her blouse.

'You know he's a voyager, don't you,' Mouse said after a while.

I was puzzled. 'Voyager?'

'Yeah, snoops pictures, you know, of girls, in the nod and stuff. Dirty perv.'

'I had heard,' I said.

Mouse looked hard at me. 'You've not got some, have you?'

I shook my head. 'No. No. Of course not.'

'Jigger knows how to get them, but he won't tell me. We ought to shop people like Dutton. It's not right.'

'No,' I said. 'But you need the evidence to shop people properly.'

Mouse frowned. 'Yeah, well maybe you could get it.' She stared at me, her eyes wide with the challenge.

Hang about, Mouse, I thought. Leave me out of this. 'Hold on, Suze,' I joked. 'This isn't Vice Squad.'

'Huh!' she snorted. 'Typical. Boys – all mouth, no action.'

She wandered off.

I stared at the screen saver: flying chickens.

Since The Water Tower thing I'd sort of seen Skaz as a brother, an older brother who cusses you and cares for you at the same time, who taunts you into defiance only to put you down again for getting above yourself. After the bombing I felt we were kind of bonded by the danger, bound by our secret crime.

Now, well, Mouse had reminded me of a different

186

Skaz. Peeper. Voyager. It wasn't something I wanted to think about. So, get lost, Mouse.

Buzz said you should swallow the truth whole. Well, just now, I was for nibbling at truth, taking it a crumb at a time.

13

Reggie the Rabbit

It was a full house for Cropper's lesson. We all wanted to know what was going to happen to Little Reggie Rabbit.

Cropper waited. Only Worm stirred, his breathing hissing behind us faint as a breeze through a keyhole.

'Listen,' said Cropper at last. 'One day a wonk rabbit was born in the warren. No fur on him. Just all-over skin. Come the winter he'd freeze, they all said. Reggie's a gonner, they said.

'But winter didn't come. Climate changed and everywhere hotted up. So hot it was only Reggie made it in his cool bunny suit. Reggie and a few likely bunnettes who fancied him now he was the only hunk around. So Reggie bunnied about and had lots of bunnikins, some with fur, some half furred, some skinless like him. And they found a new warren and lived under the hot sun happily ever after. The whole of rabbit nation saved by one raw rabbit. Just shows wonks can save the world. Evolution's all about wonking and bonking.'

Cropper grinned. Everybody cheered, especially the wonks amongst us. And especially Worm.

How was it going to work for him? I wondered as the bell rang. It wasn't fair taking your breath away. I couldn't see any advantage in having crappy lungs.

At break I scoured the usual places for Jigger, back of bikes, round the kitchen bins, under the fire escape. No Jig.

Then I saw Worm again heaving and wheezing.

'Wanna do me a favour, Worm?'

He frowned. When people asked him for favours, like airheads wanting a suck on his inhaler, he usually said no.

Waste of time asking, I suddenly thought. I'd no bike to trade him a ride.

He shook his head. He could be a right stubborn little git.

'Just deliver some stuff down your way,' I said.

'Stuff?'

'Yeah.'

'Where would someone like you get stuff from?'

'Never you mind, Worm. You're not the only smart-arse in the world. All you got to do is deliver it.'

'And get nicked. No way. I wasn't born stupid.'

'Aw, get stuffed, Worm.'

I walked off.

'If it's Hoodz Five gear,' he said after me, 'don't touch it. Once you start they'll have you by the balls for ever. Step out of line and they'll shop yer. Or smack you about.'

'Smack who?' said a voice.

It was Skaz Dutton. 'What's up, Lee?'

'Had his bike nicked by Hoodz Five,' said Worm from a distance. 'Got him delivering their stuff.'

Skaz looked hard at me. 'You prat. Just like them airheads to get a wuss doing their dirty for them. What you thinking about, Lee, messing with scum like that? What would mummy say?'

'They took my bike,' I said. 'Didn't get much choice.'

Skaz pulled a face. 'That fancy thing! Took it down The Feck? Now that was clever. Like you wanted to suicide yer bike.' He couldn't believe me.

'Got him in the lock-up,' said Worm. 'On Tanner Street.'

'Someone shopped you, Reggie boy. Could be Jigger. He's a loser. Hoodz Five got his number, head banged him with it.' He laughed.

'I get it back if I deliver their stuff,' I said, ignoring the bit about Jig.

Skaz looked at me, frowning and laughing at the same time. 'You're not believable, Lee. Get real. It's been vanned to Sheff and traded for a bunch of fiver bags on the street already.'

'No,' I said suddenly, knowing it was yes, yes, yes all the way up the M1 to Sheffield.

'And what you going to do when the cops bust you and find a bundle of envelopes –' Skaz paused and then put on his Policeman Plod voice and said – 'concealed about your person?'

'How do you know about the envelopes?'

'Cos everyone on The Feck knows,' said Worm.

'And you're the only wonking bunny who doesn't,'

said Skaz. 'If you want to survive, better start learning fast.'

'OK. You know so much about it, you deliver them,' I said.

'Cost you, wonk boy.'

'You will?' I said, surprised, not thinking Skaz would take over the biz.

He eyed me up. 'On second thoughts, no.'

'Aunty wouldn't like it,' explained Worm.

'Who the hell's Aunty?' Then I remembered Jigger talking about her.

'Sshh,' said Skaz. 'Keep your voice down. Words in your ear is how Aunty works. Clever. Whispering makes us all piss-scared.'

Even you, Skaz, I thought.

He winked at me and started to wander off.

Some help he was.

One thing was clear, if Skaz really thought Hoodz 5 were a scum load of airheads, he wouldn't have shopped me and told them about Assault so they could ambush me.

Wrong there, Mouse.

Someone else had shopped me.

Jigger?

Skaz was calling back, 'Got those silk undies yet?'

I pretended to look puzzled.

'For the party?'

I shook my head.

'OK!' He came back.

'I will do you a favour, Matthews. Since knicks aren't your thing. Go to Big Dave on the market tomorrow.

He's got these OK pendants. Dead cheap. Silvery with hearts hanging on them. Mushy, but girls like them. Say I sent you.'

I nodded. 'Ta.' I didn't like to say I was grounded and my chances of getting to Alison's party were as good as a chocolate bunny's in a bonfire.

'How much?' I said.

Skaz shrugged. 'Negotiate.' Then he wandered off, grinning. 'Offer him stuff,' he called back.

Sure, Skaz, get myself busted.

I watched him disappear amongst the playground swirl of kids.

Was I looking good!

Grounded. Best bike nicked. Kid sister in hospital. Police on my tail. Hoodz 5 hoodlums ready to juice me.

One more day in the life of normal.

Well!

Fight your corner, said Dad.

Trouble was I was in four corners at once all looking at a fight.

Then I remembered Gran's fiver. That and the few quid in my piggy bank was enough for a pendant and something for Skinny.

Surely?

I decided to go for the pressies. Something nice for Skinny might just impress Dad enough to let me off the lead so I could go to Alison's.

Worth a try.

After school I saw Jigger hanging about just outside the school gates.

I waved. He was hooded up, hands sunk in pockets.

'You not been in today, Jig?'

'No. Seen Mouse?'

'Where you been?'

He shrugged. 'Just about. Well, have you seen her?'

'Yeah. Before school. Why?'

'Got us some tickets for The Shed.'

'Can't go, mate. I told you. Anyway I've been grounded.'

'What for?'

I told him about Assault and Hoodz 5 and the envelopes.

'Brown envelopes?'

I nodded.

'Bastards,' he said. 'What you going to do, Lee? Where's the stuff now?'

I pointed over my shoulder at the rucksack.

'You bog-brain! Are you crazy or what? You know if you get caught with that lot . . .?'

He didn't finish.

I nodded. I sort of knew. And suddenly I felt like I was carrying a live bomb, with one of those trembler things that set it off at the slightest nudge. It was strapped to my back. Someone's elbow, the fickle hand of fate even, could detonate it any time.

'Look, Jigger. Do us a favour. Get rid of them for me? You know the score. I'll pay you back, honest.'

He was silent for a minute and then nodded slowly as if he was still thinking it through.

'Yer a mate.' I tried to shrug off the rucksack.

'Not here, you prat,' he hissed.

We walked down Canterbury and on to the railway path.

I held out the bundle.

He didn't take it. Instead he folded his arms and looked at me like I needed lessons.

'What?' I said.

'Is this real?' he said at last. He took one of the envelopes, pressed it with his fingers then shook it next to his ear. 'You're telling me Big Hoodie gave you this lot to deliver?'

I nodded. Jig's mood had changed. He seemed calmer and colder now we were on our own.

'Yeah. Why?'

'Exactly. Why? Why give some prat kid piddly bits of stuff? It ain't worth posting, Lee. And for all they know you could have gone straight to the cops. Whatever they are, the Hoodz boys aren't stupid.'

I said nothing. Jig was making sense. A lot for a brickhead.

'They knew I wouldn't shop them as long as they had Assault,' I said feebly.

'Maybe,' said Jig. 'Maybe they were testing you. See how you shaped up. Maybe it was just a laugh. Maybe they thought you were such a Noddy you'd get busted. Their way of smacking you back for lamming Garrett.'

'How do you mean, testing?' I said slowly.

'Recruitment,' said Jig. 'They need all the posties they can get. Ones with good cover. No one suspects nice all-over-innocent, shirt-in types to go round running stuff. Wake up, Lee. This is how it is. You do the job and they put you on their books so to speak, put a few quid in yer pocket, string you along with a promise to return Assault. And then when you get stroppy they threaten to tell mummy and daddy and the nice men on the Drugs Action Team that you're in the biz.'

I shivered. Were Hoodz 5 really trying to recruit me? Is that how it happened?

'You seem very clued up here, Jig.'

'You need to be to survive down The Feck,' he said. 'Otherwise they have you. Suck the blood out of yer life. Real time Ju Ju, mate. That's what they are.'

'Yeah.'

'Here, give 'em me.' He took the rest of the envelopes. 'Probably filled with bicarb anyway. Can't see Big Hoodie wasting A1 stuff on you for a trial run.'

'Got to be delivered tonight,' I said. 'First class.'

'Sure, Lee.' He shoved the envelopes into his rucksack before swinging it on to his shoulder.

'You know, mate,' he said, 'I've been thinking. Sounds to me Hoodz Five knew you were coming. All five of them together, dead-end street, convenient lock-up round the corner. Tell me I'm not suspicious, but who knew you were going down The Feck?'

I told him half the school.

'And Skaz Dutton?'

I nodded.

'Probably that gob mouth.'

'Not likely. He thinks Hoodz Five are psychos.'

'Doesn't stop him shopping you for a fiver.'

'A fiver? You think he'd do it for a fiver?'

Jigger ignored my question. Suddenly he said: 'Time Hoodz Five got sorted out.'

'Sure, Jig.'

'It'll happen, you watch.'

Just as he turned to leave, I said, 'You know Dutton does these videos, girls and stuff.'

Jigger looked at me, grinning.

'No, seriously, Jig, Mouse says you know where you can get them.'

'They're crap. Big Dave flogs them on the market. If you want a peepsie of Libdidi do-dah, forget it. The only one you get a good look of is Garrett. Waste of time. You can get her real time for half the price.'

'Oh!'

I pointed at his rucksack. 'You know where to deliver those?'

He grinned. 'Jamil will.' Suddenly he slapped me on the back. 'And don't try Big Dave. Get wise. Other day Worm bought a Dutton production off him. Wheezed home. Got himself all wanked up. Slammed the video in. Pressed START. A right scam. Turned out to be some bygone kiddie cartoon. Suck on that.'

Wonker Worm I thought.

'Of course. Big Dave's on to a winner. No one dares go back and complain. But that's what it's all about,' said Jigger. 'Keeping one scam ahead of the rest. See ya. And keep yer head down. Out of Hoodz way.'

I watched him wander off down the path.

My head was down and jammed. Now I really owed Jig.

I leaned against the path fence and tried to suss it all

196

out – H5, Assault, running stuff, The Feck, the ambush, Jamil, Dutton's dirty videos.

Get wise, eh!

I began thinking.

Jig, I said to myself, you seem to know a lot about Hoodz 5. Maybe they've got you too. Maybe they've logged on to your brain, man. They tapped yer skull with the company logo, didn't they? Maybe you belong to them. Maybe you're just conning me. Maybe you'd sell me down the river for a fiver. Maybe everyone is just conning everyone else Big Dave time.

Hell! Just who could you trust?

And someone had let on about Assault.

Jigger?

Skaz?

Even Worm?

One of them had shafted me. Why?

I just couldn't figure that out so I turned and started for home.

Gran was in doing a brew. She shushed me and pointed upstairs. 'Your mum's resting. She's been up all night.'

I didn't need to ask.

But I did. 'B bad?'

'I've lit candles,' said Gran. 'In church.'

I hate it when people give you a sideways answer like they don't think you're big enough to take it. Gran, give it me straight. Is Skinny going to die soon? Is that it? And candles are all we got? Fat chance they have against killer-joy cancer.

Gran lit candles in church after motorway crashes and terrorist atrocities or sometimes when planes went down if there were British on board. Candles in our family were for hopeless causes and helpless cases.

'Don't worry, Gran,' I said, 'God will listen.'

'Let's hope so,' she murmured.

Just then, Dad came in.

'White blood cells right up. Second lot of test results are back.' He slumped in his chair. Gran gave him a mug of tea.

'Up and up,' he said. 'It's a bugger.'

Up and up! How far does it go? I thought of Gran's barometer next to the mirror in her hall. That went up and up, down and down. All over. From 'storm' to 'tempest' to 'hurricane'. One night I remember it was wild wind, trashing everything. I imagined the barometer shaking, the needle shuddering past 'typhoon' and off the planet into world annihilation.

Now, inside Skinny white corpuscles were exploding everywhere, and her bloodometer was rising, rising: 10,000 per millilitre, 15,000, 20, 25, the reds falling in their billions.

'A right bugger,' said Dad again.

I looked at him warily, wondering if he was going to cry again or something or remember the bike and give me another earful.

He must have read my mind because he gave me a half grin, leaned over and cuffed me like his hand was a big friendly paw. 'Sorry about this morning, son. It's just Bea. It got me, eh!' He sighed, sipped his tea. 'It's so unfair. Why our little B? What's she done? What have

198

we done? It doesn't make sense, Lee. Does it, you tell me? Tell me, eh?'

He searched my face, frowning.

'Don't be daft,' said Gran. 'What's the lad know? You can't expect him to know.'

'I do, Gran, honest I do,' I said, not really having a clue what I knew. But I felt better for saying it. I wanted to be part of the worry, belong to the fear. For the first time in ages I was there holding hands with my family, all of us together squeezing each other tight.

After a bit Gran said, 'You got that present yet, Lee?'

'Eh, what's this?' said Dad.

Gran explained how it was my idea to get Skinny something.

Dad nodded and nodded. Like he was slowly getting used to a bit of surprise news. 'That's good, Lee. That's really good. Look,' he said after a bit of thought. 'You get me one of those envelopes for that charity, the ones you had this morning, remember. I'll give you something for it. You're a good lad. We could do with a lot more of that sort of thing.'

'I've got rid of it,' I said. 'The envelopes I mean.'

'Well, you can get some more.'

'I think they've run out of them,' I said too quickly.

'What's up, Lee? You sound like you don't want my help.'

'No. No. It's not that, Dad.'

'I mean, do you want me to sponsor this drug thing or what? I'm offering here, Lee. Bit of charity. Come on.'

'That's great, Dad. Great.'

'That's better son. Never look a gift horse in the mouth. Well, here's a tenner for starters. Put that in the box like. And make sure that form teacher knows who's done the giving here, right? Now, I'm going to see how your mum is. Take her a cuppa.' He slid a ten-pound note across the table. It was new, crisp and smooth as plastic.

'Thanks, Dad.'

Pressies no problem now.

Later, before I got into bed, I smoothed out Dad's tenner and held it up to the light. The queen's head was on one side, Darwin's on the other and in the top centre shone a sun with rays printed thin as spider silk. Like capillaries they were, the skinniest, the most fragile blood hairs of all like the ones threading through Skinny, blind alleys for reds dying, dying and gasping for oxygen.

Then I realized.

Wednesday.

I'd missed Tae Kwon Do. Forgotten all about it what with all the stuff about Skinny. Buzz would probably think I was having a sulk, taken the hump over him saying I wasn't ready for my green belt.

Well, maybe I had a plan.

Maybe I should go up to him and say: 'Yes, sir. You were right about me not being mature enough for the green. I understand what you were saying about self-discipline, about awareness of others, about facing up to your own weaknesses. Strong is the warrior who knows his own weakness.'

Then Buzz would say, 'Thus speaks the true spirit of

the master.' And I'd be a green belt faster than you could say chop *chirugi*.

I leaned over and switched off my lamp.

I just hoped Jig could deliver those brown envelopes in time and I could say bye to Hoodz 5 for ever.

It was the phone woke me up. Early.

Skinny! I thought and leapt out of bed. I went out on to the landing just as Dad opened his bedroom door. We both stopped and looked away quickly like we'd caught each other out.

'That was your mum on the phone,' Dad said, his voice croaky with sleep or worry.

I waited uneasily.

'At least the count's not going any higher.'

'So, it could start coming down today if they do this chemo thingie?' I said hopefully. I knew Skinny being ill was really hurting him so I spoke very slowly, carefully putting one word on top of another, building up a bit of fragile comfort for him. And I held my breath because I guessed it could all blow away at any moment, at the sudden ring of a bell or knock at the door.

Dad gave a bit of smile. 'Yes. Yes, Lee, it could. Well done, you.'

'And then everything will be OK.' I grinned. 'Give Rabbit some too, get him hopping and chop chopping again.'

Dad stared at me. 'Chemo's not funny, Lee. It half kills you.'

I gulped. Prat me. Now everything was flat again.

Dad shuffled off to the loo.

I went downstairs and sat in the kitchen, gloomily eating Krispies.

I bummed school for first couple of lessons. I'd told them about Skinny and they said any time I wanted to chill out, take it easy, they understood.

On my way to the market I passed New Look. Mouse had said all the girls went there for their party gear; said it was just the place for me to get Alison something.

I hung around the store entrance, trying to look like I was waiting for someone to come out, like my sister or something.

And then I found myself yessing to the boy-band stuff lamming off the walls and wondering if I should give it a go rather than try down the market. I mean, for starters, could I trust Skaz?

I swung round on my heels, cool like, see if there was anybody inside the store without anyone guessing I was swinging round and trying to see if there was anyone inside the store.

Everything was pink and silver. Glitz city.

I couldn't do it.

I just couldn't go into the girl-only bit. No way. At least, not when every other bozo kid was in school. I'd stick out like lolly-licker's tongue. They'd take me for a perv, they would, if they saw me looking. You'd have to have a brain by-pass to do that.

I turned and walked away.

Down the market I found Big Dave.

'Skaz Dutton said you have some jewellery cheap.'

'Cheap? No, sonny. This is street prices but shop quality.'

'OK. Skaz said you had these pendants. I need two.'

He leaned forward and took a card from off the stall. 'Thirty-five quid.'

I gasped.

'But to you, cos yer a mate of Dutton's, thirty.'

Thirty? It was still out of my league.

He laid one across his open hand. It was silver and the curvy heart dangled over the podge of his palm. 'And for two you get a multi-buy discount. So shall we say straight twenty? Best I can do.'

'I've only got fifteen quid,' I spluttered. 'I didn't think they'd cost so much.'

He shrugged.

'Take it or leave it, sonny. But don't leave it long. These'll be snapped up.'

'OK. I'll take one at ten quid and buy something else.'

'Er, not quite, sonny. If you have just the one you lose the discount. Cost you twelve fifty then.'

My heart sank.

'Well, you got all sorts else,' said Big Dave, sweeping his hand over the stall. 'This a present?'

'Well, it's not for me,' I said.

'Girlfriend maybe?'

'Sister,' I muttered.

'How old?'

'Seven.'

'Try this.'

He held up a bright-pink tube. '*StarDust*' it said. '*Hair and Skin Glitter*'. 'Kids love it,' said Dave.

Yeah, Skinny liked bright stuff.

'Two fifty to you.'

OK. Sorted.

'Got any wrapping paper?' I said.

'Hey, cheeky now, I'm not made of charity. You can have this. Give it a good iron. It'll be all right.'

He shoved a folded sheet of creased pink paper into my hand. 'Girlie enough for you?' he said.

I walked back towards school, found a bus shelter and sat down on the bar they put there for old fogies. You sit in there and no one thinks you're on the bum and reports you. They think you're just bus hanging, cartoon schoolboy, basic model bozo.

I peeped in the bag. Big Dave had put the pendant in a black velvet pouch. It looked dead rich.

I got the bag out, slipped the pendant on to my palm and gave it a good look. It shone dully. It didn't seem pretend. It looked real silver, dead real, not that sort of sprayed-on stuff you get, the sort Gran buys at her church fayre.

Alison would like it. I just had to persuade Dad to let me go Saturday.

Well, I thought, looked like I owed Skaz one for this. 'Bout time he did me a favour. Then I remembered the joke biro he'd given me in Cropper's class that time. It made me think again. Thing was with Skaz you never could be sure he was being straight up. You never knew where he was coming from, always kidding on with his scams and his dodges and his pocket camcorders. Everything was camouflage with him. Maybe it was all spray-on. He was like a scratch card, rub him and all you got was a few worthless numbers. Then, once in a while he came up with the goodies.

Yes, A-plus fly was Skaz Dutton, puller of tricks, switcher, morph master, chancer, biz boy, wheeler-dealer, con-king, dodger, jackladdo, nudger and winker, bomber, half-baddo, forger, snooper, spy, key-holer, girlie snapper, peeper, blackmailer, on-the-sider, half-friend, part-time pal, prankster, faker, larker, dark-horse, winner.

I put the silver back in the bag.

I wondered if Jig would be in school. He seemed to be missing more and more days. Maybe his mum was playing up, maybe he was stuffed with looking after his sister.

Maybe.

I guessed he'd delivered the Hoodz 5 stuff by now. That would get them off my back.

I thought about Assault. It was gone, for ever. I knew that now. Up to claggy Sheffield. Well, Hoodz 5 had nothing on me now. They could stuff their biz. I was in the clear. I wasn't going down The Feck again, no way, ever. Jamil could stuff his newspapers. I'd get a Saturday job down the Co-op, get Jigger to join, stacking baked beans and tins of cat food.

I was going back to normal where I belonged.

No, Hoodz 5 couldn't touch me. They were history in my book. Jigger seemed to think so too. Reckoned they were going to get sorted, he said. I couldn't see anyone giving Big Hoodie grief, clearing him off the street.

Mind, Jigger did know the score down The Feck. Maybe he knew something was coming up.

I just hoped Dad would have a blackout about charity envelopes. If he ever found out the Community Link Scheme was nothing but a Skaz-size scam, I was in for a mega roasting. I wouldn't be grounded, I'd be buried.

Despite having my big parka on, I was getting real cold in the bus shelter. It was one of those days. Wind all over you, getting right under your skin. I was shivering. I needed some warm. I needed the school library.

When I got there the place was full, bozos everywhere.

Mouse beckoned me over. She was leaning against one of the hot-water down pipes.

'Feel that,' she said, holding open a book. 'Put your hand in.'

I did, on the page, and she closed the book gently.

'It's warm!'

'Yeah, been on the radiator. Hot book.'

She smiled. Little cat smirk.

'Heard the latest?'

'What?' I said.

'We're all going down Swanwick's Saturday afternoon before the party. Skaz's idea. Then on to Alison's house.'

'Dutton's idea?'

'Yeah, he said he knows the score, knows people down there. Get us on the rides cheap and stuff.'

'He says! You believe him?'

'Yeah, why not? He works down there, doesn't he?'

I nodded but I wasn't too happy about Skaz doing deals for Alison.

'If he's messing her about I'll have him,' I said.

'Oohh, now who's getting all jealous!'

'Naff off, Mouse.'

I still had my hand in the book. Before I could get it out she'd slammed it with another, a right brick of a book, a thudding encyclopaedia, and flat-packed my knuckles underneath.

'What's that about?' I hissed.

'Being jealous.'

'Me? I'm not jealous. Of Skaz Dutton. You must be joking.'

'Who said I was talking about you?'

I eased my hand out from under *The Big Book of Knowledge* and kissed the knuckles.

'So, stuff you, Lee Matthews,' said Mouse. 'I've got work to do. Other fish to fry.'

I watched her force her way through the sprawl of kids chatting and dozing. Lots were bozoing into the distance beyond the big wall clock and into the empty hourless spaces where all kids hang out some time of the day.

What was she on about? Me, jealous? Says who? She probably fancied Skaz Dutton and didn't like me saying I'd sort him out. Well, watch out, Mouse, wolf is Skaz Dutton, a right perv, swap your tail for the farmer's wife he would.

14

The Little Ballerina

My bedroom that night. Just Gran and me in. Presents wrapped, sort of. I wasn't sure about the glitter. I mean two pounds fifty's worth of Star Dust didn't amount to much. So I found some cotton wool in the bathroom medicine cabinet and wrapped Skinny's sparkle in it to bulk it out. Then I wound the extra paper round and round to give it that big expensive look.

Still, it was the thought that counted.

Then I thought about the thought. First it was Gran's idea not mine to get Skinny the present. Then I took it over, thinking, yes, a pressie would cheer her up, I want to do that. But now I'm thinking something else: nice thoughts were OK and dead quick but they couldn't corner a single white cell and blast it.

What Skinny really wanted was some sparkle back in her blood, glitter round the bone.

And the pressie wasn't just for Skinny. It was for me. I had to admit it. To put me in Mum's and Dad's good books, convince them I wasn't the selfish wuss Mum took me for and con some charity out of Dad, the sort that took the cuffs off and magic-wanded me from boot-boy Buttons to Prince Charming at Alison's birthday ball.

Friday.

Cropper wasn't in. The whisper went round Buzz was on his way subbing for him.

Big groan.

Everyone thought we'd be doing meditation and press-ups.

Better than wonky rabbits, said Garrett.

Cheers all round.

I suddenly thought of the Ju Ju. They were wonks really. Scary wonks. How were they surviving? Probably in kids' cartoons.

Strange!

When Jigger and I fought them, they had smoky grey skins and red eyes and sometimes you couldn't sleep safe at night for fear of them. But now in my mind they were all-over red as if their skin had peeled away, like you see in horror films where someone rips off their face. They'd probably left The Swamp already and tripped to Hollywood, Ju Ju after a job in special effects.

Someone said Buzz was just coming.

Everyone settled into whispers.

I wondered what part gob-eyed Cropper played in the Game of Evolution. He kept us all quiet, herded us together like frightened rabbits, each one sitting at a his-'n'-hers hutch in classroom number eight, first floor of the bunny farm. It stopped us getting picked off one by one by Mr Fox. Safety in numbers. Mr Fox can't eat a million rabbits. Long as breeding keeps ahead of eating, us rabbits will survive and keep on going one hop ahead of extinction.

And when we can't think of what to do, wonk Worm will save us all with his big brain.

Then I thought of the fox in The Swamp the night I took Alison's Tae Kwon Do stuff home to wash. Was that a rabbit or a rat in its mouth? Did one rabbit, one rat, matter? Long as the team survived was a single rat or a single rabbit worth losing sleep over?

Skinny had jaws at her throat, sucking on her blood.

One little girl.

That was different though. She was important. She mattered. She mattered more than any other creature in the whole wide world.

She did.

To Mum.

To Dad.

To Gran.

To me too.

When Buzz appeared everyone had calmed down.

He told us to write a summary of our last lesson with Mr Cropper.

Groans.

Then he sat down at his desk to read *Martial Arts Monthly*. I knew that's what he was doing because he was moving his hands about, a bit like he was imitating the moves in the mag.

Eventually he saw me looking and called me over.

'About this green belt,' he said.

'No probs, sir,' I said. 'I understand what you're saying. I have to stop being a bozo and start being a true warrior. Bozos see no further than the nose on their crumpled faces. Warriors lift their eyes to the hills and see beyond.'

'Yes,' said Buzz slowly, obviously surprised.

'You said that bit about the hills, sir.'

'I did? Right, OK, Lee. So. You're a warrior then?'

'Yeah, sort of.'

'Warriors fight, Lee. What do you fight?'

'Demons. I used to fight the Ju Ju but not any more. That's kid's stuff. Now, I'm fighting demons all over, sir. Biggies.'

'Demons? Come on, Lee, aren't we getting a bit *Lord of the Rings* here?'

He was right. It was the Buzz effect. Sometimes when I talked to him it came out all myth and Mordor.

And yet, it was no Hobbit dream; there really were demons out there.

'They're everywhere,' I said. And I told him about Hoodz 5. And the sinister figure of Aunty. I told him about how we used to have a Ghost Baby in our house and how now we have a Great White Vampire, come to suck Ghost Baby's blood and turn her back to ghost again.

'Look, Lee,' he said after a bit. 'You've got too vivid an imagination. Maybe you should just focus on Mr Cropper's work.'

I was surprised. Surely anyone who could talk about leaping salmon could take ghost babies and vampires for real.

He noticed my frowning and leaned back on his chair and said, 'We all invent stories, Lee. Helps us handle the dirt life throws at us. In stories we rehearse real life so when it gets up and *chirugis* us we can take the hit. Get it?'

I didn't, not really. It was all bozo to me.

'And all this warrior and demon stuff,' he went on, 'makes you feel a hero, right?' Here he waved his rolled-up mag like he was Luke Skywalker swinging at Darth Vader. 'If you feel a hero,' he said, 'you act like a hero, even though inside you're confused and scared. Am I right or am I right?'

If you say so, Buzz. But to be honest, the thought of Hoodz 5 scares the living hero right out of me.

'I like the way you're handling this, Lee. Facing up to your life. The old masters call it *smiling at the tiger*. Yes, sounds like you've been doing some growing up this last week. Maybe we ought to talk green belt again, eh?' He winked.

I smiled. Gotcha!

'Now what did you do last lesson?'

'Reggie the Rabbit,' I said. 'The Hairless Hopper. And how he saved the world.'

Buzz looked gobsmacked. 'I thought Mr Cropper taught Science.'

Yes, yes, I said as I walked back to my desk.

Green belt in the bag.

Yes.

Might impress a few people roundabouts. Watch out, Alison Libidowicz. Not such a wuss now.

I looked round the class. Heads down everywhere,

212

writing about Reggie. Watch it, bunnies. I'll tiger smile the lot of you.

From now on things could only get better.

I bumped into Mouse as we left.

She said to watch where I was going.

Still had a bit of a one on her. But she didn't clear off.

She asked if I'd got Ali anything. I said yes.

What, she wanted to know. 'Go on, tell,' she said.

I told her a silver pendant and not to tell Alison. Girls want you to respect their secrets but they'll dump on everybody else's like it's lost property.

I made her swear.

She said OK and did I get it from the market.

No, I said some posh place up town. Real silver.

'Oh, nice one, Lee.'

She grinned. 'See ya tomorrow, down Swanwick's. Tarrah.'

She skipped away. Wasn't she suddenly full of a good time? Was it something I'd said? I wondered.

I got home and found the house empty.

Skeffin hell!

They'd all gone to see Skinny without me.

Suddenly I heard Dad's car outside. He dashed in.

'Come on, where you been?'

'Why? I'm not late.'

'Your mum couldn't wait, Lee. She's that mithered.'

I started upstairs.

'Where you going now?'

'Got to get B's pressie.'

'Well, move it.'

I rushed into my room and stopped dead.

It was unrecognizable.

Mum had done a tidy. More than a tidy – it looked like Dirt Buster International had been in and done it over and over. Tooth-combed it. Books, socks, CDs had been stashed or stored. Even the bed was made and tucked right up. It looked like a kid's room from one of Mum's *Good Home* catalogues, film-bright, ping-clean and perfect. It just wasn't my room any more. It needed a good trashing.

And it smelt of bleach and polish.

'Come on, Lee.'

I looked round for the pressies. I'd left them on top of the chest of drawers. They were nowhere now.

I tried every drawer, opened them up, rummaged about. Tossed this, tossed that. No sign of pressies. Nothing in the wardrobe.

Where were they?

Looked under the bed, dragged out the old play box. Tipped it.

Nothing.

Chucked the pillows.

Nothing there.

Emptied my sports bag.

Nothing.

Dad stood in the doorway.

'For God's sake, Lee. Your mum's just cleaned this place.'

'I can't find the present for Skinny,' I said. 'You know where Mum's put it?'

'No. But we gotta go. Come on. Maybe she took it with her.'

My heart jumped a beat.

Took it?

Took it?

Which one?

Both?

I couldn't think. If she'd taken Alison's present I was shafted.

Dad shoved me in the front seat and bulleted out of the drive.

'Why would she take them?' I asked. 'They were mine. I got them.'

Dad shrugged. 'Thought you might forget them?' he suggested.

I snorted.

I hated the way she tried to run my life. I wasn't a kid any more. When was she going to realize that?

I tore off my school tie and stuffed it in the glove box.

We walked up to the door. Ward 12E it said. Children's Services. Beside it stood an easel covered with a kid's drawing. It was a stick picture of a girl: skirt, arms, legs all painted in thick red lines that had run in long dribbles down the paper so it looked like she was dripping blood.

'Charming,' said Dad. 'Tuck yer shirt in, Lee. You look right yobby like that.'

Dad tapped a code into the security keypad and pushed. I stuffed my shirt back in.

Inside, the ward was divided into bays, each with

four beds all toppling with teddies and backed by walls postered with piccies and kiddie art.

Some had curtains pulled round them. I learned later that when kids were really poorly they got the curtains. Bad news when you got curtains.

B was next to a window.

At first I couldn't actually see her because Gran and Mum were in the way sitting alongside the bed.

As we entered Mum turned, smiled at me, got up and gave me a big hug.

Suddenly I was tops. Ace brother. And I knew why.

Over her shoulder I could see Skinny, head on pillow, eyes closed, a long tube running down to her neck and then disappearing inside her jamas.

She looked so little.

And around her neck lay Alison's present, the silver pendant, the heart lying flat against her chest on her bunny top.

'It's lovely, Lee,' said Mum. 'She's so pleased. And fancy getting her two presents. You must be rich,' she said joking.

'It must have cost a bomb,' I heard Gran say. 'It looks real silver. Is it?'

I nodded.

'I hope you don't mind, Lee, about me bringing them,' Mum was saying. 'I just couldn't wait to see Bea's face light up, that's all. You don't, do you? Mind? And I had to wrap them again, I'm afraid. They did look a bit, well, untidy.'

I stared at Skinny.

'What's up, Lee?' said Gran. 'Cat got your tongue?

I know it's a bit of a shock at first, seeing her like this but . . . well . . .' Her voice trailed off.

Just then I didn't know which was the bigger shock – seeing Skinny so . . . so . . . still or seeing Alison's jewellery round her neck.

Now I'd nothing for Ali.

I was stunned.

Even if I could save the glitter I couldn't give that to her. She'd go mental, getting some cheapo glit.

What the hell could I do?

'Say hello to your sister,' said Gran, 'and stop gawping or you'll catch flies.'

'Soz, Gran.'

I just stood there.

'Go on. Give her a kiss. It's not catching.'

It's not that, Gran, I thought. It's just . . . well . . . she's my sister.

Gran gave me a shove.

I bent over the bed and touched B on the lips. I'd never done that before. It was strange, kissing your own sister. She smelt of medicine. I wondered what it was going to be like kissing Alison. I wondered if our lips would match, fit together all right.

I stood up and she opened her eyes.

'Thank you for the lully necklace,' she whispered. 'I love you, Leelee.'

I felt really bad inside when she said that. Like she'd made all the effort and I hadn't. And when people are bad, dead sick, they say things they really mean, things you can't turn away from. I looked at Skinny again.

Her eyes were closed, her skin sweaty and white.

I'd never really thought of her loving me. That was scary. I wasn't sure I wanted her loving me. I thought: I'll have to love her back. There was no way out of it, what with her lying here looking so sick. I couldn't not love her back. I had a duty.

Stuff me! That was all I needed.

'What's wrong with her voice? What's this tube thing?' I said. 'Why's she speaking funny?'

'It's the medicine, the drugs they give them,' said Gran. 'It's her mouth. She's got these ulcers.'

'OK. That's enough of that,' said Dad.

Skinny tried to raise her arms like she was going to give me a hug but she couldn't make it and they fell back flat on to the white sheet covering her.

'Glad you like the necklace, B,' I whispered. 'I love you too.'

She gave a weak smile. 'That's nice. Don't leave, Lee.'

I felt her hand close over mine. It was hot.

'Bunny soft,' she said with a little smile.

'Yeah! Bunny soft,' I said quietly.

Slowly her grip relaxed.

'No need to whisper,' said Dad. 'She's not ... er ... well, you know.' He dragged a chair over and sat at the bottom of the bed. It was like he was up in the stands where it was safe to watch.

He gave me a thumbs up. 'Makes her look like a princess.'

I turned back to Skinny. 'I won't leave you, B. No one's going to leave you.'

'Keep the Ju Ju away, won't you?'

I nodded.

218

'What's she saying?' said Mum. 'What was that? Ju Ju? What's that about?'

'Just kids' stuff,' I said.

'You been filling her head with some nonsense,' said Dad, frowning from the bottom of the bed.

'No, of course not. It's just that Ju Ju is all the bad stuff that happens to us. All the dirt life throws at us. Like . . .' I pointed to Skinny and mouthed the word leu-kae-mi-a. The sounds felt soft and slimy and they squirmed slowly over my tongue like fat brown slugs.

Dad nodded.

He understood. He knew about bad stuff. Saw it every day and night back of his cab, out of his mirror.

And wasn't I a plonker. Thinking the Ju Ju had gone off to comic land where they belonged.

No way.

They'd been lying low all this time, just waiting their chance and now they'd taken it, got inside Skinny, and were wreaking havoc everywhere.

This time it would take more than two bike boys playing Tarzan to rid the world of their terrible scourge.

Gran bent down and pulled something from a plastic bag. She unwrapped the tissue around it and placed it on Skinny's bedside table.

It was her ballerina music box.

Gran held the lead in her hand. 'Find somewhere I can put this plug, Lee, will you?'

Above Skinny's bed the wall sprouted leads. No three-pin anywhere. Just holes marked 'Oxygen' and 'Suction'.

I looked down beside her little trolley and behind it.

219

Then I saw a point beneath the bed about midway along the wall. I crawled under but the lead was too short.

'Stupid,' said Gran. 'Poor mite won't be able to see it.'

I took the box, slid it along the floor, crawled after it and pushed the plug in.

I lay there, flat on my stomach, watching. The little ballerina began turning, and twinkly lights shone up through the glass floor, setting the glitter alight in her short skirts.

The dancer reminded me of Mouse with her small bright eyes and jewelly lips.

I slid backwards and stood up.

Under the bed the little dancer went round and round and round, and the twingy pingy music played on.

Skinny lay very still.

No one spoke. Not for ages.

Any time now, I thought, someone's going to crack up and start crying, Mum first.

Then the music stopped.

The box whirred.

We all froze.

Then from below the notes started up again.

'Lee, turn the thing off. It's getting on my nerves,' said Dad.

Mum frowned.

I crawled in after the ballerina and pulled the plug on her.

'You're a fairy,' I said to her. 'Wave a wand and sort me something for Alison.'

No sooner had I asked than a great idea came twing ping into my brain.

I rose from the floor. 'It's too big,' I said.

Gran looked up.

'The pendant. I can exchange it.'

What I was thinking was this: if I could get the thing back off Skinny, I could give it to Alison tomorrow for her birthday and then I had a few days to get some cash and replace my little sister's silver heart.

Mind, I thought, it was one thing having time, but where was I to get the quids?

'No exchange.'

It was Skinny. She had her hand round the silver heart. 'I like thith one.'

I sighed.

So that was that.

I was stuffed. I had less than twenty-four hours to get Alison something and no money to get it with.

Mum was stroking Skinny's hair now.

Then I remembered what Gran had said about chemo making you bald.

Bald Skinny Bunny. Wonk from the warren.

Bozo me. I'd bought her hair glitter. What a wuss.

I looked at Skinny again. Her eyes were closed and the pendant lay tightly bound in her fist.

Trust her to like the skeffin thing so much!

15

Jungle Jim's

'She is OK?' Dad kept asking on the way home. 'I mean you talked to the doctors.' He swung the car round a corner. 'What were they saying?' he asked Mum once more.

Because he kept looking across at her sitting in the passenger seat he crashed a red light so she told him to calm down.

It was raining and traffic was heavy. Brake lights were spurting red, blood glitter on the tarmac.

Dad stared through the wiper swish.

'She's still got this infection. It often happens,' said Mum wearily. 'And that's the reason they've put her back on antibiotics. They've sedated her so she can sleep. They'll do another test early in the morning. We'll know then whether the white cell count's really levelling out or whether it's . . .' Mum's voice faded to a hiss like a last release of air.

I was sitting in the back with Gran.

Thinking.

It would look bad me going out to Swanwick's and

parties while my kid sister lay seriously ill in hospital. What would that make me?

That would make me miss out on Alison, that's what.

Let's face it, I thought, there's nothing I can do about Skinny. That's for doctors. They'll fix her. She's on drugs and stuff. Then they'll do chemo and then she'll be OK.

Sorted!

Might as well get some partying done, as Jig would say.

That night, in bed, I remembered what Buzz had said about the stories we tell ourselves. How what goes on in our heads follows us into real life.

I began thinking stories.

I needed two.

I needed one to get me down to real-life Swanwick's by six o'clock the next day and one that would get me a silver pendant by eight in the evening.

I went through some options.

I could tell Dad I was doing a sponsored coconut shy for sick kids, that I was going to help on special charity stall selling candy floss, that I had an appointment with Madame Sophie, the fortune teller, to check if she could see any hope for Skinny B in her crystal ball.

But I didn't.

Some lies are better than others. How could I crack on about charity when my sister really was sick and seriously so in hospital?

I decided to tell Dad that I had to meet Jigger at Swanwick's in the afternoon because he said he knew someone down there who might know about Assault. And that on the way back I would go and see Gran.

I'd say Gran likes the company. After all, she only has the dog left now.

I also decided that on the way to Swanwick's I'd drop in on Gran and get her to cover for me while I went to the party.

I stared at the curtains shivering in a draught from my window.

Pendant! Alison!

OK. No way could I get the money for another silver heart.

So this was the story here, I said to myself.

I'd tell Ali about Skinny, lay it on a bit. Tell her about cell counts and stuff and chemo and gums going bad and bones being rubbery and the vomiting. Ali would go all soft and sorry. And I'd tell her that's where her pressie went, to Skinny. To make her feel a bit better. A dangle of silver helps when your hair falls out, I'd say. Tears will fill Ali's eyes. She's kind like that. I know she is. She'll hug me. 'That's so ... so ... YOU,' she'd say. 'You're so ... so SENSITIVE.'

I fell asleep dreaming of Alison in a short glittery skirt twirling round and round on a mirrored floor. Suddenly a crack opens up in the mirror. Smoke pours out and then the heads emerge, red and shiny, on long snaking necks.

Ju Ju.

They swirl round Alison. She goes on dancing, dancing. Then they begin to wrap themselves around her, round her legs, round her thighs, round her whole body until she disappears in the thick glistening red coils.

The coils tighten and the heads nod and knock against each other and the great knotted Ju Ju snake starts to descend, down, down through the cracked mirror, dragging the smoke with it till everything disappears and the dark fissure closes over.

I wake up shaking.

Sweaty and chilled at the same time.

A half-moon, like a lost mobile, hangs in the sky.

Ju Ju, I hate you.

Breakfast – and I tell Dad my story about meeting Jigger at Swanwick's. I know I'm grounded, I say, but give me a chance I tell him, I might be able to sort out that top-spec, top-whack bike. I know if I say 'top whack' I could be in trouble reminding him of how much I'd cost him, but I thought if I suggested there was a faint hope of recovering Assault he'd go with it.

He frowns.

'Jigger? What you going with Jigger for?'

'He thinks he's seen Assault. With a kid who works at the fair.'

'Right, I'm coming with you. Sort the little bastard out.'

Skeffin hell! Life was cocking up my story even before I'd started.

'It's OK, Dad. Jigger and I can sort it.' I nod hopefully. 'Anyway, Mum needs you.'

'For what? What are you talking about?'

'For support. Stop her cracking up.'

225

'Don't try telling me what or what not to do, Lee. You're thirteen years old, for God's sake.'

'Nearly fourteen,' I say.

He ignores me.

'And if your mum wants support, she knows she only has to ask,' he says sharply. 'She knows that.'

It's true. Whenever Mum asks, Dad is there. He'd taxi her all over if she wanted, to the moon and back if she asked. 'He's very good,' I once heard her say to Gran, 'but once in a while, I just wish he'd do something off his own bat instead of me having to ask all the time.'

'He should make you queen for a day,' Gran had said. 'Grant you every wish before you'd thought of it yourself.'

'You should make her queen for a day,' I say to Dad. 'She'd like that.'

'Wouldn't we all.' He frowns at me. 'What do you think Mother's Day's for?'

Yes, Dad.

He slaps a fiver on the table. 'Get your mother some flowers on the way back for me.'

Good one, Dad. I give him the thumbs up.

'And, by the way, Bea's still holding her own. Cell count's the same as last night.'

Good one, Skinny. Keep that silver heart safe and a-tick-tick-tocking.

'And you be safe,' says Dad. 'I don't want you getting into any more trouble. That Swanwick's place is villain city, it's full of nutters and no-hopers. I suppose Jigger knows what he's doing.'

Course, Dad.

Then I tell him about Gran wanting me to go round for the evening, keep her company and that. It will save him cooking me a meal, Mum being with B and all.

He likes the sound of not having to go down the chippie, and agrees.

Simple.

As Buzz says, stories sort your life out.

But it works both ways. Life sorts your stories out. I didn't realize that then. I do now. As Cropper says, never underestimate the unexpected.

I did that day and it cost me.

Here's how.

About five in the afternoon I slipped out of the house at the back, calling bye to Dad from the kitchen. This was so he wouldn't see I'd got my best cargoes on and new trainers and ask me why.

Swanwick's is on the far edge of The Feck and I needed plenty of time to go the long way round and avoid Hoodz 5 territory.

I was just at the end of Far Pastures when some maniac on a bike came screeching out of the shadows and nearly did a front tyre tattoo down my cargoes.

'Yer stupid prat,' I shouted as the biker squealed to a halt and wheelied round.

'Soz, soz.'

It was Worm.

I was gobsmacked. He had a bike.

'Trying to kill me, were you? Anyway, what you doing round here?'

'I said soz, didn't I?' He was wheezing heavily. 'You off down Swanwick's?'

'Yeah!'

'Well, don't.'

'Why not? What's up? Party off?'

Worm took a quick breath.

'Big Hoodie's out for you.'

'Out for me?' I said uneasily. 'What you mean, out for me?'

'After you. Jamil said. Told me to warn you.' He leaned right in my face. 'I said they're maniacs.'

The night air seemed suddenly colder. My mind was doing wheelies, racing like the brakes had gone.

Jamil had said? Said what?

'What exactly did Jamil say?'

'I was in the shop,' said Worm, dropping his voice, 'getting some mags. Jamil comes over, whispers in my ear. Says to tell you Hoodz is mad boy and wants to bad bad you.' Worm waited. 'Look, don't be a bozo, Lee. Everyone knows you fancy Alison Libidi-thingie but your face won't stand a likely if they chop you. She'll take one look after your Hoodz Five makeover and think horror comic.'

I nodded, but wasn't really listening. I was thinking, Why? Why was Big H wanting to bad bad me? Surely it wasn't biz. Jigger had sorted that out by now.

'Did Jamil say why?'

Worm shook his head. 'You know Jamil. He's still on ABC. Hasn't reached Y yet.'

Worm was always a smart-arse, I thought.

I said nothing, but my mind was peddling fast again.

The envelopes.

Jigger had promised delivery.

The bastard hadn't posted them. The punters had complained. Big Hoodie looked bad bad bizman. No biz, no trust. No trust, no profit.

He'd probably sold the stuff on and made a packet for himself. Bloody Jigger. Some mate.

'Stay home, Lee,' Worm was saying. 'Just don't think otherwise.' He turned his bike. 'I got to go. It's party time. Sort it out tomorrow but keep outta sight tonight.'

And with that he was off.

I didn't wait.

I was walking then running. It wasn't brain telling me to hurry. It wasn't common sense. It wasn't the thought of Alison.

It was something else.

Something inside that was shutting down all the other voices – Mum's saying no, Worm saying watch out, Gran saying Bozo's best, Dad's saying don't you dare, Jigger saying get real, Buzz saying bend and you won't break, Skaz Dutton saying cluck, cluck, Cropper saying bunnies the lot of you, Skinny B saying stay with me, Leelee, stay with me . . .

Something else saying: Go. Go. Go.

And yet it wasn't a voice, not like all the others, because as soon as I stopped to listen it disappeared. Like when I stood at the wide dark edge of Gants, stood and listened hoping for a word, a yes, a nudge, a nod, I got nothing. Just my heart fluttering in the breeze and the rush rush of speeding cars.

But something shoved me off that kerb and sent me

plunging across the road and heading for Swanwick's, for Jungle Jim and the Hoodz 5 boys. And as soon as I started running again round Gants, round the edge of The Feck it was there beside me, stride for stride, keeping me going.

My shadow. My mate. My *ki*. Me.

And all the time I ran I could hear the beat of his running in perfect time with the pound of my heart, his breathing an echo of mine like I was breathing for him, he for me.

The amusement park has this big entrance. A stonking great cut-out of Jungle Jim, stiff arm stretched out leaning against a giant palm tree. The leaves curve over and attach to Jim's head so that arm and leaves form a huge arch under which we jungle pigmies pass out of The Fèck into the Kingdom of Darkest Africa.

Everyone – Garrett, The Pole, Alison, Mouse, Skaz, Worm, me, all the others – have to meet outside The Zambezi Falls, Swanick's number-one attraction, Africa's biggest waterfall. In real life, the Zambezi River thrashes its way through rocks and rapids before it hurls itself, at a million tons a minute, over the cliff edge down a suicidal 300-metre drop into the jungle below.

In The Feck, The Falls are famous as Jungle Jim's bang-on bungee drop.

You climb up this scaffolding at the back and come out on a platform about thirty metres up. They harness you in and toss you over the edge. Jigger told me about it. You free-fall a bit then the elastic kicks in and jacks you back up and, while you yo-yo about, water spurts out of various holes and gives you that genuine sprayed-on Zambezi feel.

Personally, I didn't fancy it. Bombing The Tower had put me off altitude for life.

I made my way towards The Falls, pushing and edging through the crowds. It was Saturday night and Swanwick's was throbbing.

Suddenly, in front of me, all crazy angles and zigzags, stood The Haunted Castle, vampire bats with white human faces hanging from its steep pitched roof. To one side and rising high above the throng, grinning at everyone who passed, stood a giant skeleton, its white boned hand pointing at all who passed.

It was an inflatable tied to the castle wall by head and shoulder, staked to the ground at the ankle. In the breeze, the black rubbery body bulged and creased like live flesh and, as I passed, its head slowly turned so it seemed the empty eyes were following me round.

And I thought of Skinny B.

Back off, Mr D. Keep away, blood-eater.

What I really needed was Jigger's bowie knife. Slash the monster.

I'm fifty metres from The Falls and I stop to watch a couple of bozos getting strapped in ready for the drop. I watch as the minders shuffle them towards the take-off point. At the bottom, fenced off by a bit of cut-out jungle scenery, is a pond, a kind of safety pool. Beside it is a notice warning punters not to go near because it is infested with flesh-eating piranhas. The best bungee boys do the swallow dive and control it so that they just finger-tip the water, no more. They call it The Swallow Dip. Going over backwards and doing The Swallow Dip is top whack. Getting your head wet is not. That is bad news – piranhas would have it off in no time.

Then I see them, Alison and her crowd all gogging at the bungee bozos. Suddenly one of them starts going. Heads jerk up. There is a crack of silence, like all noise is switched off, and then the screams pour through, and the lights and the drum roll seconds too late.

Suddenly I'm aware of Skaz waving to me. He is standing next to Alison mouthing something and pointing at The Zambesi Falls. He wants me to go down with him. Do the bungee plunge.

No way, Dutton.

Then I see him lean over Alison and say something into her ear, all the time eyes on me.

She turns to where he's pointing and waves.

Then she starts to walk towards me.

'What you waiting for?' she says. She's got her hair ponytailed in a scrunchie the way I like it. Star Dust sparkles on her cheeks and the lights have turned her lipstick bruise purple. She's wearing a short silver parka and shiny pink trousers and looks gorgeous.

'Skaz says you're too chicken to do the bungee, but I said you weren't.'

I look over at Skaz. He's mouthing me. Cluck, cluck, he's saying.

'You've got to be sixteen or something,' I say.

And the words tumble out of my mouth and metal

clangs in my head and a ladder swings out into space and I'm hanging on to my life suspended above a black crevasse beneath the mocking moon.

'You all right?' Alison is saying, her face faintly frowning.

'Yes. Yes,' I say, the memory of The Tower suddenly vanishing.

'Great! Don't worry. Skaz will get you on. Everyone knows him here.'

She swings round and, as she does, something works loose from round her neck and falls to the ground.

I bend and pick it up.

It's a pendant. Silver with a dangling heart.

It rests in my palm, light and tickly.

'Nice, isn't it?' she says.

And I'm thinking, yes but it's the one I was going to give you and where did you get it from and maybe you bought it yourself, which makes sense because of course girls buy jewellery and stuff and why not and it's better than if I come up with a pendant just the same what a plonker I'd look then.

'Nice,' I agree.

'Pressie,' she says.

'Pressie?' I say uneasily.

'From Skaz.'

I stand there slabbed.

Bastard!

He sends me to spend quids on jewellery and then gets her the same himself. Probably got it freebie on some scam or other while I have to pay full whack.

233

Bastard!

'Look,' I say. 'I did get you something.'

And I told her about Skinny being ill and hospital and the bruises and the white cells and the green belt. It all came tumbling out.

Alison just stared at me.

'Lee, Lee! That's awful. Is she going to be all right?'

I shrugged. I could feel tears coming. I'd never cried over Skinny before. I held them back. Just stopped them in time.

'It's nothing,' I said.

Alison put her arms round me.

'I'm so sorry, Lee. So sorry. I never knew. Why didn't you say?'

I shrugged.

'You know, Lee, you're so . . . so . . .'

'Sensitive?' I said.

'No, not quite. Not that. More, more like sensible. You're too buttoned up. You need to let go. Be yourself more. If you want to cry over your sister, just cry.'

'But Buzz says –'

'Oh, stuff Buzz, Lee. This isn't pyjama time. This is for real.'

16

Aunty

Suddenly someone pushed me in the back, staggering me forward.

'Keep walking, Matthews. Let's surf the rapids.'

Dutton.

I shoved him off.

'Come on, Lee, before the queues start. You and me, show these losers how to do it.'

'Yeah, Lee. Go for it.' It was Alison. 'You can do it.'

Suddenly there was a drum roll, the PA thundered, lights flashed across the sky and swept over us as another two bozos plunged downwards screaming.

Neither got to the water.

'Naffos,' shouted Skaz.

Everyone cheered.

Beside me, Mouse was jumping up and down, glitter from her hair sparkling in the glaring light flooding the Falls ahead of us.

'Go on, Lee. Let's see you.' She gave me the thumbs up.

Alison joined in again. Then The Pole and Garrett nudged me forward.

Hell!

It looked a done deal. Maybe they'd fixed something. Mouse seemed a bit too quick with her thumbs up.

I hesitated, all thought of the pendant drowned by the bungee bozos smacking the water ahead of us.

'Cluck. Cluck.' It was Garrett.

I turned. Alison was giving her hair a right tugging.

As soon as the guy on the gate saw it was Skaz he let us through on a freebie.

'Stay with me, Matthews, and you'll get in all evening for free.'

'Why'd you get her that pendant?' I shouted as we clambered up the steps.

Through the scaffolding I could see this huge brush like the ones they have on car washes, slowly turning on a spindle and spraying water through vents in the front of The Falls.

He stopped and turned.

'Eh?'

'I was giving Alison a pendant, remember. Not you.'

'Soz, mate. Didn't I say? I got it for you, a freebie. But you were late so I gave it to Alison. Couldn't wear it myself.' He winked. 'And I wasn't going to waste it on slaps like Garrett, now was I?'

Some bozos had come up behind us and Skaz turned and clambered up the rest of the steps.

Square one again, I thought. Dutton all talk. Could I believe him? Could I like!

And here he was again, leading me on. Taking me to the edge. Seeing if I'd cluck up. And in front of his mates this time.

No way, Skaz.

We'll go over the edge together.

And you lay one clacky finger on Alison and I'll have you, Dutton. I will.

As we emerged on the gangway at the top, lights blazed at us from below. I shielded my eyes and looked out into the night. Beyond the rim of brightness, stalls glowed and their lights stuttered in the evening breeze. To one side I could hear the whirr and crash of dodgems and, above that, tearing the air, the screamers on The Boomerang, and then, underneath everything, the throb throb of generators, the beat at the heart of the fun, keeping the fairground tinselled and glittered up.

I peered over the edge, but it was too bright to see the others. I couldn't even make out the ground. If they'd moved it and put a bottomless pit in its place, I wouldn't have known.

Suddenly I felt very sick.

My mouth was as dry as a duster. I knew I had to do it. Life doesn't have reverse.

Take a deep breath and come out fighting, Dad would say.

OK, Dad, here goes. For you. For Skinny. It's tough for her. She can't wimp out.

Down below they were all cheering.

Nor can I.

*

Jutting out from the gangway were two launch pads, as Skaz described them. They were expanded metal walkways and reached about a metre or so into space.

'I'm your handler,' said a voice in my ear. 'Just do as I say. Front or backwards?'

'Just down,' I said, trying to joke a bit.

'Backwards,' called Skaz, who was about three metres to my left. 'Do the Swallow.'

God!

Stuff Swallow, I just wanted to get it down and over.

Before I knew it, I was being strapped round the feet and shackled to a long snake of black elastic.

From below, I could hear them all singing. ''Ere we go, 'ere we go.'

Bastards, the lot!

I glanced down.

The floodlights were off and only the lower lights beside the piranha pool blazed. Round it the gang were gathered.

They seemed miles below, small pale faces. Ju Ju whities. Piranha eyes, lying in wait down there under the murk of night.

I was guided to the start of the walkway. It was just like standing at the end of a short dive board in a swimming bath.

I looked across at Skaz. He thumbed me one and shouted something, but a sudden blast of rock like the roar of tumbling water blew his words away.

I'm going to die, I thought. What if the elastic breaks? Dad, Dad, I'm going to die.

'You OK?' said the handler.

I nodded. 'Course. Why not?'

'Put this on,' he said. He gave me a crash helmet. 'There's a mike inside. Soon as you hear me give you the all-clear you can go.'

'Head first?' I said.

He nodded. Like he dealt with bozos all the time.

I lowered the helmet over my head. It smelt of grease and sick.

Once inside, I couldn't hear a thing, just a tinny crackling in both ears. It was like my eggshell skull was beginning to crack.

Then I felt the handler hold my shoulder and shuffle me along the walkway.

I was right on the edge.

Faintly I could hear the drum roll.

'OK,' said a crackle in my ear. 'Go.'

Go?

Go!

I couldn't. Not just dive headlong.

Backwards.

No way.

I'd crack my skull.

My knees began to give. Oh, God! Don't. Don't. Don't let me pee. Not in my new cargoes. They'll all see.

I looked down.

It was miles.

Miles.

I couldn't do it. Dutton could call me cluck all the way to the moon for all I cared. I just couldn't.

239

I tried to penguin walk back to safety along the gang plank.

But I could hardly move, so tight was the harness round my ankles.

Suddenly there was an explosion of light. Drum rolls battered the air.

Screaming and shouts echoed up from far below.

I felt myself wobbling.

I was losing it.

I had to steady up.

No good.

Too late.

Christ!

I was going.

Tumbling.

Then everything seemed to slow down. I felt so relaxed. I was falling backwards like I was falling on to a bed, like I was drifting into dreams, like I was floating along a river of darkness.

I plummeted down, down, down into the thunderous black of the Zambezi abyss.

I came to, hanging upside down like a freaking fruit bat.

Hands dripping.

I'd done it!

Swallow dipped it.

Top whack, bungee boy.

I tried to cheer. Voice just croaked.

Everyone was waving.

I waved too and swallowed a mouthful of puke.

I had a vague sense of Mouse pistoning the air with

her little fists and the others dancing about and waving scarves and stuff.

Suddenly my whole body was flooded with energy.

Yes, I'd done it.

Yes.

Head to head with Dutton.

I punched the air.

Stuff you, Skaz.

Stuff you.

Bit by bit I was pulled back up by the safety rope. On the gangway the handler had me out in secs. He ripped the helmet off.

'What a bloody stink,' he said. 'Go on, get out of it.'

By the time I'd got to the bottom of the steps, my legs had stopped trembling.

Skaz was waiting for me. 'You great gob, look what you've done.' He pointed to where Alison stood wiping down her puffa jacket.

'What?'

'You came down puking. Nearly got the lot of them.'

I went up to Alison. 'Soz. I'm really soz. It happens every time. Me and bungee. Upside down and I start honking. Goes back to me being a baby and my mum throwing me out of the window.'

'Ha. Ha. Ha,' she said. 'This is a new puffa, I hope you know.'

But I could see she was impressed with me. Doing the bungee. Me taking Skaz on and not ducking out. Me doing the Swallow Dip.

'You were great,' said Mouse. 'Just toppling off like

241

that, like you'd fainted.'

'Thanks,' I said.

'Yeah, and doing it backwards,' said Garrett, her mouth gob open. 'Bleeding backwards.'

'Thanks. Easy really. Just thought I'd do something different.'

Skaz snorted. 'You puked because you were piss-scared,' he said in my ear. 'You fell off, you tosser.'

'No way,' I said. 'It's easy, Skaz. I'll show you how it's done sometime.'

Skaz looked at me, his eyes clenched. Then suddenly he smiled. 'OK, bungee boy, let's see you puke up on The Boomerang.'

The Boomerang!

What the hell was he on about?

I watched him wander over to Alison. He said something to her. She laughed. Looked over at me.

I stiffened.

What was that all about?

Mouse was talking again.

'You were ace, Lee. Ace.'

'Yeah,' I said, half listening, half keeping an eye on Dutton and Alison.

'Jigger seen you?' she said suddenly.

From somewhere near, music had started up on the PA system again.

'He says watch out for trouble this evening. Do as you're told, he says. Don't try it on.'

I was still feeling a bit puked out from the bungee and I wasn't quite with what Mouse was saying.

'Try it on?' I said.

Mouse shrugged. 'He just said to tell you to watch your back.'

I was listening now.

First Worm, now Jigger sounding red alert.

'Why isn't he here?' I said, wondering if he was avoiding trouble himself.

'I asked Ali to invite him, but she said no.'

I looked around.

The place was filling up. A million bulbs, sugar-lighting the night, candy flossing every face around.

No trouble in any of them.

Too much to scream about.

Too much ante in the air.

Then Mouse grabs my arm. 'Come on. Let's have fun. It's The Boomerang. Let's hit the wall.'

Skaz and Alison get the first car. That's cos his mates done him the favour and let him jump the queue. Rest of us have to wait.

'This her, yer girlfriend?' I hear one of them ask him up front.

Skaz laughs.

'Cheeky,' says Alison.

I get in the last car. Someone turns up the music. Mouse slips in beside me. 'Snuggle up,' she shouts. 'And hold on. I might get thrown out.' I put an arm round her shoulders. She pushes into me. A snug fit. Soft against me. Bunny soft.

I grab the safety bar with my free hand and lock it into place.

'I bet you scream before I do,' says Mouse. 'First to scream pays for the pizza afterwards. OK?'

I nod, but I'm not really taking any notice because I've just seen Skaz Dutton sitting in the front car with his arm round Alison Libidowicz.

Suddenly we start moving.

Each car, of the twenty cars on the Boomerang, is fixed to the end of a long metal arm that swings round and round and round. The car can also revolve on its own at the end of the arm. This creates what Mouse calls the puke effect.

I'm still looking at Dutton. I'm staring eyeballs at him because he's got his arm round her and they're kissing. Dutton is snogging Alison Libidowicz. They're at it like a pair of hot bunnies.

The speed is picking up. I can feel air pressing into my eyes, pushing up my nostrils. I'm being forced against the back of the car. Mouse's lips are all pursed like she's just sucked a lemon. Her hair is flying and its sparkle is flecking me too. I blink it away and try and catch Skaz and Alison. Their car is banking steeply and they're locked on to each other like they'd pushed the G-force button. She's got an arm round his neck, he's got his hand cupped over her backside, wrinkling the soft pink satin of her trousers.

I look at them angry, sick, lost, betrayed, and I can feel my face crumpling under pressure from the car's velocity, my sight blurring in the acceleration of everything around us. We're hitting max.

Mouse is screaming and grasping my arm.

Hitting the max is hitting the wall on The Boomerang.

At its fastest the cars ricochet right across the space and, as each one looks like it's about to crash the wall, an explosion of light blinds you and you're hurled backwards, stomach gagging for a way out your mouth.

I've now got both hands on the safety bar as we slow down and I'm trying to bend it in half.

I'm going to knot it round Dutton's neck when I get off.

Soon as the bar unlocks I'm away and pushing through the crowd to get at Skaz. Everyone around's a blur except one person.

He turns in slow motion.

I raise my fist.

I'm going to smash that bastard's face. I'm going to smash it for all the scams, all the tricks he's pulled, the crap he's put me through with his dives and his bombing and his clucking and his keyhole camcorders. But most of all I'm going to smash that sicko face for screwing me up with Alison Libidowicz and running his pervy hands all over her.

Then . . .

Someone grabs me.

'Hold on, mate. Or you'll get yerself hurt.' I stop struggling. 'That's better. Now just come quietly, nice and slow.'

I'm thrust forward through the crowd who've stopped to watch and I'm forced round the back of The Boomerang.

I hear Mouse's voice saying, 'Where you taking him? Leave him alone. Help him, someone.'

No one does.

I stumble over bits of planking and cabling and eventually find myself forced up the steps of a caravan. The steps are silver and the door shiny bright.

Inside it's dark, just a bit of stray light making shadows of the furniture. I smell cigar. It's like our house at Christmas when Dad smokes.

Then I remember what Mouse said about Jigger, and me not trying it on.

Some hope. The guy holding my arm has a grip like a plumber's wrench.

'This the kid?' says a voice from the far end of the van.

I try to see who's asking, but it's too dark.

'What's your name?'

'What's going on?' I say.

'Just answer,' says the man still holding me. He slams me on to a chair and squeezes my neck like he doesn't know the difference between threat and throttle.

'Lee,' I gurgle.

'OK, Razzer. Let him go.' Razzer slowly releases me.

I gasp.

'You Jigger's mate, are you?'

'Yeah.'

'Good. Now listen, sonny. And listen hard. Play it right and you won't get hurt. Jigger said you were OK. So he'd better be right.'

My mind races. Who is this guy? Play what right? Just what has Jigger said?

There's a pause and I can hear what sounds like lips smacking. The figure at the table leans forward.

'For a school kid you've been a bit out of order, sonny. Pushing biz for some of the low life round here.'

'Eh?'

'Look, sonny, Aunty knows everything.'

I stare at the dark silhouette.

Aunty!

I can't believe it.

This is Aunty?

'You've been delivering for that Hoodz scum. No more, sonny. We're going to take them down and you, you're going to keep that big mouth of yours shut. You're going to say nothing about Jamil and envelopes and stuff. You hear me. You never seen Hoodz, you never seen brown envelopes.'

I shake my head. Yes, yes, anything you say. I'm truly gobbed. I'm sitting in the same room as The Feck's number-one hardman honcho. Me, Lee Matthews.

Hell!

Aunty takes a puff on his cigar. I see a red brightening glow. Ju Ju mouth. Ju Ju ready to suck the life out of you. Turn you into a lost soul.

I nod, still staring at the shadow ahead of me.

'As far as you're concerned you don't remember anything. Just keep yer mouth closed.'

I nod again.

'And if you don't know how to keep yer mouth shut, Razzer will show you how it's done. Get my drift?'

I nod and as my brain thaws I know for sure now it was Jigger sold me down the line. Told Aunty about the envelopes. Gave them to him. Set me up for a Hoodz 5 makeover.

'You're going to sort out the Hoodz?' I say.

'None of your business, sonny. Now get out.'

'Will I get my bike back?'

Aunty swears. 'Sonny, forget yer sodding bike. This is biz. What do you think we are, a kiddies' playgroup? Out.'

Razzer grabs me by the neck, and leans towards Aunty. 'You wanted to know about the lippy kid.'

'Yeah, that's right,' says Aunty. 'Sit down, sonny.'

Razzer shoves me back on the chair again.

'You were trying to wop some kid just now, the lippy one. Who was that?'

'Oh, just a bozo I know,' I say.

'Oh, so why were you after him?'

'Because he's a tosser.'

'And?'

'Because he was after this girl.'

'A tart you fancy?'

'No way. She's not a tart. Get lost.'

Suddenly, Razzer is crunching me by the shoulder. I cry out. 'He's lying, boss. He was with this little bit of skirt. A matchstick Mini.'

'No, that's Mouse. I'm talking about Alison.'

'Alison?' says Aunty, his voice low like a dog growling. 'You fancy my Alison as well?'

I froze. 'YOU'RE A-Alison's . . .?' I stutter. I feel my throat closing.

'You and this lippy kid who was with her. On the Boomerang,' says Razzer.

'The one all over her,' growls Aunty.

'That's Skaz Dutton,' I blurt.

There is a big intake of breath and I see the cigar tip grow red and angry in the dark.

No one says anything. My mind is stumbling. Alison, Aunty's daughter! Stuff me!

'Well, sonny. No one takes advantage of my Alison. Got that?'

I nod like my head has worked loose.

'Now, tell me more about this Dutton kid.'

I hesitate. I could do some real damage now to Skaz. Blow him out of the picture. Tell all about pervy videos and his daughter.

'Well, let's have it,' says Razzer, squeezing my shoulder. He leans in my ear and whispers, 'I'm going to wipe him anyway, say what you like.'

'He's just this kid in my school,' I say, suddenly sick for Skaz.

'You said he was a tosser.'

'He gets up my nose at times, that's all.' I'm just trying to make it sound like Skaz is this nobody, like he's just another bozo kid the blind side of ordinary, like Razzer will decide he isn't worth planting.

There is silence.

'You buy stuff down the market?' Aunty says suddenly.

I nod. 'Sometimes.'

'From the big guy's stall?'

'No.' Then I remember Skinny's pressie. 'Yes. I bought something for my little sister.'

'Anything else?'

'No.'

Then Aunty drops his bombshell. 'You buy any dirty videos?'

I shudder inside. Skeffin hell! If Aunty knew about Skaz's piccies, he was dead meat.

'Yer did, didn't you, yer little perv?' says Razzer.

'Never,' I say. 'Perv yourself.' I turn to face Aunty. 'My sister's ill. Got leukaemia. And that's about as dirty as you can get, mister.' I think I'll get enough sympathy from the leukaemia stuff to save me a Razzer work-over.

I can feel his breath on my neck.

Then I have a really megawatt idea.

Aunty has his hand up like if he dropped it something nasty would happen. He seems to be weighing things up.

'Yeah, I remember now. I bought a silver pendant. For Alison. Birthday pressie.'

Aunty nods. The cigar glows red with approval.

Then he waves his arm. 'Get rid, Razz. And, sonny, yer right, my daughter's no tart. Don't you ever forget that. And she doesn't know about this meeting. And if you ever tell her, Razzer will fold yer legs for yer.'

17

Loves Ya Skinny

Then I'm shoved through the door and told to wait.

I wobble down the caravan steps and sink on to the bottom one. I'm vaguely aware of the din and the grind of engines and the rumble of rides.

I'm shaking and it isn't the after-effects of The Boomerang.

Could I believe it? Alison Libidowicz, Aunty's daughter!

It kind of fitted in a way because I remember what Jig said about them having Mercedes money. You don't do Mercedes on the Social. You don't do anything on the Social, except survive. That's what Gran says.

And stuff you can do, Gran. You can do stuff on the Social. Aunty sees to that.

Stuff me! And Skaz. Bad news. They're on to you, know about yer pervy cams and scams. You're for the drop, matey. You're going to come out on crutches unless I can do something.

Suddenly, even though I'm still trembling, I begin to feel sort of safe. That's because I'm thinking it's OK with me and Aunty because of the pressie and Alison and me

251

standing up for her and saying she wasn't a tart. I think Aunty liked that. It isn't that I feel protected by Aunty or anything. It was just he obviously doesn't think I'm worth bothering with. The tiger eyes are on someone else. And now I know who.

Hoodz 5.

It all fits. Jigger said H5 were going to get wiped. He knew because he was in with Aunty.

Then I laugh. I'm thinking Skaz now.

Dutton, I've got you right in the palm of my hand, I say to myself.

As soon as I think this, I feel cold regret seep into me. In a way I'd sort of shopped Skaz. Fingered him. I should have kept my mouth shut, but ... well, I just wasn't thinking straight.

Skaz Dutton. You've cut me no favours, you've twocked my girl, stuffed me enough times, but ... well ... we have done things, you and I, gone over the edge together, like.

I push my shoulders back to ease the bruising. A Razzer handshake ain't fun, Skaz.

I stood up. The ground vibrated with the throb of generators.

I needed to warn him.

Then I thought of the bungee jump. He was so keen to chicken-lick me. Why me, Skaz? There's bozos everywhere you can sharpen your image on. Why pick on me? Is it just because I'm there – wrong kid, wrong place, wrong time? Or maybe, Skaz Dutton, you're jealous.

Ever thought of that? You can be jealous without knowing it. It can make you edgy. It makes you want to do me a downer all the time because, hey, get this, you know if you don't then one day I'll swallow dive you out of it, edgy you off top spot.

Anyway, your life's in my hands now.

Suddenly the caravan door opened and Razzer came down.

'Move it. And forget what you've just seen. Tell anybody and you'll spend the rest of yer life trying to forget you ever had legs. Now off.'

We stumbled back towards The Boomerang, my heart playing solo double bass.

'And anyone ask where you've been,' said Razzer from behind, 'say with Security, right?'

I nodded.

'And if that little screamer you were with starts playing up and shouting, give her one.'

'I can't wop a girl. Not Mouse.'

'You can if I say so, sonny. And don't try warning your pervy mate I'm after him or you'll end up so yer mother won't want you. Like him.'

'Don't worry,' I said, trying to sound like I didn't care. 'He ain't my mate. He's a bozo. When you find him, you give him one for me.' I raised my fist.

He seemed convinced.

Then he grabbed my shoulder, ducked me under a loop of lights and we stepped back into Swanwick's world.

*

253

Eventually I found Mouse.

'Where you been? Are you OK?'

'Yeah, yeah. Seen Skaz anywhere?'

'No, why should I want to see that perv?'

I stared at her, surprised by her hostility. I could see her brow was furrowed and spangled with glitter. Under the yellow of the lanterns strung round the stall near us, her skin glowed. Yeah, I thought suddenly, you're looking OK tonight, Mouse. Yeah, tasty. And I remembered how soft and warm she was when she snuggled up to me on The Boomerang.

'Alison will be back in a min,' she was saying. 'Maybe she knows.' She leaned towards me. 'Jigger told me about those videos. Ali doesn't know, so don't say anything.'

I nodded.

'You OK, Lee? What did Security want?' It was Alison running up and stopping a bit breathless.

'Got scared off,' I said, looking straight at her. 'Evidently I'm a security risk.'

'Well, push my boat. That's a load of moo cow,' said Mouse.

'You're mad,' said Alison. But I could see she was hiding a smile.

'You're having us on, aren't you?' said Mouse.

Just then a flock of screams filled the air. Someone had puked on The Orbiter. I wasn't really noticing. I was thinking hard. I had thought of asking Alison to help me find Skaz but she'd want to know why and what all the fuss was about and I couldn't really tell her. Not shop Skaz again. And Mouse wouldn't help. Looked like I was on my own on this one.

Suddenly Susie was offering me a Coke.

'Kills off the Ju Ju,' said a voice.

I looked around.

Standing a bit away was Jigger.

I stared at him.

'OK. OK,' he said. 'I should have told you, but I couldn't.'

'Couldn't what?' said Garrett who had suddenly appeared out of nowhere.

Jigger took my arm and drew me away.

'Oh, same to you,' I heard her shout at us. 'Be like that. We're going in The Haunted Castle, aren't we, girls? So there.'

'You go, frighten the ghosts,' said Mouse, joining us.

'It was Aunty's idea,' Jigger was saying, voice low. 'He wanted Hoodz Five off his patch. Bad for the biz.'

Hoodz 5! Hearing the name made me stop, cold and uneasy suddenly.

What with all the stuff about Aunty and Razzer and Dutton, I'd kind of forgotten I was boy on the run, dead bait too. Maybe I should forget about Skaz. Just scarper myself. And then again, maybe not. H5 would never show here, not on Aunty's territory. Swanwick's was safe as houses, surely.

I motioned Jigger to shut up because of Mouse.

'It's OK,' he said. 'She knows what's going on.'

'How did Aunty know about the envelopes? Why didn't you deliver the stuff?' I whispered.

'Cos Razzer got me first,' Jigger hissed. 'They were staking out Hoodz Five. They knew you'd been sorted by Big Hoodie.'

'But why didn't you tell me? I've been muscled by Aunty and Razzer for this.'

'He needed the money,' said Mouse.

I looked at her. 'How do you know?'

'For his mum. He told me. She's got to have stuff.'

'And you believe him?'

I turned away.

Then looked back at Jigger. 'I bet it was you told Hoodz about Assault. For the money,' I sneered.

'No, he didn't. That's dead unfair, Lee. It wasn't Jigger,' said Mouse. She put her hand on his arm. 'If you must know, it was your friend, Jamil.'

Jamil!

I stood rooted.

'Jamil? You're kidding!' I stared gob mouthed at the two of them.

'Hoodz Five ran protection on the shops,' said Jigger. 'Jamil's was one. He was scared. They threatened to smash his place. Assault was his way of paying them off.'

'So he knew about deliveries and stuff?'

Jigger nodded. He looked at me like he was holding something back.

'What else?' I said.

'Aunty knew about the protection deal too. Offered him to take over the contract. Get shot of Hoodz Five for him. Jamil said yes and told them about the delivery system. Aunty liked that. He's taking over the Hoodz distribution. That's how Razzer got me, one hand in the letter box. Posting your stuff. Nearly broke me arm.'

I sighed.

I was mad at Jamil. I was sorry for Jamil.

Mad and sorry for Jigger too.

I looked up. Mouse was searching my face.

'He did it for his mum,' she said quietly. 'It really isn't his fault.'

I nodded. Walked over to Jigger and fisted him one.

'Mates again?'

'Mates.' He looked at me. 'You OK, Lee?'

'Yeah, I'm OK,' I said.

Mouse and he started talking rides.

Was I OK?

Was I not.

Around me the lights and the rides and music swirled. My head too. The girl I fancied had dumped me – for Dutton of all people – and her dad turns out to be the number-one Feck hardman. My friend Jamil has sold out on me. Some thug has threatened to turn me into jigsaw pieces and the H5 heavies are after me.

And behind all of this crazy traffic is Skinny B bruised and hot eyed lying on sheets, the blood squirming with insatiables, white cells devouring, devouring.

I turned and saw Alison was still there. 'Thought you'd gone on that haunted thingie.'

'Just waiting for Susie.'

'You seen Skaz?' I said.

'Yeah, why? He was on the cages.' She nudged me. 'You checking him out? Bit jealous, are you?'

'Come on.'

'It's only a bit of fun. Me and Skaz.' She started to finger the silver pendant. 'He's all right though, isn't he, Dutton? But not really my type.'

'Nor's he mine right now,' I said, half wondering

whether to leave him in the cage and let carnivore Razzer gnaw him up and down. 'But I need to find him, quick, all the same. Before something nasty happens.'

She looked startled.

'Hoodz Five!' I said.

'Skaz?' It was Jigger. 'You say you were looking for Dutton? He was on the Big Game Safari ten minutes ago.'

'See ya,' I said to Alison.

'No, wait,' she said.

I hesitated. 'I gotta go. It's important.'

'What about my party?'

'Stuff that,' I said.

'Stuff you too,' she said, frowning.

'We're going as well,' said Mouse. 'Down The Shed. Jigger and me. He's got some freebie tickets.' She linked arms with him.

Alison and I gawped at the two of them.

'With Jigger?' I said in disbelief. 'But he's a –'

'Dead brain,' said Alison.

'A what?' said Mouse sharply. 'Dead brain you.' And she grabbed Jigger and the two of them walked off together.

We watched them, gobsmacked both of us.

'Fancy going with a loser like that,' said Alison at last. 'I thought she fancied you.'

'Mouse? Me? No way,' I said, mouth still dropped in shock at watching Jigger walking away arm round Susie, alias The Mouse.

Did she really? Fancy me? Mouse? I found myself thinking. Maybe if I hadn't been so set on Ali, I'd have noticed.

Suddenly Alison flipped up this little camera hanging on her wrist.

'Smile when I say.' She fiddled about with some angles.

I was thinking hard about Mouse now.

Who was always popping up whenever I was around on my own, in the library, in the classroom? Yeah, Mouse. And who stood up for me in Cropper's class when he had me Reggie Rabbit out front? Mouse. And who got me into Alison's party? Mouse. And who thought I was cool? Mouse. And who clamped my fingers in *The Big Book of Knowledge*? Mouse. I stopped. Now why should Susie kitten face do that if she fancied me? I wondered.

'Smile!'

I tried.

'What a wuss face,' said Alison.

'Soz. Just thinking.' Then I told her about Susie and *The Big Book of Knowledge* incident.

'What did you expect? She brought you offerings. Messages of cool and comfort and you never even noticed. That's the worst thing, not even noticing. That hurts. And when cats are hurt they scratch. You just been clawed, Lee. Lucky you still got your eyes intact.'

I nodded. What a dim clucker I was. 'Look,' I said, 'I didn't mean it about the party.' Better smooth down Alison, I was thinking. I didn't want more scratch marks. 'It's just –'

'You gotta go, I know. It's your sister.'

Somebody was calling her.

She waved and then turned back to me. 'Look, we'll talk Monday, right?'

I nodded.

My heart lifted. Alison and I had a date, Monday. Good!

Not so good – Jigger going off like that with Susie. And not a word. He might have said.

All of a sudden I felt … I felt … well … let down. I felt dumped. I felt left out. I felt doored in the face.

Hurt.

Come Monday I'd tell him too. Might even slap him one.

Anyway, wait till the Ju Ju come smoking out of him – that'll scare her off, get her whiskers in a twist.

I pushed my way through the crowds, eyes everywhere – looking out for Razzer, Big Hoodie, Skaz.

But most of all for Skaz.

Big Game Safari? No Skaz. Neither at The Haunted Castle. Nowhere. No sign at The Jungle Jim Cruise.

I began to think I was too late. I should have just gone instead of listening to Jigger and Mouse and Alison. Skaz could be a right bandage case by now.

'Hey, Lee,' said a voice. 'What's up? Where is everyone?'

Skaz!

'Dutton. Am I glad to see you.'

He raised his eyebrows in mock surprise.

'You got to get out,' I said. 'Right now. I'm not joking.' I grabbed him by the arm and tried pulling him behind the canvas side of a stall, out of sight.

He pulled away.

'Hang about, Matthews. What's the big deal?'

'It's Aunty and Razzer. They know about your pervy videos and Razzer's out to get you. Jigsaw you.'

Skaz just smiled.

'Cool it, Lee. I know. I know Razzer. He's a bozo brain.'

'You know?' I said, amazed. 'Razzer's a bloody maniac. You must be off yer head.'

'Look, little Lee. It's sorted. Me and Razzer.'

I stared at him. 'You mean, you've seen him, today, now, here?'

'Yeah.'

'And he hasn't meatballed you?'

'Do I look meatballed?'

I shook my head. It didn't make sense. It never did with Skaz Dutton.

'What happened?' I said.

'We came to an agreement. He left off lamming me. I left off telling Aunty about how he was pocketing some of his street biz for himself. I told him Aunty would have his fingers in the mincer if he found out. That knocked him for the count.'

'You got anything on Hoodz Five?' I said, wishing I could jump trouble like he jumped trouble.

'No, except Big Hoodie's after you.'

I nodded.

'Better get home, bunny no-mates.'

I stiffened. There he was again. Dutton having a laugh.

'Well, you can forget Alison Libidowicz anyway,' I said coldly. 'You know she's Aunty's daughter. And when she hears you've been peeping her she'll give you a razzering you won't forget.'

Skaz smiled. 'You going to tell her, are you? Well, I'll just say you and I were in it together.'

'Together? You're joking.'

Skaz shrugged. 'That's why you were so keen on her going to TKD. You enticed her there so I could skimmy them through the skylight. Remember?' He was laughing now.

'Is that supposed to be funny? As if anyone would believe a word.'

'Lee, my bozo friend,' he said. 'I've tried but you just don't learn. Forget about trying to be smart. Go back to being a bozo. It's what you do best.'

I scowled.

'Here,' he said. 'I got a goodbye present for you.' He handed me a parcel roughly wrapped in a plastic bag.

'Present? Goodbye?'

'Yeah, I'm off out of here. Sheffield. My dad has a job there.'

I bet, I thought. Pushing bikes on the hush hush.

'What about Alison?' I said.

He shrugged. 'Bit of fun. What else is life but a laugh?' He spat on the ground. 'Fancy bombing the Big Wheel, later on, after they close? That'd be a laugh, eh?' He flexed his fingers. 'Would you really tell her, about the piccies?'

I thought for a minute. If it meant I got a crack at Alison, I would, yes.

'No,' I said, grinning.

'Says you.' His eyes narrowed. 'You know, Lee, maybe you're not such a skeffin wuss, you're a skeffin bastard.'

I laughed.

We both laughed.

The first good word I ever got from Skaz Dutton.

And the last.

Because, while I was wondering what was in the parcel he'd just given me, he smiled, stuck his hands in his jeans and wandered into the passing crowds.

I watched him go. Gradually his figure, so clear and unmistakeable at first, merged with a hundred others. Eventually I was left guessing which one of the many was his drifting among all the bozos into the anonymous darkness beyond the glitter of the fairground lights.

I unwrapped the parcel. Pulled out the pressie. It was a video cassette. 'Pinky and Perky Productions' it said on the label. There was a note attached. 'Hey, big boy. Remember I said when yer old enuff you can have a peepsie. Well, here she is!'

Perv Dutton!

Hell! I had to get rid because if Aunty found out it would make a Hoodz 5 makeover look like kiddies' playtime.

But then, I thought, Ali in the all-together. Tasty or what.

Then another video filled my head. A golden field, a beautiful girl and I tumbling through the waving corn stalks, she falling laughing to the ground, her hair beaded with grains, me beside her, both of us together, bodies kissing, lips skimming, hearts drumming and the long slow sun melting everything but us.

I dropped the cassette and, with both feet, jumped on it, smashing it and smashing it. And I didn't stop until it lay blitzed in a thousand pieces. I kicked it all over, scattered it like no one could ever put it together again, like I was kicking some of the clag out of my life.

Once I was satisfied, once I'd stamped enough pieces into the ashy earth, I looked around. No hooded figures coming my way. No hardman with pipe-grip hands groping for me. Just big kids rattling the cages, bulbs burnin' and poppin' all over, hot boys lit up, glitter girls glammed out and riding their luck.

I needed to get out. Get some fresh air into my life. I needed to climb out of the shadows and take in the stars and the sky and all the clean emptiness of the night.

It was Skaz's joke about bombing the Big Wheel that gave me the idea.

Only trouble was I had to get to Jamil's first and that was right on the edge of Hoodz 5 territory.

Next I was out of Swanwick's and heading for Gants. I thought if I entered The Feck from our side, from the Far Pastures end, it would be easier to get to Jamil's, less bandit country to cross.

At Gants I turned left and started to descend. I practised a few TKD moves. Make me feel quicker, faster. And I started trotting, get me warmed up, give me a start should I have to leg it from Big Hoodie or whatever. There was other low life in The Feck besides Hoodz 5.

A car passed me slowly. Black Merc. Brake eyes glowing red. Four figures inside. I stopped. Bent down to do up a shoelace, ready to reverse and sprint down the next ginnel and into oblivion.

The Merc idled. Edged forward. It seemed undecided. Suddenly it took off and swung into a side street.

I crossed the road and edged into the shadows. Once I was level with the street I tried to see if the Merc was still there. It was halfway up parked on the right and facing me. I backed away and decided to do a downwind. This is what Jig and I used to do hunting Ju Ju. We'd go in a big circle to get behind them. Downwinding we called it. That's how David Attenborough does it on his safari programmes. He always says he's going down wind.

Eventually I got to Jamil's. Window blazing in the dark. Open all hours is Jamil's.

When he came in from the back I was waiting for him at the counter. I laid half a dozen cans of paint spray, three Arctic White, three Midnight Black neatly in front of him.

'Lee, hellos. You good one? How Skimpy?'

'Skimpy bad. Lee good. Now, Jamil. I'm taking these cans.'

He totted it up on the till.

'Fiftins fifty.'

I said nothing.

'I talk to Aunty, Jamil. Aunty say Jamil help Lee or it be bad bad for Jamil. Aunty say Jamil did the bad bad on Lee. Sold him down the river to da Hoodz Five boys. Aunty maybe bring back the boys. You OK with that?'

Jamil's eyes went widescreen white.

'They blow my shop, Hoodz want,' he said, looking at me sideways. 'I good mans in bad times, Lee. Aunty boss now. More bads for me. More, more bads.'

He looked bad scared. 'You spray my shop?'

'No, Jamil, mate. That's an H Five habit. I'm going to bomb bad The Water Tower. I got some cluck to wipe out of my life.'

Just one prob. Had to get over Gants and beyond in one piece.

Outside on the pavement I stood for a moment in the light from Jamil's. Across the tarmac stretched my shadow, the head dissolved in darkness, the torso lean, the legs splayed like a Wyatt Earp wannabe, gun fighter from the OK Corral.

I shook the tins. I was armed and I was out of here.

I looked down the hill towards The Feck proper.

It had gone!

Blacked out.

Leccy was off.

And for one moment I imagined the jaws of earth had opened and swallowed the place whole leaving nothing but a dark crater like The Swamp, the continent of our childhood, where Jigger and I played and fought and killed.

But I knew nothing shifted places like The Feck. Like the Ju Ju, they were with you for ever. Hoodz 5 and Jigger had taught me that. I knew now about its rat-litter lock-ups and burnt-out bangers. I knew about its gutter slop and drain swill, its clagged stairwells and its bin-stink lift shafts. I knew about its dead-end alleys, its junk and filth and doped-out dogheads. And most of all I knew it was there for the duration.

And then, as if to warn me, the blocks of The Flats suddenly loomed up sullen and gigantic, backlit by a flare of illumination from Swanwick's, and with them the hulks of houses, occasionally straffed by the dashing lights of cars, crouched ready and waiting below.

I turned towards Gants, The Tower and escape.

I crossed into the gloom of the street and made for the bus route that led north. I kept to the shades and the overhang of trees gliding like a stream, as Buzz would say. Don't go with the flow, he used to tell me. You are the current not the water, spirit not body. Make your own tide.

I reached the main bus route and headed Gants way.

I'd hardly got into my stride when I noticed it.

The black Mercedes again.

It was parked in a side street just ahead of me, bonnet nosing into the main road, body blocking my way like some animal lying in wait.

I stopped.

Suddenly it began to move out, turning and edging down the kerbside in my direction.

I took a step back. Two steps. Three.

Suddenly the headlights blazed.

I stopped.

The car spurted forward then slowed.

I backtracked.

It idled after me.

I swallowed hard. Who were they? In the blinding lights I could see nothing of the occupants. Hoodz 5? Not likely. They weren't Merc boys. And, anyway, if they wanted to jump me this wasn't how to do it. What was going on?

Maybe I could do a runner across the main road, dash behind a passing car, disappear as the Merc tried a U-turn.

I moved towards the kerb.

But the Merc read me and suddenly accelerated, the roar of the engine shocking me so I stumbled backwards.

Then I saw what they were doing.

Bit by bit they were forcing me back and back, nudging me further and further into The Feck. Already the streetlights were out and I was on the rim of its shadowed world.

Maybe it was Hoodz 5 after all driving me into their territory, into the dark heart of it where no one could see them smash me. That was it. They wanted no witnesses. I was going to be slabbed and no one would ever know.

I quickened my pace, broke into a jog. Soon as I saw a side street I was going up it and away down a ginnel, a back entry, anywhere.

Then I realized the Merc's lights were off. I wasn't rabbit stiff in their beams any more.

I stopped. Looked behind.

No Merc.

Merc gone.

I breathed a huge sigh. I was off the hook. It was back to Gants.

Then they hit me.

A van came squealing on to the pavement. Doors jumped open. Three figures leapt out, grabbed and dragged me for about twenty metres on to some grassy area. My head was forced down. I could smell soil.

One of them spoke. A voice I knew too well.

'I told yous, boy. I told yous, don't ever mess with Hoodz Five. And what you do? Yous mess me up.'

'No way,' I said shakily.

'For a delivery boy, yous worse than Pony Express. Now what yous do with my stuff?'

'Mate of mine delivered.'

'Who?'

'Jigger!'

'Jigger!' he hissed. 'That dead brain. No one delivered. You shafted me, you little bastard.'

Sick slopped at the back of my throat, dropped and left it burning, burning.

'Get my stuff or your face will be wiping the wall,' he said. 'Outside Jamil's tomorrow, nine a.m., boy,' he hissed in my ear. 'Have my stuff or yous yesterday's news. I'll trash every bone in yous body. And jus to show yous I keep my promises, here's a little free sample for yous to taste.'

*

What happened next was all a blur of noise and swearing and grunts and scuffling and figures running in all directions.

I was hurled sideways and sent slithering face down. I'd hardly got to my feet when something thudded in my back and sent me sprawling again.

I got on to my backside and shovelled myself backwards as far from the action as possible.

Suddenly The Feck leccy flicked on and in the stray light from the road I could just make out, jammed beside the van, a black Mercedes. Nearby, four or five figures were smacking the crap out of somebody.

I didn't check who or what. I was out of it.

I sneaked back on to the street ready to leg it.

Then the door of the Mercedes opened and a man got out. He was dressed in a dark-blue security jumpsuit. It was Razzer.

'Nearly lost you, you little bugger,' he said.

'Lost me? What's going on?' I said.

Suddenly a figure staggered into the road, collapsed and lay face up under the streetlight. His hood was down. His eyes were bleeding something dark. I stared at the swollen face. He was dead Ju Ju. Smokey white skin, red bubbling from his rap mouth.

It was Big Hoodie.

But he was no rap boy. He was white. Just his blood came in shiny black, oozing like tar in the yellow light.

Now I recognized him. It was bullet eyes, Big Hoodie. The kid who'd wopped me one that night at Tae Kwon Do, the night Alison chucked all her *dobock* and I'd rescued it.

Well, bye-bye, rap mouth. Yous had yous life re-designed. Hoodz 5 is yesterday's boys.

I felt Razzer's hand close over my shoulder. I winced a bit. It was still tender from earlier when he'd tried clamping me to the chair in Aunty's caravan.

'That's what happens if you annoy Aunty, sonny. Now scram. And you ain't seen anything. Gob any of this and you'll be an emergency rest of your life.'

I took one last look at Hoodie lying on the tarmac. He looked like one of those war photos you get in the newspapers, all crumpled, still and death stiff.

I ran. Ran as fast as I could and never stopped till I was on the path by the railway. Eventually I slowed down.

Of course, the Merc had been tagging me, waiting for Hoodz to jump so they could do a bit of jumping themselves. I swallowed hard. Aunty had used me as bait.

Bastards.

I took in big, deep-lung swallows of cold night air. I swelled with it, collapsed with it and gulped for more.

I looked up at the moon, creamy and curdy. And at the stars all ping clean and bristling with light. I thought of what I'd just seen. Pay-off time for street scum, blood and bone smashed; Jamil, nice mans at heart, scared witless; Aunty shoving biz and shooting up lives. I needed air and life and clean things and Gran and Mum and Dad and Skinny B.

Mostly Skinny.

Because, in all the whirl of things that evening, somehow I'd forgotten her and I felt bad, real bads.

If anyone needed prime time, Skinny did. I had to up

the ante. Make the world sit up and root for Skinny. She needed news, headlines. For too long the wrong people were getting credit in my book – Hoodz 5, scam king Skaz Dutton, Alison, Jigger, Mouse. It was time to flip channels.

I got to The Tower and made my way round the back over a load of clag: burnt tyres, bits of corrugated sheeting, curls of rusted wire. From somewhere in the dark under shadow of The Tower water was leaking and pinging carelessly on some broken piping.

I found another ladder.

This was it.

I hauled myself up.

Rung by rung I climbed. I never looked down. I never looked up.

The ladder held firm because I knew it would.

I felt strangely powerful. Like my legs would never tire, my arms never ache no matter how far I went. I could have climbed to the moon and back without a wobble, without a single mis-fire in my heart.

Soon as I started up I felt someone other than me was climbing beside me, someone else climbing with me, in me, strong and undaunted. Because every time I gripped the next rung and jacked myself up, I felt the push from inside. Every breath I blew plunged through my blood and pulled me like a tidal hand upwards and upwards.

I reached the walkway and stood there gazing at the town glittering in the night. I watched the stars – Mouse glitter.

I knew now I'd never see Skaz again. Something told me he was gone for ever. No more stunts, Skaz. No more pulling rabbits out of hats. I was the last bozo bunny you tried that on.

Thing is, Skaz, I ain't your bozo any more. I've done bozo. I've done bombing. I've done Ju Ju. I've done the biz.

Sad really.

No more magic man.

I was right out of Skaz. He was right out of me. We'd parted equals. That was enough.

Time for real life.

Forget warriors and enlightenment. Forget the way. The only enlightenment was: there was no enlightenment.

Because maybe Skaz, not Buzz and the Great Masters, was right – it was all a laugh. One great big joke.

Gran thought, up there, God was snooping on each of us, holding us steady in his long cam shot, ready to record every fumble and fault.

Of course what Buzz said about God's thumbprint sounded good. Somehow out of all the dust and the clag and the grot there was something to be made, or to be found.

And Buzz could be right.

After all, clag had got Skinny, and out of that I had found something. I'd found Skinny herself in a way. Not Skinny sister. Not Skinny Ju Ju. Not sweet Skinny ballerina. Not Skinny pink bunny.

But a little girl. With pale skin and a wheeze. A seven-year-old with bad blood and a silver heart.

I began to edge round the walkway till I was standing in front of the letters Skaz and I had sprayed on the night we did the bombing.

I laid out five of the cans on the metal flooring. The sixth I held in my hand.

This is for you, Skinny B, I said. You and me.

I started shaking the can. The pellet inside clattered about.

Then something rattled in my head. I thought back to that first time we'd bombed The Tower.

'I owe you, Skaz,' I said aloud. 'On the ladder that time, you made me full front the scare inside me. You did. Without that I'd have never got back. And I wouldn't be here now.'

Soon as the can was ready I started spraying everything white. It took ages to spray out the whole of CLUCKY.

But eventually CLUCKY was no more.

Then I got the first can of the Midnight Black.

And I sprayed and sprayed, hoping the stuff wouldn't run out before I'd finished.

It didn't.

Once I was down the ladder I walked back to the bridge where Jigger and Worm and I had first seen Skaz's bombing.

I never looked back till I was there standing by the parapet.

In the dim light of the moon I could see the square of white I'd sprayed, and on it, in black letters, the words –

LOVES YA SKINNY

hotnews@puffin

Hot off the press!
You'll find all the latest exclusive Puffin news here

Where's it happening?
Check out our author tours and events programme

Bestsellers
What's hot and what's not? Find out in our charts

E-mail updates
Sign up to receive all the latest news
straight to your e-mail box

Links to the coolest sites
Get connected to all the best author web sites

Book of the Month
Check out our recommended reads

www.puffin.co.uk

Read more in Puffin

For complete information about books available from Puffin – and Penguin – and how to order them, contact us at the appropriate address below. Please note that for copyright reasons the selection of books varies from country to country.

www.puffin.co.uk

In the United Kingdom: Please write to Dept EP, Penguin Books Ltd, Bath Road, Harmondsworth, West Drayton, Middlesex UB7 ODA

In the United States: Please write to Penguin Group (USA), Inc., P.O. Box 12289, Dept B, Newark, New Jersey 07101–5289 or call 1–800–788–6262

In Canada: Please write to Penguin Books Canada Ltd, 10 Alcorn Avenue, Suite 300, Toronto, Ontario M4V 3B2

In Australia: Please write to Penguin Books Australia Ltd, 250 Camberwell Road, Camberwell, Victoria 3124

In New Zealand: Please write to Penguin Group (NZ), Private Bag 102902, North Shore Mail Centre, Auckland 10

In India: Please write to Penguin Books India Pvt Ltd, 11 Panscheel Shopping Centre, Panscheel Park, New Delhi 110 017

In the Netherlands: Please write to Penguin Books Netherlands bv, Postbus 3507, NL–1001 AH Amsterdam

In Germany: Please write to Penguin Books Deutschland GmbH, Metzlerstrasse 26, 60594 Frankfurt am Main

In Spain: Please write to Penguin Books S. A., Bravo Murillo 19, 1° B, 28015 Madrid

In Italy: Please write to Penguin Italia s.r.l., Via Felice Casati 20, I–20124 Milano

In France: Please write to Penguin France S. A., 17 rue Lejeune, F–31000 Toulouse

In Japan: Please write to Penguin Books Japan, Ishikiribashi Building, 2–5–4, Suido, Bunkyo-ku, Tokyo 112

In South Africa: Please write to Longman Penguin Southern Africa (Pty) Ltd, Private Bag X08, Bertsham 2013